Home to Stay

Linda Shertzer

JOVE BOOKS, NEW YORK

HOME TO STAY

A Jove Book / published by arrangement with
the author

PRINTING HISTORY
Jove edition / December 1996

The Putnam Berkley World Wide Web site address is
http://www.berkley.com/berkley

ISBN: 0-515-11986-5

A JOVE BOOK®
Jove Books are published by The Berkley Publishing Group,
200 Madison Avenue, New York, New York 10016.
JOVE and the "J" design are trademarks
belonging to Jove Publications, Inc.

PRINTED IN THE UNITED STATES OF AMERICA

10 9 8 7 6 5 4 3 2 1

Prologue

LESTER MARTIN HAMMERED the shiny brass knocker against the front door of Henry Richardson's huge brick mansion, and waited.

And waited.

He shifted his case from hand to hand. It wasn't heavy. It only contained the few pages of Mr. Richardson's Last Will and Testament. But he was impatient standing out in the dark, and he had to do something.

He looked out over the close-cropped lawn and the well-pruned rosebushes bordering the walk. The lilac bushes were trimmed just enough to hide the brick wall from the inside.

"This is a heck of a time to be doing business," Lester grumbled as he pulled out his pocket watch.

It was too dark to see the small hands against the face. He jammed the watch back into his pocket and debated whether to knock again.

"I'm a respected lawyer, damn it. Folks come to *my* office, not the other way around," he asserted to the silence of the evening as he paced back and forth across the porch. The heels of his shoes clunked against the white painted boards. "Of course, I guess Mr. Richardson is sort of a special case," he had to admit. He gave a little chuckle. "Not too many folks in town have his kind of money."

Then he shook his head in bewilderment.

"I never will understand why Rachel Williams chose to marry Tom Pickett instead of Richardson. For that kind of money—heck! *I'd* even marry him!"

He laughed aloud, then resumed his pacing and grumbling.

"I know Mrs. Cartwright only comes here during the day to do the skinflint's housekeeping, and Red Wilkins comes once a week to mow the lawn. But you'd think with his money, he could at least hire somebody to answer the darn door at night. Of course, it's not like the crazy coot has any real visitors. Heck, he's not so great looking that everybody wants to see him."

Lester was having a good time, amusing himself by verbally abusing Henry Richardson. The more clever insults he thought of, the louder his voice grew.

"He probably just sits alone every evening, counting all his money. Probably sleeps with it. Might even try to eat it."

He laughed harder.

"I wouldn't be surprised to find out he'd tried to—"

"Good evening, Mr. Martin. Thank you for coming."

Lester dropped his case. No fair! Mr. Richardson had opened the door and it hadn't even given a warning squeak.

"I hope you haven't been waiting long."

"No, no, not at all," Lester hurriedly assured his most important client as he fumbled to retrieve his case.

Should he try to convince Richardson that he was really talking about some other lonely, homely, rich guy? Or should he just hope the man hadn't really heard him all that clearly? This was one client Lester didn't want to lose.

When Richardson stepped back to allow him to enter,

Lester gave a silent sigh of relief. He wasn't fired after all!

As Mr. Richardson turned and made his way down the hall, Lester followed in his wake. The floors, the furniture, and all the knickknacks lying around were all spotlessly clean, as if no one actually lived in the house. Although the large mansion was full of what Lester judged to be expensive furniture and valuable pieces of art, he could hear his footsteps echoing through it as if it were completely empty.

He was a lawyer. His livelihood depended on his ability to be logical and unemotional. He figured he had as little of what folks might call "fancy" as possible. He'd heard—and scoffed at—all the tales the older kids told to scare the younger ones, about Mrs. Richardson's ghost haunting this house. He didn't hold with all that silly Spiritualist stuff. But he still had the eerie feeling he was walking through a living tomb. Or through a body that had no soul.

Richardson led him into a large office, and took his customary seat behind the desk.

Lester didn't like that, either. *He* was supposed to be in that big chair behind the desk, showing how much he was in charge, not seated in the humble chair on the other side, indicating his dependence on Richardson's payment.

But he was a realistic man, and not stupid. If Richardson wanted, he'd sit on the roof—and make sure the payment was well worth his time and effort.

He set his case on the desktop, opened it, and pulled out the long papers.

"Everything's just the way you wanted it," he said as he handed the papers to Mr. Richardson and waited while the man read.

Richardson didn't even bother to look up from perusing the document as he said, "I expect you to follow through with my other instructions as well."

"Oh, yes, sir," Lester agreed emphatically. He sat quietly while Richardson finished reading.

Suddenly Richardson looked up, pointed his finger at him, and fixed him with a narrow glare.

"If one word of this gets out to *anyone* before I'm dead, I'll see you never practice law anywhere around here ever again."

"Never happen," Lester vowed.

Part of him didn't believe Richardson could do it. No matter how much money the man had, his influence couldn't reach everywhere. On the other hand, Lester didn't relish the prospect of wasting the rest of his life trying to make a living practicing law in East Elbow, Idaho. He felt sure that if he made a mistake, somehow, Richardson would see that he did.

"But I still don't understand why—"

"No, Lester, I don't suppose a man like you would."

Mr. Richardson leaned back in his chair and steepled his fingers on his stomach. With his chin resting on his chest, he gazed into the fire and gave a deep sigh.

"My wife died many years ago. My only son lived for just a few hours. I have no other relatives." With a bitter little chuckle, he added, "At least none I'd care to acknowledge."

"You're still in the prime of life." Lester tried to sound encouraging. "You could marry again . . . have more children. . . ."

"The only other woman I ever considered marrying chose to wed a dirt-poor farmer instead. Her son, who I might have called my own, barely knows me, and doesn't particularly seem to want to."

"No, no. *That* I can understand. But I don't understand why you want to keep this a secret."

"Until now, they've all ignored me. I won't have everybody pestering me now just because they suspect I might have left them something."

With jerky, angry movements, Mr. Richardson picked up his pen and signed the last page with a great flourish. When he looked up again, Lester almost fell off his chair in shock. Richardson was grinning like a Cheshire cat.

"Besides, I like surprises," Mr. Richardson said.

"Oh, this'll be a *big* surprise, all right." Lester chuckled as he refolded the papers and replaced them in his case. "I don't think *anyone* will believe you've left your entire fortune to Wendell Williams."

1

"*Why*, MIRANDA, MY darling!" Charles Madison Lowell III exclaimed as he peered out the open window of the speeding train. He was trying his best to lean over her without actually touching her. "I had no idea this country was so . . . so wild."

Oh, just wait until we put on our war paint and feathers, Miranda Hamilton wanted to remark.

But she'd spent the past two years at Mrs. Bigelow's exclusive Finishing School for Young Ladies in Boston, learning *not* to make that kind of remark anymore. It wasn't the kind of reply a wealthy, well-bred young lady made to a gentleman. It wasn't like anything she'd ever heard any of the proper young ladies of Charles's acquaintance say at any of the elegant parties they'd attended. It certainly wasn't the sort of thing a lady said if she wanted to remain engaged to her fiancé, and maintain family harmony.

So instead, she just giggled and gave his arm a playful tap, just as she had seen the other young ladies at other parties do.

"Oh, Charles, you do exaggerate so! But truly, it's not as bad as you might think."

"It couldn't be," he muttered. "Are you sure there aren't any wild Indians on the rampage in the vicinity?"

This time she almost forgot and laughed aloud. She stopped herself just in time and giggled. "You've been reading too many penny dreadfuls."

"You mean like the ones Captain Jackson Armistead writes?"

"Precisely!"

He sniffed with derision. "You know I don't read those preposterously contrived things."

She smiled sweetly. "No, of course not. How silly of me to suppose that you might."

What was Charles's problem with Captain Armistead? *She* always enjoyed reading his exciting tales; she had for many years.

"But I've read the newspaper accounts. . . ."

She grimaced. *Oh, yes, and we all know how extremely accurate they are.*

Instead, she tried to assure him, "You needn't worry. I haven't seen an Indian around here since I was just a little girl."

Charles tugged at his starched collar with obvious relief. But he still kept careful watch out the window.

"I don't suppose I could blame them for leaving."

Leaving? It wasn't as if they'd had much choice in the matter, she thought, but again remained silent.

"It's pretty barren out there."

"Barren?" she repeated, trying very hard to keep the disbelief from being too evident in her voice.

Your brain is barren if you can look at this countryside and think that! She wisely kept her mouth shut.

"There's nothing but fields of corn and wheat, and herds of cattle."

There are also tall cottonwoods, sunflowers as high as an elephant, purple and white wildflowers springing up along the sides of the roads . . .

He gave a derisive laugh. "We haven't seen too many houses, but what we've seen is certainly different from what we've built in Boston."

"I'll admit there's a big difference between cattle barns and Beacon Hill mansions."

In the barns the cows don't talk. Stop it, Miranda! she scolded herself. And don't you dare laugh out loud at your own jokes.

She continued pleasantly, "You'd have to go pretty far to find a mountain or the sea—I suppose," she added quickly. She shouldn't appear more versed in geography than he.

Of course Miranda had admired the beauty of the rolling countryside she'd traveled through on her way to Boston, and the drama of the rocky New England coast when she'd visited the seashore. But deep inside, she couldn't help maintain that, to her way of thinking, nothing rivaled the pure beauty of flat waves of green and gold, as far as the eye could see, rippling with the wind under a wide blue sky.

But she'd succeeded so far on this endless, exhausting journey, in being pleasant and agreeable to Charles and his mother. She certainly didn't want to ruin things now by expressing an opinion.

So she just nodded and said, "Indeed."

"Aha!" Charles exclaimed, pointing out the window. "At last, some more buildings are coming up in the distance."

"That must be Grasonville," she informed him in calm, ladylike tones. But the impatient little girl inside was trying her best not to bounce up and down on the seat and shout with glee at the excitement of coming home.

"Grasonville. Now arriving in Grasonville." The strident voice of the conductor, passing down the aisle, confirmed Miranda's assertion.

Charles released a huge sigh of relief. Then he turned to the elegant, elderly woman who was seated across the aisle.

"Mother. Oh, Mother," he called softly, rousing her.

"Oh, dear. I must have dozed off momentarily," Mrs. Lowell said.

You've dozed the entire trip. Instead, she replied, "Travel by rail can be so wearying."

Mrs. Lowell sat more erect and adjusted her hat atop her head. She brushed the long ostrich feather back from her face. "I hope you don't think me rude, my dear."

"Oh, no! Not at all," Miranda, smiling pleasantly, hastened to assure her future mother-in-law.

She thanked her lucky stars the formidable woman had slept most of the way and spared her the monumental effort of not dozing off while Mrs. Lowell rambled on and on. The elderly lady's idea of conversation was recounting scintillating tales about anyone who wasn't in the room at the time. Riding out West in a train filled with complete strangers, the field was pretty much wide open to her.

Mrs. Lowell glanced around at the ragtag conglomeration of passengers. "I don't relish being stared at."

Everyone could've ignored you if you hadn't started snoring.

"It would have been so much more comfortable—and discrete—if we had been able to hire a private car," she added with a stifled yawn. "Or even our own compartments."

"There weren't any available on this run," Charles reminded her.

"Margaret Cabot warned me," Mrs. Lowell lamented with a forlorn shake of her head. The feather waggled from side to side, just like the thin skin under her chin. "The farther west one travels, the more primitive the conditions become. That is, until one reaches San Francisco—or so I'm told. But I ignored her, much to my sorrow. After all," she added, gazing pointedly at Miranda, "I did so want to please you by meeting your parents."

"I do appreciate it, too." If Miranda had been able to reach her across the aisle, she would have given the older woman's hand a reassuring squeeze. Instead, she beamed her her most sincere look. "I truly, truly do."

Mrs. Lowell smiled serenely and raised her chin. "Yes, I know, my dear."

"Never fear, Mother. Relief is in sight." Charles reached over and patted his mother's hand in consolation.

Well, at least one of us got to her, Miranda thought with a bit of satisfaction.

"Although I cannot fathom why your parents couldn't make the trip back East instead." Mrs. Lowell sounded just a bit peevish.

"It's terribly difficult for them to leave the farm this time of year," Miranda tried to explain.

Mrs. Lowell raised her eyebrows as if to indicate her continuing puzzlement. "Why your father, with all his money, continues to farm as if he had none . . ." She left her sentence unfinished, as if the forlorn shaking of her head would say it all for her.

"He likes to farm," Miranda answered.

Better than he liked digging in that mountain. She knew Mrs. Lowell looked askance at her father's farming activities, but she positively loathed talk of his mining days.

"Besides, they've promised to come visit us this Christmas."

"I'm looking forward to that so much," Mrs. Lowell replied, but Miranda didn't think she sounded very excited at all.

Charles turned to Miranda and asked, "How long before we actually arrive in Grasonville?"

"Very soon," she replied breathlessly. She grasped the window ledge with such anticipation that her kid gloves stretched tightly across her knuckles.

Not soon enough. If I could get out and push to make this darn train go faster, I would.

However, considering she was wearing her best traveling suit of dove gray gabardine, and considering she didn't want to embarrass Charles or Mrs. Lowell, she decided to sit and quietly wait.

At last, with a sharp blast of the whistle and a belch of steam, the train screeched to a halt. The other passengers immediately rose and, in a babble of excitement, began scrambling for their baggage. The conductor called directions up and down the aisle while the porters outside shouted from the platform, seeking travelers to assist for a sizable tip. Workmen loading and unloading boxcars farther back yelled to each other.

"Miranda!"

Above the noise of the crowded platform, she heard her father's voice calling to her.

"Miranda!"

Frantically she searched the platform for her parents. It had been so long since she'd seen them—a whole year! At last she spotted her father, tall and red-haired, standing in the middle of the platform.

Proper young ladies don't shout in public, she admonished herself. *Oh, hogwash! It's my daddy!*

"Papa!" She waved her lace handkerchief in front of her, trying to attract his attention. "Papa! Over here. We're over here."

Sam Hamilton turned in her direction. His tanned face expanded into a wide grin at the sight of her. He looked as if he'd just jumped down from the hay wagon, pulled on a jacket, and come to town. No matter how many times he put on a fancy suit and went to his office in town, this was the way she liked to see him best. She'd never seen her father looking more handsome.

Standing beside him was her plump little mother in a brand-new pink and green plaid dress.

"Mama!"

Bertha Hamilton bustled toward her across the station platform and enveloped her daughter in a warm embrace. Then, still holding both of Miranda's hands, she stepped back and looked her over.

"Have you been eating right?" she demanded.

"Yes, Mama."

"Plenty of meat and gravy?"

Miranda wavered.

"Good bread and butter?"

Miranda nodded.

"Good, but you still look too thin." Her mother shook her head.

"Oh, Mama, I'm fine," Miranda protested. "Don't worry so much."

"I can't help it. You're my baby."

"Oh, Mama. I'm twenty years old."

"I don't care how old you get. You'll always be my baby."

Miranda knew better than to argue that point.

Mrs. Hamilton sighed deeply as she examined her daughter. "You look so beautiful. I'm so proud of you."

"You look pretty, too, Mama," Miranda returned. "That's a new dress, isn't it?"

Mrs. Hamilton smiled and stepped back to show off her latest creation. "Do you like it? I made it myself— just for the occasion."

"You did a wonderful job. But then, you always do."

"Oh, just wait till you see what else I've made for all the parties everyone has planned for you."

"You look quite charming, Mrs. Hamilton," Charles said.

"Well, aren't you sweet!"

"Mama, Papa, this is my fiancé, Charles," Miranda quickly made the introductions.

"I sort of figured that. And oh, aren't you a handsome young man! Now I see why you want to marry him," Mrs. Hamilton added in a loud aside to her daughter.

"You sew your own clothing?" Mrs. Lowell asked. "How quaint."

Miranda had seen that same stiff smile pasted on Mrs. Lowell's tight lips at dozens of formal receptions and equally boring parties. But one thin eyebrow was raised to a more haughty angle than Miranda thought was usual. Obviously, Mrs. Lowell was not pleased. But if Mrs. Lowell's criticism of her mother's fashions was her biggest problem during this visit, Miranda decided she'd consider herself lucky.

"I myself have never been so . . . talented," Mrs. Lowell continued, "and have always found it more convenient to resort to the services of a quality dress-maker."

Mrs. Hamilton looked Mrs. Lowell over. "Well, the one you've got has done a pretty good job so far. I don't see much reason to change."

Miranda gave a quiet little chuckle of pride at her indomitable mother. Mrs. Lowell maintained her stiff smile.

"Mrs. Lowell," Miranda interjected, making all the appropriate gestures, "may I introduce my mother, Bertha Hamilton. Mama, Eunice Lowell."

"*Enchantée*." Mrs. Lowell gracefully extended her hand.

"It's good to finally meet you, too." Mrs. Hamilton seized the other lady's hand and started pumping it.

"A pity you couldn't have made the acquaintance of my husband." Mrs. Lowell continued to smile while she tactfully pulled away from Mrs. Hamilton's friendly grasp. "The late Mr. Lowell was descended from the Plymouth Lowells, and related on his mother's side to the Bradfords and the Hawthorns. Of course, my father, the late Harold Kittredge Madison, was from Quincy, Massachusetts. My mother was a Wilson—one of the Danforth Wilsons."

Mrs. Hamilton was staring blankly as Mrs. Lowell continued to rattle off her extensive genealogy.

"Miranda didn't mention much of that in all her letters. But she's told me so much else about you," Mrs. Hamilton continued with undaunted cheerfulness. "I'm glad to have the chance to get to know you better before the wedding."

"Indeed," Mrs. Lowell replied. "I greatly doubt we shall see much of each other afterward."

"Oh, I wouldn't say that." With a broad grin Mrs. Hamilton glanced up in the direction from which the train had just come. "Those tracks run both ways."

Miranda watched Mrs. Lowell's smile grow stiffer.

"We'll be coming at Christmas. We can't wait to meet

all the Lowells, and the Wilsons, and the Bradfords, and all your friends, too."

Her father stepped up and clapped Charles heartily on the back.

"I'm especially glad to meet you, young man." Mr. Hamilton gave a deep chuckle. "After all, I have to make sure you're the right fellow for my little girl."

Miranda wanted to laugh again as she watched her father assume his most stern, intimidating look. He'd managed to wrestle a fortune in silver out of the side of a mountain with all the determination behind that glare. He'd even managed to make her behave—occasionally. Now she was having a good time watching Charles learn to deal with it.

"You will be able to support her in the style in which she's become accustomed, won't you?" Sam demanded.

"Oh, yes, indeed, sir. I assure you, sir, I certainly have the means. I desire nothing more than your daughter's complete happiness." Nodding his head vigorously, Charles vowed, "I shall take very good care of your daughter."

"I shall see that he does," Mrs. Lowell pronounced with great seriousness. Then she turned to Miranda. "And vice versa."

"Oh, there'll be no vice in my daughter's household," Mr. Hamilton declared sternly in what Miranda knew to be his best mock hayseed accent.

"We raised her proper-like," her mother chimed in.

Miranda could see the orneriness dancing in her father's eyes. She watched her mother's eyes twinkling with shared mischief. She'd always had a strong suspicion that their sense of humor was one of the things that had kept them together—and happy—for so many years.

But Charles and his mother didn't laugh. Didn't they get the joke? Miranda wondered. She knew that they had a sense of humor. At least, she thought they did. She'd seen them laughing at parties.

Maybe they were reserved in public. Maybe they were reserved because they didn't know her parents very well yet. Maybe it would all improve once they got home. I hope, she added, and tried to cross her fingers on both hands.

Well, if Mrs. Lowell's criticism of her family's fashions and censure of their sense of humor were the only things she had to worry about, she'd still consider herself lucky, Miranda decided. But she feared she was clutching at straws.

Mr. Hamilton cleared his throat and placed his arm across Charles's shoulder. "Well, Charlie, my boy—"

"Charles," he corrected cautiously.

"I guess we ought to go see to the baggage. If I know my Miranda, she'll have brought along enough trunks to fill a whole boxcar. I've got a sneaking suspicion your mother packs about the same way, too, doesn't she, son?"

"Well, sir, I didn't actually count. I . . . I think her maid packed for her anyway."

He was still smiling, but Miranda could see the uncertainty in his eyes as her father drew him off toward the rear of the train. Was he doubting the wisdom of going off with Sam in an unfamiliar town? Or was he doubting the wisdom of marrying her?

Her mother and Mrs. Lowell were standing there, staring at each other. She was certain her mother didn't know any of the people Mrs. Lowell enjoyed gossiping about, so they wouldn't have much to discuss there. She greatly doubted that Mrs. Lowell could offer her mother any helpful hints on putting up this year's crop of pole beans.

There ought to be something she could do or say to relieve the awkward silence.

She ostentatiously looked at her surroundings. She pointed out the large brick train station, with its green roof, lots of white gingerbread trim all around, and a huge clock set up on top. As she recalled, it was one of the loudest clocks she'd ever heard.

"I can't believe it," she said, and heaved a very audible gasp of awe and wonder. "Nothing's changed since I left."

"What did you expect, Miranda? You were back here only last summer," her mother reminded her.

"Oh, yes . . . well . . . well, a lot of things can change in a year's time, but nothing's changed here," she asserted, still looking around as if to prove her point.

Then suddenly she spotted him!

No, it couldn't be. Wendell Williams had left Grasonville three years ago. Occasionally, he'd sent a letter to his family, and his half sister, Sally Pickett, had passed the news on to her. But Sally hadn't mentioned anything about his return in any of her letters. Del had never written to her personally. Maybe he hadn't wanted her to know he was coming home. Maybe he didn't want her to know anything more about him ever.

Miranda could only stand there and stare silently after him. When she was little, she thought she'd be spending the rest of her life with him. Then she'd feared she'd never see him again. Yet, there he was, big as life, boldly striding across the station platform.

His face was much tanner and his fair hair appeared lighter than she remembered. Was that what Texas had done for him? His shoulders seemed broader. He'd worked hard enough on his family's farm before. What else had he been doing while he was away?

But he looked directly at her and then moved on without the slightest hint of recognition.

Her heart plummeted into the cold pit of her stomach. She knew she'd been a real pest to him when she was little—following him around all the time. She was chagrined to recall that she'd ever done anything so foolish. She took a little consolation in the fact that she'd been a mere child at the time. But she never thought she'd been such a nuisance that he'd want to pretend he'd never even known her.

Miranda pressed her lips together. She felt the muscles of her jaw clench. She blinked hard. It was the bright sunlight after the darkness inside the train car. That was why her eyes were threatening to tear.

Del just kept walking. Well, if that was the way the

narrow-minded, unforgiving, ignorant farm boy wanted it, she thought with a proud lift of her head, well, then, so be it. She had a perfectly wonderful future ahead of her. She didn't need him.

She began to turn back to her mother.

"Del! Del Williams!" Mrs. Hamilton shouted, and waved her hands high over her head. "Halloo! Over here! Del!"

Mrs. Lowell stared at her with disbelief.

Oh, mother! Miranda wanted to bury her head in her purse—or throw herself onto the train tracks.

Del's head lifted and he looked around. As soon as he spotted Mrs. Hamilton, his face broke into a wide grin. He shouldered his way across the crowded platform directly toward her.

"Mrs. Hamilton, why are you . . . ?" Out of the corner of his eye he noticed her. He left his question incomplete. His jaw dropped. He stared at her. "Miranda! Is that you?"

She nodded.

"Well, I'll be dipped!"

He appraised her from head to toe. In all the years they'd known each other, he'd rarely paid her that much attention. Back then she'd have appreciated it more than he'd ever know. Now it didn't matter at all.

"I didn't even recognize you," he told her. He chuckled as he gestured up and down her body. "Your hair, your clothes." He laughed. "That hat!"

She thought she looked very stylish, even if she was a little bedraggled after traveling all day. Oh, what did Del know, anyway?

Had her appearance surprised him that much? Perhaps he was telling the truth. Perhaps he really had ignored her because he hadn't recognized her, not because he wanted to avoid her and found it impossible after her mother had caused such a ruckus.

"What are you doing at the train station?" he demanded.

He was still smiling, but there was a cold caution in his

eyes. Was the foolish man expecting her to jump around his neck right there on the platform?

"What have you been up to for the past three years without having me around to pester the living daylights out of? What are you up to now? Probably no good. Definitely trouble."

Shut up, Del, before I throw you onto the train tracks. She smiled stiffly and replied, "I just arrived from Boston."

"Boston? What were you doing in Boston?"

Making beans and tea, you fool.

"I've been going to school there for the past two years," she informed him.

Obviously, none of his letters to his family had included any questions about her, she thought with just a touch of pique, or he'd have already known that. And why hadn't Sally mentioned her, anyway?

"School, huh?"

"Yes."

"Gee, Miranda, I thought you already knew everything."

I knew enough to get over caring for you, you big waste of time. Instead, she smiled and replied coolly, "There's more to learn than you've ever considered."

Del cleared his throat. "So, they've taught you everything they could—or that you'd let them—and you've come home to impress everyone?" he asked with a chuckle.

"Not exactly," she told him. She could feel her smile stiffening, even as she spoke. She had a bad feeling about announcing this to Del. "I've returned home to be married."

"Geez, Miranda!" he exclaimed. He gave a humorless bark of a laugh and backed up several steps. "I should've known you wouldn't take long, but this must be some kind of record. After all this time, are you still threatening me with marriage?"

Miranda could feel the hot color rushing to her face.

Maybe they'd all think the redness came from the heat of
the day or the excitement of this happy reunion.

"No."

She tried to keep the tone of her voice as flat as
possible.

"My appearance isn't the only thing that's changed in
two years."

She was bound and determined to make sure he knew
this in no uncertain terms.

"I'm not the goggle-eyed chatterbox infatuated with
the boy next door that you remember," she told him with
cold condescension. "You make me sound like such a
sinister, conniving vixen."

Thank goodness Charles wasn't here to witness this
embarrassing exposure of her childish infatuation!

She didn't want to laugh in the face of Del's rude
question. She wouldn't want him to think she had ever
taken her feelings for him as a joke. To her, her girlish
affection for him had been all too real.

She didn't want to appear too angry, either. Then he
might mistakenly believe she still cared about him. Not
at all. Not anymore. No, indeed!

His rude outburst only served to reinforce what she
already suspected. What had she ever seen in him
anyway? she wondered. He was just a poor farmer—
unschooled and uncouth. His boots were scuffed across
the toes and worn at the heels. His trousers were
threadbare at the knees and the tops of the pockets. His
hair curled around his ears and hung down the back of his
neck just a little longer than he'd usually worn it. He
probably hadn't even opened a book since he'd left
school.

"Uh, yeah . . . sure, Miranda. So, what are you
doing here?"

"I've come home to be married in my own church,"
she explained. "That's what's customary in polite
society—in case you weren't aware."

"Even my cousin Adelaide and her husband Joshua are

arriving from Ohio just for the wedding," Mrs. Hamilton said excitedly.

Miranda maintained her composure. "Then I'll be moving back to Boston to reside with my husband— Charles Madison Lowell the Third."

"Who?"

"Charles Madison Lowell the Third," Miranda repeated more slowly.

Del reached up and scratched the back of his head. "*All* of them?"

She assumed the haughtiest demeanor Mrs. Bigelow had ever taught her students in Deportment Class.

"Don't be absurd," she said icily.

Mrs. Lowell gave a polite, yet quite noticeable cough. Miranda turned to her.

"Mrs. Lowell, may I introduce Wendell Williams? Just a friend from my childhood," she told her with a stressed lightness. "His family owns the farm that borders my family's property."

"Pleased to meet you, ma'am," Del remarked, doffing his weather-beaten hat.

Mrs. Lowell gave Del a polite smirk and a slight nod of the head.

"Del, this is my fiancé's mother." Maybe he'd behave himself better if he knew this, Miranda thought.

He still didn't waste much time on the reserved lady. He turned again to Miranda.

"So, this Lowell fellow's the lucky man, huh?"

His manners didn't improve much, either. "Yes, Charles is the lucky man."

She wanted to smack Del alongside his hard head and yell, *It could've been you, you big dummy! But you were too stubborn, too thick-headed, too eager to go out and make your own way in the world, to see what a really great wife I'd have been for you!*

But she'd rather eat live, crunchy, squirming bugs— antennas and all—than to let Del know how he'd broken her heart when she was just a little girl.

So she stood there with her hands folded politely in

front of her waist. She realized, with overwhelming horror, that she was wearing the same rigid pasteboard smile as Mrs. Lowell. Was this required attire for all society matrons? she wondered. She wouldn't turn into the aloof, elderly lady, she determined—well, at least not until she was much, much older. But, well, right now, she figured that was the best that Del deserved.

She and Del stood on the crowded platform, watching each other warily for what felt to Miranda like an eternity. He didn't seem to have much to say to her, but then again, he never had. She certainly didn't have anything to say to him, not anymore. How odd to realize that, without pestering him about marriage, she really had very little in common with Del Williams.

"But enough about us. What brings you back to town, Del?" Mrs. Hamilton broke in.

Del shrugged. "Just a visit, I guess."

"When you left the farm after your mother—Lord rest her soul—passed away, we all thought . . . well, boys need to become men the best way they know how—without getting the tar beat out of them. But when you were gone so long, we thought we'd never see you again."

Miranda had felt the same way. She'd determined then to put him out of her mind for good. He should certainly be able to tell from the way she was acting that she'd succeeded rather well.

She looked around the platform. "Where did Papa and Charles go with our baggage? Shouldn't we be searching for them? Isn't it time to go?" She'd had quite enough of Del for the time being. She had to find some way to escape from him.

Mrs. Hamilton was glancing around the platform, too. But she was more intent on her own questions. "Where's your family, Del? Didn't they come to meet you?"

"They . . . they don't know I've come back yet."

"Didn't you wire them?"

"Well, no. That takes money, and . . . well, there was the train ticket to buy."

"Oh, I understand completely," Mrs. Hamilton said. "But since you're going in that direction anyway, can we offer you a ride?"

Oh, Mother! Just when she was trying to get away from him!

Miranda watched Del hesitate. Did he hate her so much that he didn't even want to ride in the wagon with her the short distance from the town to their farms?

"We're going that way anyway," Mrs. Hamilton urged.

"I appreciate your offer, but I've got some business in town I've got to see to first. I don't want to hold you up."

"Oh, well," Mrs. Hamilton replied, with a shrug of her shoulders. "I guess you've got to do what you need to."

"Oh, yes, indeed, Del," Miranda said. "Don't let us keep you from your pressing business."

What business in town could possibly be more important to Del than seeing his own family? she wondered. It used to be nothing was. Apparently she wasn't the only one who had changed a lot by going away. At least her changes had been for the better.

"Are you back to stay, Del?" Mrs. Hamilton asked.

Miranda held her breath as she waited for his answer.

"I guess it depends on a lot of things."

She waited to see if he'd elaborate on his reasons.

But he just said, "I guess I really ought to be moving on, and let you all get home and get settled in." He started to back away. "I'll be seeing—"

"Del, before you go," Mrs. Hamilton said hurriedly.

He paused, but Miranda didn't think he looked as if he wanted to stop at all.

"You know, there are going to be a lot of parties for Miranda and her fiancé. You're certainly invited to each and every one."

"Thanks, Mrs. Hamilton."

Miranda noted that he didn't say whether he'd be attending or not. She also noted that she was way too concerned with finding out the answer to that question.

"Please tell Mr. Hamilton I said hello," Del said.

"Oh, you'll see him enough when you come over for

all the parties," Mrs. Hamilton told him with great certainty.

He just nodded. Miranda doubted he'd be showing up at any of her parties.

Don't put yourself out for me or anything.

"Nice meeting you, Mrs. Lowell," he added.

Well, he could be polite, Miranda noted with surprise. He waved at them, then turned to leave.

What? She watched him with shock and—no, not dismay. She refused ever to admit to feeling dismay where Del was concerned. Not a "Nice seeing you again," or "Best wishes on your engagement," or even a "Don't trip over your own shadow, stupid." Not one word to her.

The miserable, ignorant clod! Even after she'd made it abundantly clear that she had no more interest in him than she might have in old Mr. Carter, who still ran the barbershop, he was still avoiding her like the plague.

Well, after her wedding, she'd never see Del again. She'd managed to survive without him so far. She could live without him forever.

Then he stopped and looked directly at her. His eyes appeared even more blue than she remembered. But his eyes still held a coldness that made her spine shiver and her heart contract with the slightest twinge of sorrow and regret.

"I guess I'll see you around then, too, Miranda."

She had the awful feeling he spoke to her as a mere afterthought. She smiled pleasantly at him anyway, and nodded.

Not if I see you first.

2

LESTER MARTIN'S TELEGRAM hadn't told Del much—just that the man had something really important to tell him. He couldn't imagine Mr. Martin having anything important to say—let alone to say to him. And why had the lawyer insisted that he could only tell him in person?

All the while he'd sat waiting in the man's office, Del had worried. This had better be good—darn good, he'd mumbled to himself as he fidgeted with the brim of his battered hat. The job he'd left hadn't been much, but at least he was working. He could only hope they'd hire him back when he returned.

Now? Heck, he'd tell that grouchy, penny-pinching, cantankerous ranch foreman what he could do with his spurs! Sideways! He'd buy the ranch and fire the ornery cuss!

In all his born days he'd *never* expected to receive the kind of news Mr. Martin had just told him!

"But . . . but I . . . I didn't even know the man," Del protested, stammering badly in his shock. Not only was it difficult to speak, it was hard to see straight and keep breathing.

"Are people you don't know in the habit of leaving you an estate worth almost a million dollars?"

"Well, barely," Del amended.

Mr. Martin grinned smugly at him over steepled fingers. There had been a hint of a laugh in the lawyer's voice, but Del could see the envy still flashing in his beady little eyes.

"The last time I saw Henry Richardson . . ." Del reached up to scratch his head, as if that would help him to remember. "Heck, I guess the last time I took any notice of the man was maybe twelve, thirteen years ago."

"Well, he certainly kept you in mind."

Del shook his head.

"I can't imagine why. I mean, I can't imagine why he ever felt there was any kind of bond between us."

"Me, neither. But apparently he did."

"He courted my mother when I was just a little kid," Del offered what explanation he could. "But after Ma married Tom Pickett, he never came around anymore."

"Can't say as I blame him," Mr. Martin said with a laugh.

"Yeah, I guess not."

"Being in town, I guess I saw him a bit more than you did," Mr. Martin said. "I'd watch him sometimes, just going back and forth, from the bank to his mansion, and back again. As the years went by, he became more and more of a hermit. But these last couple of years I don't think anybody but Mrs. Cartwright saw him."

"Who?"

"His housekeeper, for years and years."

"See, I didn't even pay that much attention to anything he did," Del pointed out.

Mr. Martin just shrugged.

"Wait a minute. Now I remember. Didn't Mr. Richardson have a gardener, or handyman, or something like that?"

"Something like that," Mr. Martin replied.

"Yeah, Mr. Wilkins. Red Wilkins. That was his name."

"Heck, Red Wilkins died years ago, Del."

"Oh."

Del was still feeling a little guilty. He was glad to have

the money, no doubt. He'd be plum nutty not to! But how could he take money he hadn't done anything to earn?

"Didn't Mr. Richardson have any family?"

"His wife and only son died a long time ago."

"I know, but did he have . . . well . . ." Del hesitated. What he was about to ask really wasn't the sort of thing to ask about the man who had just bequeathed him almost a million dollars. "Did he have maybe . . . a child he didn't talk about in public?"

Del's suggestion met with the heartiest laugh he'd ever heard from Mr. Martin.

"Yeah, I guess that was a pretty dumb question, considering it's Mr. Richardson we're talking about." After a pause to let Mr. Martin catch his breath, Del continued, "How about brothers or sisters? Nieces and nephews?"

"He mentioned some a long time ago, but I don't think they got along very well," Mr. Martin said. He chuckled. "I can't imagine why. I don't think he ever tried to write to any of them. In all these years none of them ever showed up here for a visit. He didn't bother to leave them anything, so I guess it doesn't much matter now."

"I guess not." Del shrugged. "I . . . I just wanted to be fair."

"He left everything to you, Del. Lock, stock, and barrel. I guess that's about as fair as life gets. Hell, more than fair! I suppose you could say he considered you the son he never had." Mr. Martin gave a hearty laugh at his own joke.

Del gave a weak chuckle. He'd always sort of felt sorry for Mr. Richardson.

Then, gradually, he began to realize that all his questions had been answered, all his uncertainties banished, all his reservations abolished. He also began to realize very clearly exactly what Mr. Richardson had done for him. He looked down to study the floor between his feet.

"Gee, I wish I'd known about this sooner."

"He didn't want you—or anybody else—to know while he was still alive."

"Why not? I'd have maybe mowed his lawn . . . or shoveled his walk . . . or just gone for a visit . . . played some checkers or dominoes."

"Oh, come on, Del. This is Henry Richardson we're talking about. He didn't want any of that maudlin, sentimental, sociable stuff."

"Yeah, I guess you've got a good point there," Del admitted. Then he shook his head. "Still, I wish . . . but, well . . . It's too late now. Too late even to let him know how very grateful I am."

"With all that money, why don't you hire a medium? Have a séance?" Mr. Martin suggested with a laugh.

Dell laughed, too. "Heck, I don't believe in all that bell-ringing, candle-burning, wall-rapping, table-turning, emanations from the ether, spirit stuff."

"Me, neither." Mr. Martin kept the smile on his face, but his eyes grew sharp and calculating. "So, what do you intend to do with your newfound fortune instead?"

"After paying your fee?" Del asked with a wry chuckle.

"You're a wealthy man, Del. You don't have to work for your money anymore. You need to make your money work for you. I'd be real happy to handle any investments— stocks and things."

He watched Mr. Martin's eyes brighten with greed. He thought he looked like a little banty rooster, just waiting to pounce on some poor, unsuspecting worm. Del didn't have any intention of being that worm.

"Oh, right now, I think I can find a few other things to do with my money."

Like repaying the friend he'd borrowed the money from to buy the ticket to Grasonville.

"I don't want to sound like a Dutch uncle or anything, but I'd like to warn you against throwing it all away on foolishness—whiskey and wild women."

"Oh, no, sir." Since when did a lawyer get to sound like Reverend Knutson?

Del eyed the worn toes of his old boots. He could feel

through his sock where the sole of the right one had split. He'd be able to buy a new pair now. Two pairs. Three! That wouldn't be foolish. Not at all.

He could see his knee beginning to poke through his trousers. It wouldn't hurt to buy a new suit of clothing.

Not to mention buying the biggest steak he could find, smothered in onions, with fried potatoes and apple pie, at the finest restaurant in town. Heck, he'd take his whole family! He'd missed them all so much. That wouldn't be foolish, either.

Trying to make his own way in the world hadn't turned out as easy as he'd thought it would. But he'd sooner eat live bugs—antennas and all—than admit it to anyone.

Del was sorry anybody had to die, but as far as he was concerned, Mr. Richardson couldn't have chosen a better time.

"What do I have to do to get the money?" he asked.

"You don't have to do a thing," Mr. Martin answered. "Just go see Mr. Hendricks—he's the bank president now—anytime you need it. I'm sure, once the news gets out, every merchant in town will be delighted to extend you credit."

Del laughed. "My mother'd turn over in her grave if she could hear you even mention my buying anything on credit."

Mr. Martin coughed. "Ah, yes, well. At any rate, what do you intend to do with the house?"

"I haven't decided yet."

"If you should decide you want to sell it, I'd be more than happy to handle all that for you."

"I'll bet you would."

Sell that big old house, Del pondered. When he was very little, he recalled riding past the place with his mother every Wednesday on their way into town to buy groceries at what used to be Pete Finnerty's General Store, until Mr. Finnerty tried to shoot some of the townspeople—his parents included—just so he could own the land the railroad was coming through on.

Del remembered Mr. Richardson always patting the

top of his head, and how much he hated it. Nevertheless, he still hoped his mother would marry Mr. Richardson just so he could move into the huge place and have lots of other children over to play with. Even now, it might be fun to live there—for just a little while.

He chuckled. "No. I don't think I'll sell it just yet. I think I might see what I've gotten myself into before I go jumping out of it right away. After all, I've never owned a mansion before."

"Well, I guess I ought to warn you then, Del. Mr. Richardson didn't do much these past couple of years to keep up the place."

"I appreciate the warning, but I think I'd still like to see the house for myself first."

"Suit yourself." Mr. Martin reached into his desk drawer. "I guess you'll be needing these, then." He pulled out a ring with several small keys, and one large brass key, dangling from it.

Grinning, Del took the ring. He didn't put the keys right into his pocket. He hefted them up and down for a moment, just enjoying the jingling sound they made—an audible reminder that he now owned the house.

Then Del rose and extended his hand. The lawyer's hand felt all cold and slimy, like a peeled potato, and he didn't seem to want to let go. Del had the feeling Mr. Martin believed if he could hold on to him long enough, he might be able to squeeze more money out of him.

"Thanks, Mr. Martin." He pumped the man's hand hard, then slipped out of his grasp. "Right now I think I need to go see my family."

As he left the lawyer's office, Del wondered if seeing his family after all this time was going to be as difficult as seeing Miranda again.

The pesky little hoyden hadn't grown any taller, but then, she'd always been a tiny little thing. Her hair was still as blond as ever, but she had it fixed up on top of her head, and she'd perched a goofy-looking little hat on top. She probably thought it made her look all grown up and sophisticated.

That dress she'd had on certainly was fancy-looking. It made her waist look so tiny. He didn't recall her bosoms being so . . . so evident, either.

However, he did seem to recall her once warning him that he'd pay a whole lot more attention to her once she got bosoms. He had to admit, she did look a whole lot more appealing with them. But no, he'd never admit he was paying the pesky little show-off the least bit of attention—for any reason!

He had to admit, no matter how much she'd changed, one thing about Miranda always remained the same. She was still full of surprises.

"Well, isn't this a surprise!" Sally Pickett stood on the front porch and greeted Del with a wry grin.

He pushed open the gate of the whitewashed picket fence covered with bright blue morning glories. He flung down his weather-beaten carpetbag and broke into a run toward her. He took the front porch steps two at a time. He grabbed his half sister around the waist, lifted her, and spun her round and round.

"Put me down!" she exclaimed, kicking her legs and pushing with both hands against his chest. "You're acting like a consarn fool!"

"It's good to see you again, too, Sis."

He set her on her feet and planted a big kiss on her cheek.

"Why didn't you warn us you were coming?" she demanded, pushing him away.

He shrugged. "I'm assuming you were the one who told Mr. Martin how to get a hold of me down in Texas."

"Yeah."

"Well, then, you should've also figured out I was coming home."

Sally propped her fists on her hips and glared at him. "I've been figuring you'd be coming home *sometime* ever since you left. But it still would've been nice of you to let us know, *personally*, exactly *when*. Wouldn't it?"

Del shrugged. "Yeah, I guess so."

"Anyway, what makes you think Mr. Martin let me know why he wants to talk to you?"

He couldn't believe his own sister didn't know about his inheritance. Considering Mr. Martin, he couldn't believe the entire town didn't know.

Before he could reply, his younger sister bolted out the door and flew into his outstretched arms.

"Del!"

Alice planted a kiss on his cheek.

"Boy, you don't put up nearly the struggle Sally does," he commented as he disentangled himself from her embrace. "You laugh a lot more, too. Not to mention how much you've grown up."

Alice laughed again and preened her long blond hair.

"Yahoo!" the young man charging across the barnyard exclaimed. "Del! Hey, Del!"

"Hey, Will!"

Glancing back over his shoulder, Will called, "Horace! C'mon, Tommy, you slowpoke. Del's home!"

A lanky adolescent and a young boy burst from the barn. Laughing, they raced each other toward the house. Del readily recognized his half brothers' faces. But he'd never imagined they could grow so tall in the short time he'd been gone.

Horace, with his long-legged stride, reached Del first and threw his arms around him. "Del! You're home!" His voice cracked with excitement.

"Dang!" Del exclaimed. He held his hand up to the top of the boy's head. "You're almost as tall as I am." He turned to Tommy. He was so tempted to ruffle his fingers through the boy's fair hair, but he remembered how much he used to hate it when anyone did that to him just because he was short and they were tall. "You're catching up fast, Tommy."

The boy grinned bashfully and scuffed the toe of his shoe through the dirt.

"Pa! Pa!" Will called into the house. "Come on. What's keeping you?"

"I'm going as fast as I can," Tom Pickett replied as he

emerged from the house. He threw both arms around his stepson. "It's good to have you home."

"It's good to be home again."

Even though the older man clapped him heartily on the back, Del couldn't help noticing how some of the hardness had gone out of his hardworking stepfather's arms. Well, Tom had always maintained it was better to wear out than to rust out. It looked as if he were trying to live up to his own philosophy.

"Come on. Let's go inside." Tom motioned to him. "Sit down. It's been so long. . . ."

As Del followed him into the house, he noticed how Tom's hair had gotten a lot grayer. His stepfather also eased himself a little more slowly into his usual chair by the fireside. Del didn't remember his energetic stepfather wanting, or needing, to sit so frequently, either. Three years had brought a lot of changes to everyone.

He felt the familiar pang of grief as he eyed the empty rocking chair by the fire. While he was working in Texas, it was easy to imagine his mother still alive and sitting there at the end of the day, doing her mending. Now that he was back, it struck him all the more deeply that she really was gone. But the curiosity of his brothers and sisters wouldn't allow him to dwell too long on his grief.

"What was it like working on a cattle ranch?" Horace demanded.

"We read all your letters," Tommy said.

"*Dozens* of times," Sally added sarcastically.

"But what was Texas like?" Horace repeated.

"Did you punch cows?" Tommy demanded eagerly.

"Did they punch you back?" Alice asked with a little giggle.

"You don't know *anything* about cowboy talk, you silly old girl," Tommy scolded. Turning back to Del, he asked, "Did you brand the cattle? Can you work a lasso like in the Wild West show?"

"Will you teach us?" Horace asked.

"Hey, hey!" Tom exclaimed to get his curious children's attention. "Give the man a chance to wet his whistle before you drown him with this deluge of questions."

Sally poured coffee from the enamel pot on the back of the big black cast-iron stove into a thick mug. From the way she shoved it toward him, he had a sneaking suspicion maybe she was still just a tad irked at him.

He glanced toward the front door. There was a lingering suspicion in the back of his mind. Something was still missing. He just couldn't figure out what it was.

"You're not going back there, are you?" Alice asked. Del could see the apprehension in her blue eyes.

"Why'd you come back anyway?" Sally demanded.

"Sally!" Tom exclaimed. "What a question!"

"Oh, Pa, you know darn good and well he wouldn't be here now if Mr. Martin hadn't sent for him."

"That's not true," Del protested. He should've remembered Sally was pretty good at carrying a grudge. But what was she still mad about?

He glanced toward the doorway again, as if he was expecting something to break the tension.

"You know I'm right, Pa," she insisted.

"Sally, be fair," Tom admonished.

"Was it fair when he left you to run this farm without him?"

"But . . . we talked about all that before I left," Del offered his excuses. "I thought I'd make my fortune. It sure worked for Mr. Hamilton."

"But it took seven years! And it worked for him. Did it work for you?"

"Not . . . in Texas," Del replied hesitantly. "Anyway, I didn't leave Pa all alone. He and Will . . . and Horace. . . ."

"They were just kids." She gave her own finish to his numbled excuses. "Tommy still is."

"Am not!" Tommy protested. "I'm nine!"

"And you and Alice," Del continued.

"We've managed," Tom interceded. "We've managed very well."

Del tried not to look again at his mother's empty chair.

"Anyway, you know it was hard for me to stay here after Ma died."

Sally stalked closer. She glared directly into his face. "It was hard on *all* of us."

Del detected very little sympathy in her voice, and an awful lot of coldness in her eyes.

"Do you think it was easy for me to take over the running of the whole house when I was just seventeen? Do you think it was easy for me to stay home, cooking and cleaning, taking care of everyone else, when I could've been out having fun with my friends? When I could've found myself a husband?"

"But . . . but . . ."

"Did you ever stop to think about anybody but yourself?"

"Enough, Sally," Tom declared.

Sally shrugged and stomped off to stand closer to the stove, as if the hard cast iron would give her support. Or maybe, Del thought, she'd spent so much time by the stove, her heart had turned into the same material.

At last Tom's question broke the silence. "So, what does Mr. Martin want with you?"

From her corner Sally offered, "I'll bet it's got something to do with those rotten friends of yours."

"*My* rotten friends?" Del repeated. "What rotten friends?"

"Allen Douglas and Jimmy Walters." Sally grimaced with disdain.

"They're no friends of mine!" Del declared as emphatically as he could.

"Horse puckies! They've been declaring you were their best buddy ever since that time you beat the living daylights out of both of them."

"They deserved it," Del defended himself. "They'd been picking on me—and every other littler kid—every time anyone of us came into town."

"Fat lot of good you did," Sally complained. "The only person they stopped picking on was you."

"Yeah, they were a pair of persistently ornery cusses. It's a wonder they weren't thrown in jail years ago."

"Or shot. But, no." Sally gave a little snort of disgust—or maybe disappointment. "They're still hanging around the saloons—"

"Sprinkling sawdust on the vomit," Horace elaborated enthusiastically. "Sweeping up the broken glass after fights."

"I guess they've got to do something to earn a living," Del offered.

"They're usually the ones who start the fights," Will told him.

"I guess they haven't changed much." Del figured they were probably the only ones who hadn't.

"They're always in some kind of stupid trouble," Will continued.

"Stupid trouble?"

"You know, the kind you've got to be really, really stupid to get into and not be able to figure your way out of."

"Oh." Del nodded.

"So, if it doesn't have anything to do with your rotten friends, what could Mr. Martin want with you?" Sally asked.

"Well, I stopped in to see him on the way home from the train station," Del admitted.

"Yeah, I sort of figured we wouldn't be your first priority," Sally grumbled.

Del decided not to go into that all over again.

He reached up and rubbed the back of his neck. He decided he ought to break this kind of news very slowly.

"It seems that Mr. Richardson mentioned me in his will."

"Why on earth would he do that?" Sally demanded. "I wouldn't even mention you in *my* will."

"Considering you've got next to nothing, I don't see much of a loss there," Will offered.

Sally met her brother's ridicule with a sneer. "I don't know what you're all laughing about," she grumbled, tightening her arms over her chest. "None of you has any more than I've got."

"So what did he leave you?" Will asked.

Del took a deep breath before answering. "Everything."

Complete silence.

Tom cleared his throat and asked, "What exactly does 'everything' entail?"

"Everything," Del repeated more slowly, and with great emphasis. "The mansion, the money—"

Alice let out a squeal of glee and began to dance around the table. Will, Horace, and Tommy whooped and took turns clapping Del heartily on the back until he was afraid they'd kill him before he had the chance to spend all his money.

Sally leaned against the wall, one hand clutching at her heart. Her mouth hung wide open. At last she managed to murmur, "You lucky bastard!"

Del joined in the laughter. "Yeah, I guess so."

He glanced toward the front door again, but he still couldn't figure out why he'd want to do a thing like that at a time like this.

Tom was smiling and shaking his head with disbelief. "Well, if that isn't the darnedest thing I've ever heard. I sort of wish we'd have known. Maybe I'd have been a little friendlier to the man."

"I don't think he would've wanted you to," Del offered.

Tom chuckled. "Yeah, from what I recall of him, you're probably right. When I married your mama, he was sort of a poor loser."

"So, I guess you'll be taking yourself over there to live," Sally muttered. "I can't say I blame you. Don't let the screen door hit you on your way out."

"I don't think so."

"Why not?"

"At least, not yet." Why in the world was he watching that darn door?

"Why not?"

"Why?" Del countered. "Are you that eager to get rid of me again?"

"Tarnation, no!" Sally exclaimed. "Now that you're back, I figure you owe us. There's a whole lot of work around here—three years' worth—for you to catch up on."

"Don't worry. I'll do what I can," he promised.

"What you can?" she repeated angrily. "You'll do what you owe us."

"All right. I will."

"Doggone right you will," Sally muttered, turning away from him.

Del glanced at the door once more. At last he realized why he'd been staring at the empty doorway.

Wait a minute! Shocked, he called an abrupt halt to his thoughts and gave himself a stern mental shake. He was *not* looking for Miranda Hamilton!

When they were children, it would have to have been a really bad storm to keep her from rushing over the field from her house to his. She'd probably spent more time at his house than at her own. She was a pest, but he'd gotten kind of used to having her around.

Wait! Stop! he corrected himself. He was *not* disappointed that she wasn't here.

Miranda had changed a lot. The cold, elegant young woman he'd seen at the train station today would never rush anywhere—and especially not to *him*.

"Okay, then. The first thing you can do is get that tattered bag I guess you call a suitcase off the front step," Sally ordered.

"Huh?"

"You heard me. Stop daydreaming and get to work."

Del rose quickly and made for the beat-up carpetbag. By the time he came back, Tom, his brothers, and Alice had scattered to other chores.

"Where should I put it?" Del asked, holding up the bag.

"Don't tempt me, Del," she warned. "Just put it in Will's room for the time being. I guess you can stay here till you get Mr. Richardson's house in some kind of shape to move into."

"What makes you think I'll be moving in there?"

She laughed. "You are, aren't you?"

He could hardly argue with her when she spoke the truth.

Coming back from Will's room, he stood in the middle of the kitchen, grinning at her. "Now what?"

"Go out to the barn and help Will set the bales aside and lay out the tables," she directed.

He stood there for a moment.

"Go on. Go on," she urged, shooing him out the door. "I don't have all day, you know. That little intrusion of yours already put me way behind schedule."

"We only used to push back the bales and lay out the tables for parties and things—to make more room for dancing."

"Yeah, I know," she replied.

His face broke into a wide grin. "Sally, I thought you were mad at me. This is mighty nice of you—"

"Don't get all teary-eyed now. It's not for you, you big dummy," Sally told him. "Maybe I'd have had time to get something together if you'd given me a little more notice."

"So, what's the big occasion?" he asked cautiously. He had a sinking feeling in the pit of his stomach that he already knew the answer.

"Tonight's our turn to have a big welcome-home party for Miranda Hamilton."

Del looked around. There was no way out of this one.

3

MIRANDA THOUGHT SHE had recovered completely from the first shock of seeing Del again. But the aggravating son-of-a-gun was standing right in the doorway to the barn. She couldn't even attend her own party without having to walk directly past him.

Since the party was at his family's home, she also supposed it would look awful rude, at the very least, not to greet him.

But she refused to speak to him any more than she absolutely had to. After all, he was the one who had wanted her out of his life in the first place.

As she approached him, she tightened her grip on Charles's arm. He was safe, stable, and secure. *He* was always there for her. *He'd* never go running off to Texas.

"Hello, Del," she said in the coolest tones she could manage. "It was so gracious of your family to invite my fiancé and me this evening."

It's for darn sure you never would have been smart enough to think of it on your own.

Del laughed and glanced around the crowded barn. "You and just about everybody else in town."

He looked different somehow. She knew he'd had a bath because he smelled a lot better than he had at the railroad station. His tanned cheeks were smooth from a recent shave. He'd gotten a haircut, too. Was that the pressing business he'd had in town? she wondered. Considering Del, that was about as intense as his life got.

He'd changed his clothes, too. They looked brand-new. So did his boots. Had he brought them along with him? He hadn't been carrying much baggage. Or had he just bought them at Nichols's Haberdashery, or at Thompson's across the street? What did it matter? You could dress him up, but you couldn't take him out.

Well, she'd done her duty by acknowledging him. Now it was time to move along.

"Come, Charles," she said directly to him, completely ignoring Del. "There are so many people—"

"So, who's your friend there?" Del asked, nodding toward Charles.

Del was actually initiating a conversation with her! She was surprised—and suspicious. He was a quiet fellow, and he obviously didn't want to have much to do with her, but he never did anything without some reason.

"You've already made the acquaintance of Mrs. Lowell."

"Ma'am." He nodded.

"But I don't believe you've met my fiancé, Charles Lowell the Third."

"Oh, yes." Del extended his hand. "It's nice to meet all of you."

Geez, Del, that joke's staler than the crackers at Quinn's General Store, she silently admonished.

He pumped Charles's hand until Miranda was afraid he'd pull it right out of his wrist socket. Charles just stared at him.

"Oh, Del, you always were such a wit," Miranda said with a stiff smile. She could think of a lot of other names to call him.

She began to pull very subtly on her fiancé's arm.

"So, what do you do, Charlie?" Del asked.

"That's Charles," he corrected, at last managing to free himself from Del's grasp.

"So, what do you do, *Charles*?"

"Well, I'm usually busy seeing to the running of my family's shipping company."

"You don't say." Del reached up and stroked his chin. "Yes, indeed."

"What do you ship, Charlie—er, Charles?" He corrected himself very quickly. Miranda could tell from the gleam in his eye it was no mere slip of the tongue.

"Anything and everything. Mostly importing raw materials from less fortunate lands, then exporting some of the fine manufactured goods produced in the Northeast."

"Yeah, I guess that would keep you pretty busy," Del agreed. "But, you know, they say all work and no play makes Jack a dull boy."

What was Del getting at? Miranda wondered.

"Oh, I have ample time to pursue my favorite pastime."

"Which is?"

"I am very fond of playing polo."

"Polo, huh? You don't say."

"Indeed, I do say."

"So, I guess you're a pretty good horseman then, eh, Charles?"

"Yes, indeed. As a matter of fact, I am."

Oh, no. At last she could see where Del was going. Maybe she could head him off at the pass.

"Charles is the captain of his polo team," she interjected proudly. "They've won the trophy at the local Country Club for three years in a row."

"Well, now, that is impressive." Del clapped Charles on the back. "Myself, I've never captained anything. As a matter of fact, the only team I ever played on was the Reds in the annual Reds versus Blues Grasonville Independence Day Baseball Game."

"The Reds always lose," Miranda remarked.

"I've never played baseball," Charles admitted.

"Never? You don't say!" Del exclaimed. "Well, Charlie—"

"Charles."

"We've got to see about correcting this oversight in your experience."

"I'm not sure—"

"Well, then, we'll have to see about going for a ride instead while you're here."

"By golly, that could be quite pleasant," Charles agreed.

Over my dead body.

Miranda pulled again, a little less subtly, on her fiancé's arm. "But, Charles, my dear, I believe we're going to be so very busy with other planned engagements that you simply won't have time for impromptu excursions."

He nodded. "Perhaps not. Quite a shame."

"But it was kind of you to extend the invitation, Del."

"Oh, yeah," Del replied. "Too bad impromptu excursions can be so . . . imprompt."

You're being an ass, Del.

"I take it you ride a good bit then, too, Mr. Williams," Charles ventured.

Oh, geez, Charles, don't prolong this any more than necessary!

Del nodded. "A bit."

"What do you do when you're not riding?"

Del rubbed the back of his neck. "You know, it's funny. There was a time, not so very long ago, when that was all I did. Just ride. Now? I have a really strong feeling all that's going to change drastically."

He laughed. It was just a laugh, Miranda told herself. Then why did she have the strangest feeling there was a lot more meaning behind that laugh than either she or Charles was aware of?

Del was a farmer. She knew he'd gone to work on a cattle ranch in Texas. All he'd done was ride. But what in the world was this change he was talking about?

What did it matter? she decided. It was only Del, just talking to exercise his jaws. Was this rude behavior something he'd learned in Texas, or had he always been this annoying and she'd never noticed it while she'd believed she was in love with him?

It was time to be seeing the other, much more important, and much more pleasant, guests.

"Now, come with me, Charles," she said, urging him along. "There are so many other people here who are just dying to meet you."

She hurried away from Del as quickly as she could without actually running and dragging poor, unfortunate Charles along behind. She had the strangest sensation of feeling Del's eyes on her, watching her.

She wanted to look back. No, that would only admit she was still concerned with him and his opinion of her. She wasn't. And she certainly didn't want it to appear that way.

Should she look back? she puzzled. What would she see? Del standing there in the doorway all alone, the way she'd left him? Watching her with longing in his eyes? The same kind of longing that used to be in her eyes every time she looked at him?

If only she could see that look for her in his eyes. Then she'd turn her back on him, the same way he'd turned away from her. She'd do it, she determined. Yes, she would.

At last her curiosity overcame her caution. She glanced back over her shoulder.

But Del was not alone. Far from it. Eager guests clamored about him so tightly she could hardly see him. Why, she could barely see the top of his head. He certainly hadn't bothered to look after her.

"When did you get back?" someone asked.

"How'd they treat you down there in Texas?" someone else wanted to know.

"Are you back to stay?"

"Nothing like being back home again, huh?"

Well, Del was certainly busy, Miranda noted. Much too busy to be giving a dang about her. She turned away. She wasn't disappointed he hadn't actually been staring after her. Of course, she wasn't. She was used to having him ignore her.

Miranda spied Sally working diligently by the tables of food set up on the other side of the barn. She pulled Charles along with her. Mrs. Lowell followed behind.

"Sally, thank you so much for all this," Miranda said. She took her friend's hand. "You've set everything up so wonderfully."

"Thank you."

Sally was busy, Miranda decided. That's why her answer was so curt.

"You certainly know how to have a party"

"Quite nice, quite nice indeed," Charles agreed.

"I suppose you've done the best you could under the circumstances." Mrs. Lowell's upper lip curled as she looked up to the rafters.

"Oh, Mother," Charles scolded jovially. "Actually, Miss Pickett, I find the rustic atmosphere to be quite charming. How innovative of you to hold your party in a barn."

"Thank you," Sally answered anyway. Now Miranda knew for a certainty that her friend hadn't really been listening too closely to anything they'd said.

Yes, she certainly must be extremely busy.

Charles lifted his head and sniffed. "Don't you just love the smell of fresh hay?"

Yes!

Mrs. Lowell sniffed, too. "If one can find it among the other odors."

Miranda gestured at all the cakes lined up on one of the trestle tables. "My goodness, Sally, you must have worked all week."

"It looks quite delicious," Charles said. "Doesn't it, Mother?"

Mrs. Lowell shrugged. "It's not exactly Delmonico's."

"Precisely," Charles said. "I can't abide Delmonico's. Far too rich for my digestion. Honestly, Miss Pickett, I can't wait to sample each and every one of these marvelous dishes." He patted his flat stomach. "I intend to do just that."

Miranda gave silent thanks that Charles was very little like his picky, demanding mother.

"You always were the best cook in town," Miranda assured her friend.

Sally gave a weak little laugh. "I think Mrs. Cartwright, Mrs. Nichols, and Mrs. Stanley might disagree with you."

"Nonsense."

Sally laughed again, but this time it was tinged with bitterness. "It's a darn shame I only have my brothers and sisters to cook for."

"Oh, Sally, don't worry. You're so pretty and sweet—" *When you're not griping about not having a husband.* "Someone's bound to come along and sweep you off your feet."

"Yeah, any day now."

Sally was as sour as Del. She'd had her vapors now and then, as every lady did, but not like this. What was making her so cantankerous? Miranda wondered. Was it something in the water around here?

"Yes, you're very busy," Miranda told her. "We'll have to have tea—"

"Tea?" Sally was trying to keep smiling while one corner of her mouth threatened to turn up in a sneer.

Well, Miranda reconsidered, she guessed not too many people did tea in Grasonville.

"Just the two of us, while I'm still here. For now, perhaps it would be better for us to move along to the other guests."

"It's your party," Sally replied. "You can do whatever you please." Then she smiled a little more broadly, and her eyes softened. "I do hope you enjoy yourself."

That was more like the Sally she knew. Miranda laid her hand on her friend's arm. "If you planned it, I'm sure I will."

Miranda, with Charles in tow, and followed by Mrs. Lowell, began to make her way around the barn. She was grateful when her mother latched on to Mrs. Lowell and dragged her off in her own direction.

"Miranda!" Flora Baker exclaimed.

Flora flounced up to her, followed by Sophie Baldwin and Dorothy Halstead. Several other girls in town that Miranda had only been slightly acquainted with followed them.

"It's so good to see you again!" Flora declared.

"I've missed you all so much," Miranda responded.

"I hear you're getting married in a few weeks," Dorothy said.

"You're all invited, of course," Miranda assured them.

"I hear you'll be going back to Boston to live," Dorothy continued.

"That's right."

"Oh, I can't bear to think that we'll never see each other again!" Sophie wailed.

"But we will. We *have* to!" Miranda insisted. "I'll come back for visits—and of course you'll come visit me, too. Won't you?"

"Of course," Flora and Sophie responded weakly.

Dorothy gave a snide little laugh.

What a foolish thing to say, Miranda realized. Chagrined, she pressed her lips together in disappointment. In this town, only her father and Mr. Richardson, and of course Widow Janet Crenshaw and Miss Catherine Barber, had so much money they could travel any distance with any frequency. How bizarre to imagine that, after the wedding, she would return to Boston, perhaps never to see any of her friends again.

Flora grabbed both of Miranda's hands in hers and stood back to examine her outfit. "You look wonderful. What a beautiful dress!"

Thank goodness Flora had the presence of mind to change the subject, Miranda thought.

"Thank you," she answered in what she thought was a very modest manner. It ought to be stylish. It had cost enough.

"Very beautiful," Sophie agreed. With a wistful sigh,

she added, "I wish I could wear those straight lines." She leaned closer to Miranda. "I'll bet you don't even need a corset."

"Don't be silly. I'd feel naked without one," Miranda said with a giggle.

"It's almost too beautiful," Dorothy commented, her wide blue eyes narrowing. "You certainly won't see anything like it around here."

"No, I don't suppose you will," Miranda replied, raising her chin proudly. She didn't want to hurt Flora's or Sophie's feelings, but she couldn't let the spite in Dorothy's remark slip by. "I tried to bring dresses from Boston that I would still be comfortable in here. Only my wedding gown is truly fancy."

Dorothy gave a little sniff and turned away.

Marvin Platt perched up high on a bale of hay and started tuning his fiddle. Hal Danvers settled down beside him and started picking his banjo. Isaac Stanley repeated on his guitar every bit of melody Hal played.

"I'll allow you the first dance with your fiancé," her father warned her. "Then it's my turn to dance with my little girl."

Carvel Marsh's grinning face peeked at her over her father's shoulder. "After that, all the other gentlemen here are lining up to wear out your dancing shoes."

Marvin's fiddle squeaked one more time. Then they set out playing in earnest.

Charles bowed to her. She offered him her hand. As they whirled around the floor, she glanced over his shoulder. Was Del lined up with all the rest? She couldn't tell in this crowd. She supposed she could compose herself long enough to dance with him without kicking him in the shins or stomping on his toes. She'd just have to wait and find out.

While she was busy wearing out her shoes, poor Charles was suffering trampled toes from every unmarried lady there.

While the musicians took a few much-needed rests, she and Charles sampled every pie, cake, and casserole, and told each cook that hers was the absolute best dish.

The trip had been exhausting enough. She should have waited a few days, and gotten some rest, before agreeing to attend any parties. But Sally had given this party. She could hardly disappoint her. Why, they'd been best friends since they were very little.

So Miranda had danced every dance with every man there—except Del. Every time she looked for him—and, mind, she didn't look for him hardly at all—she could barely see him, he was so besieged by curious old friends. All she really noticed was that each man who took her hand and wrapped an arm around her waist was not Del.

At last most of the food was just scraps, and some of the guests were hunting for their wraps. Miranda was more than ready to go home.

But her mother was still parading Mrs. Lowell around to every lady of her acquaintance, as if she were some sort of a trophy. Some of the men had lured Charles off to sample their homebrew. If Mr. Nesbitt and Mr. Baldwin had managed to talk him into a tasting contest between their rival "corn likker," heaven only knew when he'd be back, or if he'd be in any condition to attend any more parties.

So she'd have to stick around a little longer. But she really needed to take just a little rest from the noise of the crowd. She found a quiet spot and leaned against a stack of hay bales and waited.

"That fancy finishing school in Boston sure has improved her."

"It couldn't have made her any worse."

Miranda's ears perked up. She wouldn't have recognized Will as the first speaker if she hadn't recognized Del's answering comment. There was no doubt in her mind who they were talking about.

"Come on, Del. Her father's rich. Why wouldn't her parents send her to a real expensive special school?"

"I'm surprised they didn't send the little pest away years ago."

*Not everyone's as hard-hearted as you, Del. Most
people actually like me.*

She crossed her arms more tightly over her chest and
leaned closer to listen harder. She just prayed no one
would notice her standing there. She didn't think she'd
mind so much having Del discover her eavesdropping,
but she'd really hate to have to leave now and miss the
rest of their conversation—especially one that started
out like that.

"I thought you used to like her." Will gave a wicked
little laugh. "I always thought you two were going to get
married."

"Shut up, Will," Del ordered grumpily. "That was *her*
idea. Not mine. No man in his right mind would shackle
himself to that smart-mouthed little wiseacre."

"Aw, she's not so bad. She just talks too much, that's
all."

Thanks, Will, I think.

"She manages to say all the wrong things in all the
wrong ways at all the wrong times," Del complained.

*I don't recall you winning any prizes in oratory in
school, either.*

"She's the spoiled only child of a very rich man."

"Hey, that should happen to all of us," Will replied
with an envious laugh.

"She's always gotten everything she's ever wanted."

I was never greedy about it.

"Daddy's money always bought it for her."

"That's not necessarily a bad thing, Del," his brother
pointed out.

"She made up her mind from the start to get me."

"Miranda usually gets what she sets her mind on."

"Well, I can be just as stubborn as she can. I made up
my mind a long time ago to be the one thing her daddy's
money couldn't buy."

"In case you haven't noticed, nobody buys or sells
anybody else anymore. Mr. Lincoln freed the slaves a
couple of years ago."

"Yeah, I noticed something about that in the newspaper," Del grumbled.

"Anyway, something that wasn't in the newspapers, but that might be even more important, and you seem not to have noticed—you don't have to worry about her anymore. She's apparently changed her mind completely about you and decided on someone else."

"Yeah. Mr. Charles Not-bad-enough-to-have-one-of-them, he's-got-to-be-the-third Lowell."

"What?"

"He's welcome to her, the pompous little stuffed shirt. Polo, can you believe that?"

"What?"

"I'll bet he doesn't dunk his bread in his soup. I'll bet he doesn't even make a noise when he burps."

"Oh, come on. He still puts on his pants one leg at a time."

"Imagine having to spend time with that sour old lemon."

"Who? Charles What's-his-name?"

"No. The mother."

"Oh. Yeah, she is a little chilly."

"That's just what Miranda's going to be like in a few years," Del predicted ominously. "Heck, she's already turning into a little icicle."

"Ha! She's been very pleasant to everyone tonight."

Del made no reply.

"Except you, huh?"

Del still didn't reply.

"Huh?" Will insisted.

"Shut up, Will."

"You've got no right to complain. When were you ever nice to her?"

"Shut up, Will."

"Do you know what your problem is?" his brother demanded. "All your life, Miranda's followed you around like a lovesick puppy every waking moment, swearing she was going to marry you. Heck, you couldn't hardly go to the outhouse without her following you, and waiting outside till you were done."

"She only did that once. Then her ma gave her what for."

"But now, for once in your life, she's not following you around. As a matter of fact, she's found someone else she wants to marry. She's ignoring you, and that's making you sore."

"You don't know what you're talking about," Del growled.

"Maybe I don't. But then, why are you getting so hot under the collar about it?"

"I . . . I don't like being unjustly accused."

"Or you don't like being read like a book," Will suggested.

"Shut up, Will. Or maybe you'd like to be black and blue like a bruise."

At last Will was silent.

"Come on," Del told him. "It's late. Just about everyone's heading on home anyway. We'd better help Sally or she'll have our guts for garters."

"Yeah, I think I'd rather risk a bruise from you than face Sally in a snit."

Del and Will emerged from the other side of the bales. Miranda flattened herself against the hay, so as not to be seen.

Del thrust his hands into his pockets as he walked away. She couldn't see his face completely, but she did notice the furrowed brow and the belligerent set of his jaw.

Just then, her mother came rushing up to him.

"Oh, Del, we've been so busy this evening, I barely had a chance to say hello to you. Every time I looked for you, you were surrounded by people welcoming you home. We didn't even get a chance to have a nice chat."

"Oh, that's . . . that's okay, Mrs. Hamilton. I know you've been real busy."

Miranda could hear him trying to make his voice sound lighter, not so grumpy. She hoped he'd wiped that awful scowl off his face before he spoke to her mother.

"Did you get all of your business taken care of this morning?"

"Yes, ma'am."

He must look more pleasant, Miranda decided. Otherwise, her mother would be questioning him about that, too.

"I hope it wasn't too troublesome."

Oh, Mama, why don't you stop beating around the bush and just come out and ask him?

"No, as a matter of fact, it was rather . . . pleasant." Will cleared his throat.

"Well, I guess it's no secret now," Del admitted.

"Oh, yes. *Do* tell everyone, Del," Sally urged as she joined the circle.

"I . . . I had some business with Mr. Martin."

Miranda grimaced. Who in their right mind would voluntarily see a lawyer—unless they'd just found out they were dying and needed to make up their will? Apparently others had the same opinion.

"Why on earth would you do that?" Mrs. Hamilton demanded.

"It seems that Mr. Richardson mentioned me in his will."

Overcome with curiosity, Miranda peeked out from behind the bale of hay.

"It seems he, um . . . well, he left all his money to me."

"*All* his money?" Mrs. Hamilton repeated.

Miranda didn't care what kind of good resolutions she'd made to avoid Del. She didn't care who else was gathering in the little circle her mother, Will, and Sally made around him. She didn't care if they knew she'd been eavesdropping.

She wasn't even afraid of making what Mrs. Lowell would call "a scene." She'd been making "scenes" in front of the people of Grasonville all her life. They were used to her. The only people who'd agonize about it were Charles and his mother. She wasn't exactly sure where they were right now, and she didn't think she really much cared. This was something much more important to worry about.

That house had been in her life a lot longer than Charles had, and she had to make sure exactly what was happening to it.

Boldly she stepped out from behind the hay.

"And the house?" she asked, breathlessly. "What about the house?"

"He left me the house, too," Del answered.

"Well, bless my soul!" Mrs. Hamilton exclaimed. "Or rather, bless yours, Del."

"Yeah, I guess so," he responded, smiling.

"Oh, no. Not the house, too," Miranda protested. "That was supposed to be *my* house!"

4

"WHAT IN THE world are you talking about?" Del demanded.

"My house. What else?"

"You mean Mr. Richardson's house?" her mother asked.

Mother was looking at her as if she'd gone completely mad. Del was just coldly eyeing her again, as if waiting for her to utter one more outlandish thing.

"No. I mean *my* house," she insisted, shaking her head vigorously. There! That wasn't so outlandish, was it? She didn't think so.

"No, *my* house," he quickly corrected.

He wore a self-satisfied smirk that was making her miserable. She was itching to slap it right off his face. She might as well kick at the loose straw strewn across the dirt floor of the barn—she couldn't kick Del. It wasn't the ladylike thing to do. So she just stood very still and glared at him.

He thought he was so grand, now that he had inherited a little money. Well, she'd like to tell him it hadn't changed him a bit. He was still the same old stubborn, hardheaded, obnoxious Wendell he'd always been.

She could hardly believe he was telling the truth. How

could Mr. Richardson have left everything to someone he hardly knew? It just couldn't be.

"Del Williams, you know darn good and well that's always been 'my' house."

"Mr. Richardson might've been pretty surprised to find that out."

"I mean," she said very slowly, and with great stress, "I had always dreamed of someday owning or living in that house. I should have known all the while I was talking, you were never listening."

"But you always talked so much, my ears had to take a rest some time. That must have been the part I missed."

Go to blazes, Del Williams! she wanted to tell him.

But she kept remembering Mrs. Bigelow's lesson— "The test of good manners is to be gracious in the face of bad." Oh, very well, Mrs. Bigelow. If you insist. But just this once, and only because I'm at a party his family's giving me. Any time after this he's fair game!

So Miranda just raised her eyebrows and laughed lightly. "Oh, Del, you're still the clever boy you always were. Ha, ha."

"I still managed to hear part of what you said. And yeah, I heard all your silly claims for that house," he told her. "But I don't know how you ever figured you'd manage it."

"I don't, either."

She turned away from Del and began to pace up and down in front of him.

"I didn't know Mr. Richardson and he certainly didn't know me. Even if I'd known him, I don't think I'd have liked the old miser."

"He probably wouldn't have liked you, either."

No, Del. You're the only one who never liked me.

She spared only a sullen glare at him for his very rude comment to interrupt her pacing back and forth.

"I realize I never had the ghost of a chance of actually inheriting the place." She gave a bitter laugh. "I didn't think you did, either. But that really doesn't have anything to do with Mr. Richardson, anyway."

She stopped pacing right in front of him. Pointing her finger directly under her nose, she glared at him.

"You know I've always loved that house, ever since I first laid eyes on it."

"Yeah, I know. You told me at least a million times." At least he acknowledged that much.

"But you forget, I've been interested in that house since Mr. Richardson was courting my mother—long before you were ever born." Del chuckled. "I guess that sort of makes it first come, first served, doesn't it?"

"Don't be stubborn."

"Stubborn? Isn't that the pot calling the kettle black?" *Go stick a pot on your hollow head, Del!*

"You know I always said I'd live in that house some day."

"Yeah." He chuckled. "You also said you were going to marry me some day."

She took a single step closer to him. Even though she'd always had to look up at him, that had never stopped her from confronting him before. She'd always managed to stand toe to toe and stare him down.

Now, when she stood so close to him, and looked up at him, she was struck again with how blue his eyes were. She noticed how he somehow managed to smell like the fresh straw he'd been leaning against and the bay rum he always used.

Now when she'd confronted him, she felt a new sensation she'd never known before. Her heart beat faster, and she felt a wild tingling around it that spread through her stomach, making her legs weak and her arms shiver. She wanted to get closer to him, much closer.

For support. Yes, that was it. Del was very strong and could hold her up if she fainted.

She shook her head. She couldn't think about that now! She had a much more important point to make.

"If . . . if you bring that up in public one more time," she warned in a coarse whisper, "I swear, Del, I'll turn your life into worse than perdition."

He wrapped his hand about her finger and grinned down at her.

"You're not going to be around much longer," he reminded her. "You're going back to Boston."

She tried to slip her finger out of his grasp, but couldn't manage. How could he know his presence was unnerving her so, and the dirty rotten scoundrel was just doing this to keep her close to him, to make her suffer more.

"I haven't left yet. I think you ought to have figured out by now that I've . . . I've changed my mind about you."

At last she managed to free herself.

"So I'll kindly thank you to stop bringing up a dead subject."

Having said what she needed, she backed away from him quickly. She couldn't bear to be near him any longer than necessary.

He didn't bat an eyelash at her threat. He'd always been so easy to intimidate. Now he just shrugged and grinned.

"Looks as if you're going to have to change your mind about that house now, too."

She should have known better than to expect any sympathy from him.

She took another step back, a little closer to her mother. She knew she could get the sympathy she needed from her. The devil take Del Williams!

"How could Mr. Richardson die and——?"

"I don't know how he died."

"I don't mean that!"

He knew it, too. Why was he teasing her? Del didn't have a sense of humor. At least, he'd never laughed at any of *her* jokes.

He was goading her—that's what he was doing. He was just trying to make her look foolish. He was succeeding very well at it, too. Somehow she had to regain the upper hand in this argument.

"How could he die and leave it all to you?"

"I've been wondering the same thing ever since Mr. Martin told me about it this morning."

"Mr. Richardson must have had *some* other family! Why didn't he leave it to one of them?"

Del shrugged. "I've been wondering that, too."

"Don't you know anything? Do you have to wonder about everything?"

He shrugged again. "I guess I'm just wonderful."

"Well, it's a free country," she said with a careless wave of her hand. "I suppose even *you're* entitled to an opinion, no matter how foolish and unfounded."

She started to pace again.

"Why couldn't he leave it to some relative from out of town, who wouldn't want to live in it anyway, and then they'd sell it to me, and go away forever?"

"Why would they want to sell it to you, anyway?" Del asked. "Just because your daddy's rich and can afford it?"

"Uh-oh," Will murmured.

"Just because your daddy's always managed to buy everything else for you you've ever wanted?"

She stopped in front of him again. This time she had enough sense to stay far enough away, and *not* to point her finger at him.

"How dare you accuse me of . . . of . . . well, I've never been greedy in my entire life! I can't help it if we've got money. You're just jealous because you don't—or didn't. That has nothing to do with my liking that house."

"But it definitely has something to do with you *owning* that house."

She was half tempted to stamp her foot in anger, but she was just too tired to argue now. It was definitely time to leave. And she was too big and grown-up—and way too well dressed—to go running across the field to her home. And she was far too grown-up to fit into her old hiding place.

She spun about on her heel, colliding with Charles. He placed both hands on her arms to stop her escape. Oh, she was so glad to see him!

She breathed a sigh of relief. Charles was steady and strong. She felt safe with him. She didn't feel safe with Del—not anymore.

On the other hand, with Charles she never felt the thrill and shiver she'd felt when she stood close to Del. She had to stay away from Del. Far, far away.

Mrs. Lovell stood behind Charles. The old lady was glaring as her. How much of this conversation had she overheard?

Charles, on the other hand, wasn't glaring at her. Wonderful, dependable Charles! He took his place at her side. She almost expected to see him spring, arms akimbo, between her and Del, like the hero from some bad melodrama. On the other hand, most heroes from melodramas probably didn't smell like corn liquor. She wondered if Mr. Baldwin or Mr. Nesbitt had won the tasting contest.

"What seems to be the problem, my dear?" Charles asked.

"Problem? Oh, there's no problem," she answered quickly. What a stupid answer! Anyone with only half a brain—even someone who was half full of homebrew—could see there was indeed a problem here.

"Well, then, my dear, what seems to be the subject of this rather animated discussion?"

Miranda stood there for a moment, undecided. How could she explain her childhood fantasy to Charles, a man of very sharp business sense—and very little imagination?

"Del has just inherited some property—a house—that I had . . . well, had once hoped to own."

"Which house would that be?"

"It's this big mansion, the last brick one on the way out of town. There are roses and lilacs and—"

"The one we passed on the left on the way to your parents'?"

She nodded. "That's the one."

Charles nodded and smiled at her. It wasn't exactly a happy smile, though. It was more along the line of the condescending smile of some great patriarchal figure who'd come to settle his erring children's disputes. Of course, when she looked a little closer at his eyes, he looked as if the patriarch had come by way of the nearest tavern.

He raised a single finger heavenward. "Aha! Never despair, my dearest."

I knew you were going to say that. It's a line of dialogue from the same bad melodrama that awful pose came from.

Charles turned to Del and offered his hand.

"My heartiest congratulations on your recent windfall, sir," he declared.

"Thank you."

"You must be quite elated."

"I'd be a dang fool not to be."

"Indeed, indeed."

Charles tucked his thumbs into the top of his trousers and began rocking back and forth. He didn't have a paunch yet, but somehow, she could see it coming, as clearly as if she were gazing into a crystal ball. All he needed was a big Cuban cigar stuck in his mouth to complete the picture of opulence and prosperity.

Quite a far cry from the picture she had of Del. Standing there in faded jeans, removing the straw hat from his head so he could wipe the sweat from his brow as he dug in the garden, the sweat trickling down his spine, and down his bare chest.

She blinked, snapping her attention back to Charles and Del's conversation. That was one heck of a crystal ball, even in her imagination. One she better get rid of awfully darn quick!

"I see now to what you were referring earlier, when you said your situation was about to change," Charles said.

If she lived to be a hundred, Miranda swore she would never be able to understand men. She was ready to smack Del silly, and here Charles was, congratulating him on falling, by sheer dumb luck, into something she'd had her heart set on since childhood.

"I'm certain that, coming into your inheritance so recently, you haven't yet had the opportunity to form a really strong attachment to the house," Charles continued. "Therefore, I'm sure you won't think me out of place in offering to buy it from you—at a price I'm sure you'll consider quite appropriate."

"Oh, Charles!" Miranda exclaimed as he named a considerable sum.

"Yes, my dear. Just call it a little wedding present from me to you."

"But you can't just buy it sight unseen!" she protested.

"But you want it, my dear. That's good enough for me."

"Oh, Charles!"

It wasn't gratitude, but desperation, that prompted her outburst. Charles had just managed to supply Del with more ammunition for his attack on her family's wealth. Now he'd be berating her for marrying a rich man, too.

Miranda couldn't take her eyes off Del, watching him, waiting for what he would say or do next. What happened next all hinged on Del.

Del stood there for a moment, his hands still jammed in his pockets and his lips tightened, as if he were actually considering the offer.

Miranda pressed her lips together and clenched her fists, too, trying very hard to keep her growing temper under control. Del might have Charles fooled, but he didn't fool her one bit.

"It's more than a fair price, sir." Charles reached into his breast pocket for his billfold.

Thunderation, Charles, do you have to be so ostentatious? It's not as if you actually carry that much money around with you.

Del took a deep breath. "Well, now, Charlie—"

"Charles."

"That's where you're wrong."

"Wrong?" Charles repeated, withdrawing his empty hand from his breast pocket. "You think it's not a fair price? I doubt anyone else would offer you that amount for that house, especially in the condition it's in."

"No, no, you're more than generous."

"Then you think I'm out of place in offering to buy the house from you?" Charles asked. "Well, I'm quite chagrined that I neglected to follow proper procedures, although I never would have thought you'd be a stickler for that sort of thing. Of course, I'll have my attorney send your attorney a letter of intent immediately."

"No, no," Del protested. "Not that. It's not that at all."

"Then what—?"

"You're wrong in thinking I haven't formed an attachment to the house."

"Forgive me if I fail to understand. . . ."

Obviously still puzzled, Charles watched Del, as if waiting for an explanation.

What was the matter with him? Miranda wondered. Couldn't he put two and two together and get four? She could already see Del's answer coming a mile away.

"You forget that I was born and grew up in Grasonville, too," Del explained. "When I was just a little boy, my mother and I used to ride past the Richardson mansion every time we went into town."

Miranda could see realization dawning on Charles.

"I know it might not make much sense to you, Charlie—"

"Charles."

"I guess, being rich and all, you grew up in a house just like that."

"Not really," Charles answered with a slightly haughty sniff. "But our summer cottage in Newport is about that size."

"Oh." Del paused just a moment. "Well, Charles, I

didn't grow up rich like you. All my life I've wondered what it would be like to live in a house—heck, a mansion—like that. Now's my chance. I don't intend to let it go."

"I understand better than you think I do. However, when it comes down to it, one large house is just about as good as any other. Take my word for it," he added.

"I'd rather not."

Unaffected, Charles continued, "For the amount of money I've just offered you, I'd say you could find any number of houses just like this one. You might even be able to build a brand-new one, to your own specifications."

Del reached up and scratched the back of his head.

"And you must admit, no one else would offer you a similar price for such a dilapidated heap of lumber," Charles said in an effort to seal the deal.

"You're probably right, Charles. On the other hand, I don't see much sense in going to all the trouble of finding another house when I've already got the one I want."

Charles frowned. "Well, then, are you sure there's nothing I can say to change your mind?"

"Nothing I can think of."

"If by some chance you should change your mind—"

"Not a chance."

Charles extended his hand to shake Del's. "Perhaps we can do business some other time."

"Maybe."

"How dare you! Both of you!" Miranda protested.

She glared at Charles. She wanted to show Del how angry she was with him, too. But she wasn't about to get near him again—not when his closeness made her feel so strange.

"I don't believe this!" she exclaimed. "There you two stand, haggling over my house as if you were a couple of horse traders bargaining for a nag." She gave a grunt of disgust.

"Oh, come now. Don't be upset, my dearest," Charles said. He patted her shoulder lightly in consolation.

She waited for Del to say something. He didn't. Oh, she should have known better than to expect anything out of him in the first place!

"Don't worry, my dear. I'll find another equally wonderful wedding gift for you."

She shook her head.

Nothing like that house. Nothing like it—ever!

"What would you want with a house in Grasonville, anyway? I mean, it's not as if you'll actually be living here, is it?"

"Well, no," she answered slowly.

He offered her his arm, to escort her from the party. Giving Del a scathing glance, she slowly and very deliberately placed her hand in the crook of Charles's elbow.

"We'll be living in our own lovely home in Boston," Charles said as he began to lead her toward the barn door.

"Yes, of course, you're right."

"A stately manor, no doubt," Del grumbled as they passed. "And probably very expensive."

"Yes, it is," she replied.

"Filled with antiques."

"Of course."

"And objects of art," he said, affecting a very bad French accent.

"Wonderful things you'll never have any concept of."

"Worth every penny then, huh?"

"Undeniably."

His voice was a little deeper, and much more serious, as he asked, "Is that what you're worth, Miranda?"

Just in time she managed to stop herself from gasping at his rudeness. She was *not* marrying Charles just because he was rich. If she'd merely been seeking a rich husband, she'd have set her sights on a Rockefeller or a Roosevelt or a Vanderbilt, or gone off to England to marry a duke or something.

But her father hadn't inherited anything. He'd worked hard by the sweat of his brow to earn his fortune. Her mother had done her best to raise her to be a lady. She owed it to her parents not to disappoint them.

Perhaps Charles had inherited his business, but he didn't lounge about the club or lie about in the country doing nothing. He worked in his office very hard every day, making sure that he kept and increased his wealth.

She had an obligation not to waste her parents' money, and her own education, on a man who had simply been someone else's hired hand, on a man whose only recommendation was that he'd been darned lucky.

She'd made the correct choice in becoming betrothed to Charles.

Anyway, Charles had proposed to her. Del never, ever had—and had turned down her proposals numerous times. It wasn't really as if she'd had the chance to make a choice.

With a flip of her chin, she abruptly turned her back on Del.

She tried to keep her tread steady and her head held high. She and Charles might be making a proud, sedate exit, but there was no doubt in her mind that Del had won this round. She wouldn't look back. She wouldn't let him think for one minute that she acknowledged this victory, or that she cared one bit what he thought. She certainly didn't want to see the look of triumph she was sure he was wearing.

"Of course, we'll be spending summers at the cottage in Newport," Charles continued.

"Yes, Charles," she answered, almost automatically.

He was right about that, too, But he still wasn't cheering her up much.

"Mother so adores the climate there. Don't you?"

"Yes, indeed." She'd never been to Newport, but she was too weary to disagree with anything.

Right now she was way too exhausted to do much thinking at all.

"We might even visit London or Paris. Would you like that?"

"Oh, yes, Charles."

"On the few occasions when you do return here to visit your parents, I'm sure you'll be staying with them, won't you?"

"Yes, definitely." She had to admit, he was right there, too.

"Then we'll just let Mr. Williams have the dilapidated old building, won't we?"

No!

She gave a sad little laugh saturated with resignation. "I don't suppose I have much choice."

Charles reached over and patted her hand. "That's my sweet, sensible Miranda. There's no earthly reason to worry your pretty little head about that worthless old house. Is there?"

Yes!

"Well, no. I suppose when you put it that way, no," she was forced to admit.

Gradually, in the cool air of the summer night, Miranda's head stopped aching. The fresh air helped clear her head. She could actually think much better again.

Charles was right, of course. She had been about to verge on the ridiculous in her childish obsession with the Richardson house. She was so glad she had him to stand up for her in front of that aggravating Del Williams. She was so glad he could calm her when her temper was about to get the best of her. Del only seemed to irritate her more.

She had no need for a house in Grasonville. The mansion she had once thought was so grand and wonderful was actually pretty small. Especially when she compared it to some of the homes of her friends that she'd visited while she was away at school, and with the house she and Charles would live in after their marriage.

When they'd ridden past it on the way to her parents' house, she was surprised at how unkempt the lawn and garden looked. She could only suppose the rest of the house had been equally neglected. She wouldn't be surprised to find that, on her next visit to Grasonville, the city council had condemned the building and had it demolished.

Charles was quite, quite correct. As they made their way to their carriage, she lifted her head with pride.

Pretty little head? Wait a minute. She almost stumbled over an invisible rock. She frowned, and her head began to ache again, just a little.

Was that what Charles had told her? Don't worry your pretty little head about it? She'd been so upset it had been difficult to listen to everything, and it was still difficult to recall it all clearly.

But, no, that's exactly what he had said. Don't worry your pretty little head about it.

All right, she could easily admit she was pretty, without being conceited about it.

Yes, as with most human beings, she could hardly deny that she had a head.

But little? Her head wasn't any larger or smaller than the normal variations among humans. Neither were its contents.

There was something about his advice that bothered her very much. She'd have to discuss this with Charles, at length—when she wasn't so very exhausted.

Del stood just inside the ornate wrought-iron gate that provided the only opening onto Main Street in the brick wall around the property. There was another, less fancy gate around back for delivery wagons, but the first time he approached the house as his own, he was determined to come in by the front.

He stared at the huge mansion looming up before him, and grinned with pride.

"Not Mr. Richardson's anymore," he said to himself. "*My* house."

All right, maybe the roof was missing a lot of shingles, and seemed to sag in that one corner. Maybe a few of the shutters—the ones that weren't missing—were hanging at odd angles. Maybe the morning sunlight could have glinted a little more brightly off the windowpanes—the ones that weren't broken—if they weren't so coated with dirt. But all that could be repaired.

He battled his way through the tangled rosebushes and across the overgrown lawn, heading toward the porch. Any minute now he half expected to see the ghost of Red Wilkins pop out from behind one of the overblown lilac bushes, brandishing a scythe, and scaring the bejeezus out of him.

Nope. He'd traveled all the way from Texas for this. He wasn't going to let a little ghost, or a little vegetation, stand in his way.

Each porch step screeched like a banshee as he tread on it. Cautiously he made his way across the porch to the wide, ornately carved, mahogany door, fully expecting the rotted boards to cave in beneath him every step of the way.

He pulled the ring of keys Mr. Martin had given him from his pocket and separated the largest one. It took some jiggling to get it to fit into the keyhole. It took a lot more jiggling to get the key to budge the stiff tumblers. At last, with a screech, the key turned in the lock.

Del reached out and turned the badly tarnished brass knob. It came off in his hand.

He stood there staring at it.

"Not exactly what I'd expected." He shrugged. "Then again, lately, nothing has been."

He was glad nobody else was around to hear him talking to himself. They might think he was as nutty as old Mr. Richardson. Was that what living alone did to a person? Made them talk to themselves?

He tried to fit the knob back onto the bolt. It slipped on easily enough, but it still wouldn't turn.

"I'm not going to let this stop me," he muttered.

He bent closer to examine the doorknob in the early morning light.

"Ah, just a loose screw."

He dug in his pocket for his knife. The edge of the blade served well enough to tighten the screw.

With a loud squeak, the knob finally turned. The bolt shifted back. He gave a push. Nothing happened. He pushed harder. The door still wouldn't open. He shouldered the door. At last, groaning and protesting, the door swung inward.

Del coughed from the swirling dust. He waved away the cloud from in front of his face. At last he was able to look around.

"Wow! Mr. Martin wasn't lying after all. This place is a dump!"

The floor creaked with each step as he made his way to the center of the shadowy vestibule. The only light came from the sunbeams streaming through the open front door.

He looked up at the cobwebs hanging from the high ceiling and the animal head trophies Mr. Richardson had collected. Those grisly things would be the first change he made, he decided. The cobwebs clung to the banister and all the statues, paintings, and curios Mr. Richardson had collected. It all looked like gray bunting left over from some long ago Independence Day celebration.

He looked down at the piles of mouse debris littering the corners. He could hear little critters scurrying around in the walls, hiding from the human intruder.

"Maybe the kids in town weren't so wrong, either. If any place would be haunted, it's this one."

He wasn't a superstitious man, or one given to flights of fancy. He sure didn't believe in ghosts. The thought of encountering the shade of bad-tempered, redheaded Gertie Richardson haunting her old house wasn't what sent him heading into the parlor in search of a window. He just figured it would be a whole lot safer walking around if there was more light in this place.

He wouldn't have been surprised to see big puffs of dust rising up from under his feet as he stepped across the carpet toward a window. The carpet must have had some kind of pattern to it once. Maybe it still did. But right now, it all looked gray.

He had to be careful where he stepped, dodging the

occasional pile of shattered glass, and the telltale rock, where someone had broken a window.

He never expected to be coated with the landslide of dust that fell from the curtain as he pulled it open. Coughing and wheezing, he brushed the dust from his face and the front of his shirt.

He pushed the faded curtain aside. He remembered they had once looked dark red as he watched them from the road. As he and they both grew older, he sort of remembered the curtains fading to a dull brown. Now, they were the same awful shade of grey as the rug. He hoped, as he grew older, that he held up better than these draperies had.

He reached up to push the lace curtain aside so he could look out the window. The lace must have been white once, but now it was brown, too. At least, what was left of it was. Most of it, dry rotted from the direct sunlight in this front window, just crumbled into tatters as he pushed it aside.

He tried to look out the window. Even without the high bushes growing wild outside, he could barely see the front lawn because of the grime and spiderwebs covering the window.

"Dang," he muttered as he continued to brush the dust from his face. "I shouldn't have gone to the trouble."

He started rubbing a clean spot with the cuff of his shirt. He peered intently out of the little clean circle.

Through the grime on the outside and the branches of the lilac bush, he could see someone approaching.

"Who in tarnation is that?"

Even if everyone in town now knew that he owned the place, few people would suppose he'd actually try to live in this pathetic ruin. Even fewer people would come calling.

Except Miranda Hamilton. She was the only person he knew who'd have the grit to come here.

He rubbed harder, trying to widen the clear spot. He frowned and squinted, trying to see who it was through the filthy glass.

Definitely a woman, he judged from the skirt, and the heaving bosom as the squarish figure chugged up the walk. Definitely *not* Miranda.

Still only halfway up the walk, the woman called, "Mr. Williams! Mr. Williams!"

"She knows who I am. I wish I could say the same thing about her."

He kept watching her approach. Maybe when she got close enough he could recognize who she was. And if he couldn't . . . ?

"What does she want with me?"

He kept watching. Maybe he could pretend he wasn't home.

"Oh, shucks!" He snapped his fingers in frustration. "I left the darn front door wide open. She's got to know I'm here. Even if I try to hide, she can waltz right in and search for me."

Or who knew what else this crazy person might try to do?

He pushed the curtain back, hoping to make it stay open and continue to admit sunlight. Then he hurried to the front door to head her off. He had a feeling it would be a lot easier to keep her from entering the house in the first place than to try to get her out once she'd managed to worm her way in.

"Might as well greet my guest," he told himself with a rueful chuckle. "I just wish I knew who the heck she is."

Even through the shadowy vestibule, she spotted him as he approached the doorway.

"Mr. Williams," she called again. "Mr. Williams, I'm Nadine Cartwright," she announced as she puffed up the steps.

She stood on the porch in front of him, bearing a broad smile that was warmer than sunshine. Her two front teeth were missing. Her gray hair was pulled back in a slick bun.

"I've come to work for you."

5

"*I*'VE COME TO work for you, Mr. Williams," Mrs. Cartwright announced, still smiling broadly. "Just like I did for Mr. Richardson."

Del stared at her in bewilderment. "Did Mr. Martin send you?"

"Who?"

"Mr.—"

"That weaselly little lawyer fellow?" The bright smile began to fade. "Land sakes, no! I couldn't pay him nothin'. Why would he bother to do somethin' for me?"

"Good question," Del admitted. "Then how'd you find out I'd inherited the place?"

She chuckled. "Are you jokin'? Everybody in town knows by now."

"Who told you I need a housekeeper?"

"A man tryin' to live alone?" She laughed, but the brightness of her smile was completely gone. "I don't need nobody to tell me you need a housekeeper."

"I'm sorry, Mrs. Cartwright, but I don't."

She peered over his shoulder and nodded at all the mess behind him. "From the looks of things, you sure as shootin' need *somebody*!"

He turned around and surveyed the room. Having let

in more light by opening the window, too, he could see the dirt and debris were far more extensive then he'd at first supposed.

"Speaking of the looks of things, exactly what happened here?" he asked. "If this is any example of your skills as a housekeeper, I don't think I want—"

Mrs. Cartwright slammed her fists onto her ample hips and stamped her foot.

"Don't you dare accuse me of not bein' a good housekeeper!" she ordered, and snorted with disgust. "Mr. Richardson passed away two months ago. It must've took Mr. Martin a while to find you, send you the telegram, and a while longer for you to travel here. And in all that time, that bald-headed little banty rooster never breathed a word of who'd inherited the place—not even to me. Never told me to keep workin', nor if'n I was goin' to get paid for doin' it, nor if'n I was still goin' to have a job when the new owner got here. He never told me nothin'. So what was I supposed to do? Keep workin' all that time for no pay?"

Del reached up to scratch his head. "No, ma'am. I don't reckon you would."

"You're doggone right!" she declared emphatically. "I might not be educated, but I ain't no fool."

The sturdy woman looked as if she could take him two falls out of three. He wasn't about to suggest that the mess left in the house looked as if it had been accumulating for a lot longer than the two months Mr. Richardson had been dead.

"I'm sorry, Mrs. Cartwright, but—"

"If I only knew if I still had a job!" she muttered pathetically.

Mrs. Cartwright heaved a gigantic sigh and started to sniff. She reached up and wiped her nose with the back of her hand, then rubbed it on the side of her skirt.

"But, Mrs. Cartwright—"

"It ain't right, I tell you. You never did a thing for him, and you get it all. I worked and slaved for the old miser for thirteen years, always there to do his biddin', and what do I get? Not one gol-darned, consarn, egg-suckin' dime!"

"Nice language." He'd heard ranch hands talk with more eloquence than that!

"That old skinflint gypped me out of my money when he was alive, and out of my house when he was dead."

Her house? Miranda would be mighty perturbed if she was to hear this.

The hefty woman dabbed at her eyes with the edge of her sleeve and sniffed again. "I really could use the job, Mr. Williams."

Before Del could refuse, she continued.

"Course, it's goin' to take a lot of work to get this place back into shape, a lot more than it would've took to keep it lookin' nice in the first place. You can blame Mr. Martin for that."

Apparently Mrs. Cartwright wanted to blame Mr. Martin for all her woes.

"Take a whole lot o' sweepin' and scrubbin'," she pronounced ominously. "These carpets are goin' to need a devil of a beatin' to get 'em clean again. Them curtains, heck, you might as well just throw 'em away. I guess you can afford to buy new ones."

She reached up and stroked her chin as she surveyed the damage.

"Course, with all that extra work, I'd say I was goin' to have to charge you a bit more than I did Mr. Richardson—at least a dollar a day."

"A dollar a day!" Del exclaimed.

"Don't try to be like that stingy, heartless old curmudgeon and tell me you can't afford it. You know darn good and well you can."

"No, I guess that's not the problem," he confessed with a little chuckle. "Although I've got to admit, even being able to say that is going to take a little getting used to."

"I wish I had that kind of problem," she grumbled under her breath. Then she snorted. "Well, get used to it fast, is all I can say."

"I'll try, Mrs. Cartwright." He really didn't see much

problem there. "But, you can see, the real problem is, I just don't need a housekeeper. I've been trying to tell you. I . . . I don't plan on doing a lot of entertaining."

She made a noise that was something like a laugh and a snort at the same time. "Do you think that old hermit Richardson did?"

"No. But it's going to be me here—"

"It was just Mr. Richardson here, too, but he still needed to have his cookin' and laundry done."

Del chuckled. "But, well, you see, I'm pretty used to taking care of myself. I don't need a housekeeper for that."

She looked around the big dirty room again. "Are you used to takin' care of a house?" She reached up to run her pudgy fingers across the surface of a fine vase sitting on a dusty tabletop. "Do you know how to take care of all these nice things?"

"But I . . . I still haven't decided whether I'm going to be living in this house or not. Whether I'm even going to be staying in Grasonville. So, no offense, but I really don't need you."

She took a step closer and shook a plump finger under his nose.

"You're goin' to need me, Mr. Williams, mark my words. If you do stay, you'll need me to clean this place up. If you don't stay, how do you expect to sell this place in the condition it's in? I'm the only one who can really take care of this house. Mark my words, I'm the only one."

"I don't expect so, Mrs. Cartwright," Del told her, shaking his head emphatically. "But thanks for stopping by."

Mrs. Cartwright crossed her arms over her generous bosom and stood her ground.

"You rich people are all alike—never willin' to give a poor old, hardworkin' woman a chance to better herself."

"Mrs. Cartwright, I just don't need a housekeeper—" Del began, but the woman was too angry to listen.

"No, you just don't need *me* as a housekeeper," she

countered. "I suppose you're plannin' on hirin' that cute little blond, dressed up so fancy, just waitin' on the sidewalk outside the gate, thinkin' I don't see her eavesdroppin' on our private conversation."

"Who?" Del's head shot up and he started scanning the grounds around the gate. "What the heck are you talking about?"

In all of Grasonville there could only be one cute little blond, dressed up fancy, who'd bother with what was going on at the old Richardson place.

Miranda.

"Thanks for stopping by, Mrs. Cartwright," Del said as he pushed past her. As he rushed down the overgrown walk, he called back, "I'll let you know if I change my mind."

She just grunted.

He pulled to an abrupt stop at the gate. Slowly he peeked around the corner.

No one was there.

Del looked up and down Main Street. He wasn't really surprised they called it Main Street this far out now. There was a lot more traffic going back and forth. They'd actually extended the sidewalk out to Mr. Richardson's place now, too, and more stores and houses lined the walk on both sides of the street. The sidewalks were pretty crowded as well.

But even though he searched for her in both directions, Del couldn't spot Miranda.

Maybe Mrs. Cartwright had been mistaken about her peeking into the grounds. Or maybe he had misunderstood Mrs. Cartwright. Maybe he'd wanted to see Miranda here so much he'd mistaken the mention of any little blond for her.

No! In the first place, he wasn't that eager to see the bothersome little pest again. In the second place, there was only one Miranda.

Miranda thought her shoes were awfully heavy. She'd grown very used to wearing the well-designed leather shoes for day wear, or the tiny cloth pumps for evening wear. She hadn't worn her old walking shoes in over a year.

But she could hardly wear that delicate footwear now. They just wouldn't stand up to the dirt road into town. Even if the sidewalks did start right past the Richardson house, well, heck, that was as far into town as she was going anyway.

She'd have rather eaten raw worms than ask anyone for a ride. She couldn't let them think she was still interested in that old house. She especially couldn't let them think anything Del did could hold any interest whatsoever for her any longer.

It wasn't Del. She just wanted to see that house.

Apparently he was planning on living there after all. Why else would he be there, opening doors and windows, unless he was airing the place out, getting ready to live there? Why else would Mrs. Cartwright be there if not to clean the place for him like she had for Mr. Richardson? The next thing she knew, he'd be looking for Marvin Platt to do his yard work for him.

He didn't really want to live there, she told herself. He was just doing it to spite her. He'd live there just until she got married and moved back to Boston. Then he'd sell the place to a complete stranger—someone who didn't even care about the house—and move away back to Texas. And they'd never see each other again for as long as they lived.

Feeling very disappointed and very dejected—not to mention completely betrayed by Del—Miranda made her way quickly back to her own house.

She was glad they hadn't moved away from here when her father had struck it rich in the Nevada silver mines. She liked the sprawling house with its big cottonwood tree in the front yard and the barn full of cows and horses in the back. She even liked the chickens, even though she could do without the rooster waking her at dawn every morning. The only thing she'd never been too wild about was the outhouse.

Of course, the place was a good bit different now from the house she'd spent the first six years of her life in. The money had enabled them to make a lot of much needed improvements.

The roof didn't leak anymore. The porch rails hadn't fallen down in years. They had a brick walk going all the way up to the house from the road, and going all the way around the house. One of these days, her father would add one of those new telephones, if they could think of someone else to call.

They even had indoor plumbing! With a bathtub, a sink, and a commode! She'd always sworn she'd live in a house with a bathroom inside, so she'd never have to use an outhouse again.

Of course, she'd also sworn she'd marry Del and live in Mr. Richardson's house someday, and look how badly that had turned out.

She crept quietly up onto the back porch. Very slowly she reached out and pushed open the kitchen door.

"My goodness gracious! Where have you been?" her mother demanded, confronting her right at the doorway.

"Ooops."

Even if she'd taken the heavy, noisy shoes off, her mother would have caught her. It was almost as if she was waiting there for her. Unfortunately, so was every-one else.

"We've been very concerned for you, my dear," Mrs. Lowell said. Her cardboard smile was very stiff. She must be very upset about something.

"I was afraid the Indians had gone on the warpath and taken you captive!" Charles exclaimed. "I couldn't bare to think of them scalping you, my dear."

"I was afraid you'd taken to running off and hiding again," her mother finished, with a wry smile.

"Hiding?" Charles and Mrs. Lowell repeated simulta-neously. Mrs. Lowell's eyes were wide with alarm.

Oh, Mother!

She was as bad as Del for bringing up all the stupid

things Miranda had done when she was a child, especially in front of Mrs. Lowell.

Miranda forced a little giggle. "Why would I ever do anything as silly as that?"

Mrs. Hamilton shrugged. "I gave up trying to figure you out a long time ago, Miranda. I just thought you'd gotten upset because of Del being so darn stubborn about the Richardson place."

"Oh, that old house?" she said with another giggle.

She hoped this one didn't sound as forced as the other. She hoped they'd believe she wasn't anguishing over it anymore.

"No, no, no. I've put that unpleasant little incident completely behind me—along with Del."

"Good," Mrs. Hamilton muttered, and moved away.

"I'm so sorry I worried you all," Miranda said. "I just went for a little walk around . . ."

She waved her hand about in the air, with no particular direction in mind. Let them make their own suppositions.

"The day was so nice, it seemed a shame to waste it indoors."

"Don't worry. You'll get enough time outdoors at the party this afternoon," Mrs. Hamilton told her. "I was afraid you'd lose track of the time, or completely forget. We're going to the Widow Crenshaw's and Miss Barber's today. We shouldn't be late."

Miranda grimaced. "You're right. I'd completely forgotten." She leaned a little closer to her mother and whispered, "Are you sure there's no way we can send our regrets?"

"Not at all!" Mrs. Hamilton declared. "Janet and Catherine are two of the most prominent citizens of our town."

"No, they're not," Miranda protested. "Neither one of them ever did one constructive, beneficial thing in their entire lives. The only notable thing about them is Miss Barber's father and Widow Crenshaw's husband—and they're both dead."

"We couldn't possibly not go," her mother pronounced with great finality.

Miranda scuffed at the floor with the toe of her old shoe. "I just don't see how you can stand to be around them after what they tried to do to you and Daddy— and me."

Mrs. Hamilton laid her hand firmly on Miranda's shoulder and looked her directly in the eye.

"That was many years ago when they tried to have me declared an unfit mother and take you away from me and given into your father's custody. It might not have seemed nice at the time, but I'm sure they meant well."

"Yeah, I'm sure."

"Anyway, it all turned out just fine," Mrs. Hamilton continued lightly. "Your father and I might never have reconciled if we hadn't had to argue over who gets you."

If Del were here, he'd have some wiseacre comment to make about neither one of them wanting her. She was glad he wasn't here to embarrass her further.

"Still . . ."

"Forgive and forget," Mrs. Hamilton preached.

Miranda decided she could be forgiving where the two old busybodies were concerned. After all, they were giving this very nice party for her and her fiancé. But she wasn't about to be that forgetful.

"Then why can't you forget I used to run away whenever I didn't get my way?" she asked.

"Because I'm your mother. I worry about you."

Miranda's expression softened. She could argue with her mother over almost anything else, but not about that. There was nothing anyone in the world could say to make Mrs. Hamilton not worry about her daughter.

"Now, come along," Mrs. Hamilton said, urging Miranda toward the back stairs. "Let me help you get ready. You've got to wear your absolute best outfit there today. And you can tell me what you think of the new dress I made just for this occasion."

"I'm sure it's stunning," Miranda assured her.

"I'm sure it's uniquely you, Mrs. Hamilton," Mrs. Lowell commented.

Mrs. Lowell turned to Charles. She glanced at the stairs once more, just to make certain Miranda and her mother were out of earshot. Then she turned back to Charles.

"She runs away?" she demanded with a censorious lift of her thin eyebrow.

"She *ran* away, Mother," Charles corrected. "In the past. Apparently she doesn't do that anymore."

"She ran away whenever she didn't get her way." Mrs. Lowell shook her head. "Oh, my dear boy, this bodes ill for the type of behavior one looks for in a Boston Society wife."

"She doesn't do it anymore, Mother," Charles repeated with more emphasis. "After all, she only went for a walk. She didn't actually run away this morning. And when did we ever hear of her running away in Boston?"

Mrs. Lowell thought a moment, her lips pursed more tightly than usual.

At last she replied, "Well, this could signify one of three possibilities. One, she has indeed outgrown that childish response to frustration."

He nodded.

"Two, we simply never heard of her doing such a ridiculous thing in Boston."

"Considering your exalted standing in the gossiping community, Mother, I highly doubt that," he replied with a chuckle.

"Thank you, Charles. Or three," Mrs. Lowell continued, "she never had to deal with not getting what she wanted in Boston and therefore had no need to run away."

"I'd like to believe the first," he said brightly.

"Indeed, so would I," Mrs. Lowell said, with much more foreboding. "However, all things considered, I am more inclined to believe the last. I must also warn you that, in the general course of married life, a wife frequently finds that she does not always get what she wants. In light of all these facts, I must caution you to be on the alert with Miranda—both here and once we return to Boston. It simply will not do to have a runaway wife."

"Nonsense, Mother," he protested. "Miranda would never—!"

"Of course not," Mrs. Lowell responded without much true conviction. "And we have plenty of servants to keep an eye on her just to make sure that she doesn't."

"Goodness gracious!" Miranda exclaimed when she saw the crowd gathered in the street.

"What is it?" Mrs. Lowell demanded.

"Sam, stop!" Mrs. Hamilton ordered, tapping on her husband's arm to get his attention.

"Are you sure that's wise?" Charles asked. "It might be some sort of riot. Miranda—or any one of us—might be harmed."

"No, they look pretty peaceable to me," Mr. Hamilton said as he reined the wagon to a halt. Apparently, he tried to get as close to the crowd gathered outside Liz Engle-meyer's Millinery Shop as possible.

"What is it? What happened?" Miranda asked as she began to climb down from the wagon without assistance.

"Miranda, watch your dress!" Mrs. Hamilton scolded.

But she was already down and heading toward the crowd. She wasn't about to stop now.

"Aren't you coming?" she called back.

Mrs. Lowell sat staring straight ahead. "I do not stand milling about with the riffraff on street corners. I shall be waiting here."

"Mama?"

Mrs. Hamilton grimaced. Miranda could see her mother wanted to be polite and remain with her guests. On the other hand, she was also just dying to find out what was going on.

"I think I'd better wait here—to keep Mrs. Lowell company," she answered at last.

"I'll tell you all about it when I get back," Miranda promised as she headed toward the crowd.

"Oh, Miranda, imagine meeting you here!" the Widow Crenshaw exclaimed as she headed her off on her way to the crowd.

"We were on our way to your party for me," she exclaimed. "What are you doing here? Why aren't you—?"

"Oh, the party's not going anywhere until we get back," Miss Barber replied.

After a few clumsy grabs Miss Barber managed to seize Miranda's hand. Her little brown eyes were squinted up tight as she tried to make out the indistinct shapes that wavered in front of her.

Apparently, the weak-eyed Miss Barber set her course in a straight line toward Liz Englemeyer's store. Miranda, for her own safety and that of the other people gathered there, could only maneuver the determined elderly lady through the crowd.

The poor dear's eyesight had never been good, Miranda rationalized. That could be the only reason she was heading straight for Del. Miranda didn't need to see his face. She'd recognize even the back of his head anywhere.

She wished she could have steered her around in a circle and back to the wagon again. But Miss Barber was the driving force behind their locomotion, and she wouldn't be stopped until she'd brought Miranda directly beside Del.

"And anyway," Miss Barber added as they came to a stop, "this is so much more exciting!"

"It doesn't take much to make Catherine happy," the Widow Crenshaw remarked. "Although I'll bet Liz Englemeyer isn't half as happy."

"What happened?"

"We're trying to find out, too," Widow Crenshaw said.

"Excuse me for breaking into your conversation—"

"Oh, not at all, Del!" Miss Barber gushed.

"Apparently, there've been a series of burglaries in town," Del told them.

"Burglaries?" Miranda repeated.

She turned around quickly. She shouldn't have done that. She hadn't judged him to be standing that close beside her when she'd first gotten there.

She was so near to him now, she could feel his warm breath on her cheek. He smelled like peppermint. She stepped back quickly.

"What are you doing in town?" she demanded.

Her heart thudded against her chest. Was she more surprised by his presence or unnerved by his nearness?

"I'm on my way to a party."

"Someone's throwing a party for you? How nice."

It should be a going-away party.

"Nope." He grinned at her. "I'm on my way to *your* party."

Miranda did not return his grin.

She knew her mother had extended some sort of open invitation to him to attend all her parties, but did the uncouth lout have to take her up on every single one of them? Or had Widow Crenshaw and Miss Barber invited him deliberately? She knew she shouldn't have trusted those two old busybodies!

"We just had to invite him, Miranda," Miss Barber explained. "We haven't had a party in so long. But we figured we sort of owed it to your mother and father after . . . well, after our suspicions . . . *completely unfounded* suspicions, so long ago . . . to do something really special for you."

"Oh, honestly, Catherine," Widow Crenshaw protested. "That was thirteen years ago. Everyone's forgotten everything by now. I certainly have. Sam and Bertha graciously have."

Widow Crenshaw turned to Miranda.

"Don't pay any attention to Catherine. Her memory isn't any better than her eyesight. And they're both getting worse."

Undaunted, Miss Barber leaned a little closer to Miranda, as if to include her in her confidence.

"There really are so few people in town we would truly feel comfortable entertaining," she said. "I mean,

can you imagine us inviting all those Stanleys—
seventeen at last count? Or those awful foreigners—
Swedish or Norwegian or something—who live over on
the other side of town? Why, they can barely speak
English. Always sound like they're clearing their throat
or sucking lemons when they talk. Or Jimmy Walters or
Allen Douglas? Why, they're real born Americans and
can barely speak English." She gave a little giggle.

"We couldn't force you to suffer through a party with
just us old fuddy-duddies," Widow Crenshaw said with a
little laugh. "We tried to invite all the young folks in
town about your age."

Del's seven years older than I am. That's not my age.

"That way you young people will have something in
common to talk about while we old folks just sit around."

I have absolutely nothing to talk to Del about.

"And we remembered how taken you were with him
when you were just knee-high to a grasshopper," Miss
Barber added with a little giggle.

Miranda wished Miss Barber's memory wasn't so poor
about some things and so darned good about others. She
also wished that, in all her years on this earth, somewhere
along the line, the elderly lady would also have learned
when not to open her mouth.

"How very considerate of you both," Miranda replied.
Boy, she was certainly giving Mrs. Bigelow's rules of
conduct a real workout here today!

The crowd shifted. Widow Crenshaw and Miss Barber
had to move around into a little circle, forcing Miranda to
stand closer to Del.

He was dressed in yet another outfit—trousers and a
starched white broadcloth shirt that stretched across his
chest. Even the nubby wool of the new jacket he wore
couldn't disguise his broad shoulders.

"How do you know about these burglaries?" she
asked.

Del chuckled. She watched little crinkles form at the
corners of his eyes as he smiled.

"How does anybody find out anything in this town?" he countered.

Miranda grinned back at him. "I guess you're right."

He reached up and smoothed back the hair on the side of his head. She felt the tips of her fingers tingling as she imagined doing the same thing herself. Coming closer to him, reaching up, touching him, feeling the softness of his hair, the roughness of the stubble of his beard, the softness of his lips. Coming closer to him.

"I got a haircut at Mr. Carter's."

Miranda roused herself from her provocative daydream and nodded. All the gentlemen in town went to Mr. Carter, for their daily gossip, and the ladies went to Miss Englemeyer's for theirs. Somehow, the information all got exchanged in the middle.

"Who else has been robbed?" Miranda asked.

"Mr. Carter said someone broke into Quinn's General Store about a week ago," Del answered.

"What did they take?"

The sun-browned, auburn-haired young man sauntering toward them answered, "Twenty dollars, a hammer, and two pounds of sugar."

"Max?" Del demanded. "Max Douglas. Is that you?"

"Yep."

Oh, no! Not Max Douglas. I hate Max Douglas. Always have. Always will.

Max tipped his hat. "Morning, ladies. Morning, Miss Hamilton."

Miss Hamilton? What happened to his usual greeting to her? "Hey, Miranda, you scabby-kneed, nose-pickin', bugger-eatin' runt!"

Miranda tried to smile cordially, but it only came out as a crooked grimace. Maybe if she said something, moving her mouth would hide the horrible grimace.

"Good morning, Max."

No, she could not bring herself to call him Mr. Douglas, not even if he became the mayor, not even if someday he became President of the United States of

America, not even if God and all His angels commanded it.

Widow Crenshaw and Miss Barber shifted places in the circle to make room for Max to fit in. Darn it! Why couldn't they wiggle to the other side? Miranda silently lamented as she was forced to move closer to Del.

And no, Del couldn't be like other, polite people who moved out to allow the new person into the circle. The unfeeling clod had to stand his ground. Miranda was forced to stand so close to him that their shoulders almost touched.

Well, not exactly their shoulders, she amended. The top of her shoulder only came up to about the middle of his upper arm. She could have very easily rested her head on his shoulder though. She could have felt his muscles under his shirt, and his body moving as he breathed.

"Welcome back to Grasonville," Max continued. "My best wishes on your upcoming wedding."

"Thank you very much."

No sense in letting him believe he was more polite than she was. After all, *she* was the one whose parents had spent all that money to make certain she had a good education in Boston. Max had been the only student in Miss Porter's third grade who was late every morning because he had to shave.

"Hey, Max," Del said, pointing, "what in tarnation have you got on your shirt?"

She blinked several times as she peered at the five-pointed glint in the morning light.

"That's right, Miranda," Miss Barber said. "Do you know who you're talking to?"

Instead, Miranda just turned to the elderly lady and smiled

"Miranda," Miss Barber announced, "you are now talking to the new sheriff of Grasonville."

"Max, that's great," Del responded immediately.

Miranda knew it was going to take her a little more time to recover from the shock.

"That's *Sheriff* Douglas to you, Williams," Max responded with mock bravado. The corners of his mouth twitched as he tried not to grin with obvious pride.

Miranda wanted to laugh out loud. Max Douglas was the sheriff, Widow Crenshaw and Miss Barber were giving her a party, and Del Williams was one of the richest men in town. Next thing she knew, the cows would dance into town wearing pink and purple tutus and singing "The Camptown Races," and Reverend Knutson would preach a sermon on "The Joys of Overindulging in Rum and Indiscriminate Copulation."

"How'd that happen?" she asked. "What happened to Sheriff Duncan?"

"He retired right after Christmas last year," Max explained.

"He moved out to California," Widow Crenshaw explained.

"We do miss him so. He gave us his address, but it takes so long for the letters to go back and forth, and sometimes we need answers now," Miss Barber finished with a little sigh.

"Hush, Catherine."

"But Max is such a nice young fellow . . . such a help."

"Hush, Catherine."

"I ran for the office, and dang if I didn't get elected." Max grinned broadly.

Who ran against you? Lucifer? That was probably the only candidate who would be worse than Max. Except maybe Del, but he'd been out of town at the time, and hadn't run, anyway. What in the world had possessed the good people of Grasonville to elect Max Douglas sheriff?

Of course, even in her surprise, she didn't forget her good manners. "Congratulations on your successful campaign."

"What made you run for sheriff, Max?" Del asked.

"I'll tell you when I see you later," he replied. "Right now I got a heck of a lot of business to take care of. A couple days ago somebody broke into Nichols's Haberdashery, too."

"Are you sure it wasn't Mr. Thompson?" Miranda offered. "Those two have been feuding for years."

Max shook his head.

"What'd they take from Nichols's?" Del asked.

"A pair of gloves? A walking stick? Bowties?" Miranda offered. What else would someone take from a haberdashery?

"Not exactly," Max corrected. "But they did manage to make off with two new hats and sixty dollars."

"Apparently Mr. Nichols is doing better than Mr. Quinn," Del remarked.

"And now someone just robbed Englemeyer's?" Widow Crenshaw asked. She looked around furtively, then leaned closer to Max to ask, "Does this incident expand the list of suspects to include some of the ladies in town?"

"Either that or Gus Masterson has finally decided to stop hiding when he puts on his wife's dresses," Miss Barber replied.

"I guess it depends on where the stolen goods show up, doesn't it?" Max returned.

"What did they take from Miss Englemeyer's?" Miranda asked.

"Nothing."

"Nothing?"

He nodded. "They rifled through the cupboards and drawers, and broke open the cashbox. But apparently Miss Englemeyer is too sharp to keep her day's proceeds in the shop."

"Good for her," Miranda cheered. "But that's still so bizarre."

"You're right. Everything they've taken has been really out of the ordinary. The weirdest thing is, if they were really after a lot of money, they'd have tried to rob one of the saloons."

"Nobody's robbed the saloons?"

Max shook his head. "That's why, at first, I thought it was just a series of pranks some of the ornerier kids in town were playing since they had nothing else to do now that school's let out for the summer. Now I don't think so."

"Do you know who's been doing this then?" Miss Barber asked.

"Don't be dumb, Catherine," Widow Crenshaw scolded. "If he knew that, we wouldn't be standing here thinking what a shame it is that Miss Englemeyer's place was vandalized."

"That's horrible!" Miss Barber wailed.

"Terrible!"

"Appalling!"

"What is this world coming to with all this senseless violence?" Miss Barber lamented.

"Can you think of any sensible violence, Catherine?" Widow Crenshaw demanded.

"Do you believe it'll extend to private homes?" Miranda asked apprehensively.

"I don't blame you for your concern, ma'am," Max said. "These burglaries used to be just annoying, petty theft. Causing that much damage to personal property means the thieves are growing bolder. You might just want to take some extra precautions with your property and valuables."

Miss Barber and Miss Crenshaw exchanged furtive glances.

"Did you hear that, Janet?" Miss Barber asked. "Don't you just love it when he talks sheriff-talk?"

"Don't get carried away, Catherine," Widow Crenshaw admonished.

"How close are you to catching these two, Max?" Miranda asked.

"Close, very close, I hope," Max replied.

Widow Crenshaw and Miss Barber exchanged another of their conspiratorial glances.

"Miranda, what makes you think there are two of them?" Widow Crenshaw asked.

Miranda shrugged. "They took two hats. One person wouldn't need two, and three people probably would have taken three."

Widow Crenshaw stroked her chin. "She's got a good point there, Catherine."

"Do you think she might . . . ?"

"Oh, hush, Catherine!"

"Those are turning out to be some mighty dangerous pranks," Del commented.

"That's nothing compared to the trouble we're having a little farther west of town," Max replied.

6

"*TROUBLE?*" MIRANDA REPEATED.

"Farther west of town?" Del asked.

"Yep, right around your neck of the woods," Max answered.

Del glanced toward Miranda.

Well, what's he looking at me for? Does he think I'm responsible for it? Why not? He blames me for everything else.

"What kind of trouble, Sheriff?" Widow Crenshaw asked eagerly.

"They're holding up stagecoaches, trains—"

"They're robbing trains?" Miss Barber exclaimed.

"They killed three men when they took the Army payroll two weeks ago."

"Oh, that's horrible!" Miranda exclaimed.

"I guess you can see why most of the efforts of the lawmen in this part of the state are directed toward finding these bandits."

"I suppose so."

"I can't get much enthusiasm from the federal marshals for a bunch of kids who take hats and break windows."

"I guess not," Del said.

"But as soon as we catch them, I'll be able to concentrate on stopping those rotten kids from playing their dirty tricks." Max shrugged. "Or maybe they'll have done some growing up by then."

"Or their parents will have caught them and whaled the tar out of them," Widow Crenshaw said.

"I think they might have to stand in line behind Mr. Nichols and Mr. Quinn. That is, if anything's left of them after Liz Englemeyer gets through with them."

"Wow! This sounds really great!"

Miranda and Del turned to the sound of shattering glass.

"Hey, Del, ol' buddy!"

Del groaned and turned away.

"Hey, hey! Wendell! Ol' drippy-pants Wendell! Don't try to turn away from us!"

"Yeah, we see you standin' there! You can't hide from us."

Miranda cringed. Jimmy Walters and Allen Douglas. If there were any two people she hated more than Max, they were his older brother and his idiot sidekick.

On the other hand, if anyone could publicly embarrass Del in exchange for all the times he'd embarrassed her, she figured suffering their company now was fair enough exchange.

Miranda knew Allen was about ten years older than Max, but they used to look so much alike they could have been twins. Now she could see huge purple bags hanging under Allen's eyes. Where the sunlight had tanned Max's cheeks so that the freckles hardly showed anymore, Allen's had only popped out darker in the sun. Red and purple wasn't a good combination to begin with, but on his face, it was really bad.

Jimmy and Allen stopped crunching the broken glass strewn along the sidewalk just long enough to make their way up to Del and Miranda. Allen threw his arm around Del's shoulder.

"Criminy! Why'd you go away? I missed you, man," he blubbered. "It's good to have my best buddy back."

"I thought Jimmy was your best buddy," Del reminded him.

"Yeah, yeah, I am," Jimmy insisted.

Jimmy just *had* to stand too close to her.

She hated when someone did that, but especially someone who smelled like Jimmy. She sniffed a curious combination of horse manure and whiskey and some other unidentifiable odor that she decided it was best if she didn't know what it was after all.

She couldn't tell if it was butter or lard slicking down Jimmy's blond hair. She just wasn't curious enough to want to get any closer to find out. There was just no room to back away from him, either.

"Hey, Miranda, you scab-eating water rat," he declared as he looked her over from head to toe. "What'd you do, steal your mother's dress?"

"Why? Do you want to borrow it?" Oh, she was so glad Mrs. Lowell wasn't there to hear that.

Allen laughed. "Don't need you for that. Looks like we can just waltz into Englemeyer's and take whatever we want."

"No, you can't," Max said sternly.

Jimmy elbowed Allen and giggled. "What? Is your little brother going to try to stop us?"

"Cripes, Max, we knew you was a nelly when you stopped hanging with us at the Last Chance and started reading," Allen accused.

Max shrugged. "I guess I got tired of the smell of whiskey and vomit."

"Now you're no fun at all."

Jimmy elbowed Allen again as they both laughed.

"Betcha he got tired of visitin' Miss Sadie's, too."

"Naw, he don't even know what them gals is good for."

"Move along now. Move along," Max ordered. "We've got to clean this mess up so upstanding citizens can walk down the street."

"Naw," Jimmy complained. He started crunching the

shards of glass under his boot heels again. "This sounds . . . yeah, um, good. Yeah."

Max headed toward them.

"Yeah, yeah, we're going," Allen said, starting to move away. He elbowed Jimmy. "If we don't, he'll tell Ma on me, the little bugger-eatin', pants-wettin' snitch."

"Yeah, we got better things to do than hang around a dress shop all day," Jimmy said.

Allen tugged on his elbow, moving them both along down Main Street. Were they heading for Sullivan's Last Chance Saloon, the Lonesome Whistle Saloon, or Miss Sadie's? Who cared, as long as they left.

"Oh, thank goodness they're gone!" Miss Barber exclaimed.

"Hush, Catherine," Widow Crenshaw scolded. "After all, he is Max's brother."

"Oh, more's the pity."

"And we have a party to get ready for," Widow Crenshaw reminded her. "After all, our guests of honor are on their way right now."

"They are?"

Widow Crenshaw seized Miss Barber's hand. "Come along, Catherine. You've been out in the sun too long."

Miranda waited until the two elderly ladies had made their way a little bit along the sidewalk. It wouldn't be proper to reach their house before they did.

She turned to go.

"I guess I'll see you there, Miranda," Del said.

Not if I see you—

She stopped. She'd already thought that once before in reply to his remark, and it hadn't worked. She'd seen him everywhere.

Once, not so long ago, she couldn't bear not to be near him. Now she just couldn't seem to get rid of Del Williams.

"Miranda, it's good to see you again so soon."

Dorothy Halstead flounced toward her across the neat

front lawn of Widow Crenshaw's house, her naturally curly hair fluffing up in the breeze.

Miranda had always been so grateful for her own poker-straight locks that stayed exactly where she pinned them. Then she noticed several young men seated on Widow Crenshaw's big wrap-around porch couldn't manage to keep their eyes off Dorothy. Several more of the bolder ones actually came up and gathered around them as they spoke.

Maybe Mother Nature hadn't been so unkind to Dorothy after all.

"Now we'll have the chance to have a nice long chat, catch up on old times," Dorothy said.

"I can't wait. I've missed you, too."

Holding Miranda's hand, Dorothy led her around to the back of the house, where the tables of food were laid out under the wide elm trees. The young men sitting on the porch followed like sheep.

"You can tell me all about your school in Boston, your engagement, *and* your fiancé."

Miranda looked behind her to see what was happening to Charles and Mrs. Lowell. She should have been able to predict it. Her mother and Widow Crenshaw were silently and politely battling over who would have the honor of showing off Mrs. Lowell at this party.

Her father had commandeered Charles and was hauling him off toward where the men usually congregated, just inside the barn door.

"Did you happen to notice the uproar as you were coming here?" Dorothy asked.

Miranda smiled at Dorothy with forced sweetness. "Something so exciting right in the middle of town. Why, who could miss it?"

"Exciting? It's downright scary!" Dorothy stopped in her tracks and clasped her hands over her bosom. Her blue eyes grew wide with horror. "Why, just suppose, some dark and rainy night, while I was slumbering peacefully in my solitary bed, one of those horrid bandits should sneak into my room—and ravish me!"

"The cad!" Carvel Marsh stoutly declared.

"Heaven forbid!" Hal Danvers gasped in affront.

"You've only to call, and I'll save you, Miss Halstead," Arthur Baldwin vowed.

She tossed her hair about and flashed them all a beaming smile. "I just knew I could count on you gentlemen to rescue a lady in distress."

Dorothy, you've got to stop going to see those silly melodramas. That dialogue is worse than Charles's.

Dorothy batted her long eyelashes prettily at them all and tossed her mane of curling hair around to best effect.

But Miranda noticed that Dorothy wasn't watching a single one of her would-be heroes. She only had eyes for the group of men standing by the larger of the two elm trees—and only one of them in particular. Del.

"I don't think they'd be out on a dark and rainy night, Dorothy," Miranda said. "You'll have to wait for better weather."

"Oh, you won't get much better weather than this," Miss Barber said, looking upward at the clear blue sky.

Everyone else just stared at her.

"You're quite right, Miss Barber," Miranda eventually said.

"In fact, the day is so warm and lovely that I do believe I need a glass of punch," Dorothy remarked.

"Oh, I'll get it for you," several young men declared at the same time.

"Why don't you get some, too, Miranda?" Dorothy suggested.

She probably supposed she was darting furtive glances at Del, but Miranda thought the girl was being painfully obvious.

"I'd be pleased to escort you, Miss Hamilton," Hal Danvers said.

"I'm not thirsty, thank you anyway," Miranda said in one breath.

Oh, Dorothy, I've managed to find a husband in spite of Boston debutantes. Your ploys are so transparent. You're no challenge at all.

Dorothy's would-be suitors sped for the refreshment table at the far side of the yard.

Undaunted, Dorothy reached out and took Miranda by the arm.

"Oh, I thought I'd never get rid of them," she said with a sigh of relief. "I've known them all my life. I've been to school with them. I remember what they looked like with snot frozen to their faces. I've seen them when their mothers scrubbed them up every Sunday for church until I'm plumb weary of each and every one of them."

"I think I know what you mean," Miranda said.

"Perhaps," Dorothy reluctantly conceded. "But *you've* had the opportunity to go elsewhere. And just look what you came home with, you lucky little minx. How nice for you."

"I like him," she replied modestly.

"I, on the other hand, can't afford to go anywhere and must wait here in dull old Grasonville and see what comes to me," Dorothy said with a pretty pout.

Don't waste it on me, Dorothy.

"It took three years, but they do say all good things come to the one who waits."

"Just what exactly have you been waiting for for three years, Dorothy?" Miranda managed to ask without clenching her jaws.

Dorothy really didn't need to say a word. She was taking Miranda directly toward the answer. Slowly, inexorably, Dorothy was drawing her toward the tree where Max, Will, and Del were standing. Miranda would rather lie down on the railroad tracks!

But she could hardly go digging her heels into Widow Crenshaw's nice lawn and leave two long ruts, so she just continued to follow Dorothy's lead, like a lamb being led to slaughter.

Wait! Maybe she was going about this all the wrong way. Maybe she could speed up and plunge Dorothy, naturally curly hair and all, into the trunk of the tree. No, that would probably only knock her unconscious. Then she could bat her eyelashes prettily at Del as she came to.

Miranda had no choice but to continue her death march toward Del.

His brother Will was a nice fellow. She figured she wouldn't mind chatting with him for a while. She still hated Max for all the nasty things he'd said to her over the years, but since he was now sheriff, and seemed to have turned his life around, she supposed she could tolerate him for a little while—until he did something else to irritate her.

But Del *always* irritated her. All the man had to do was stand there and she felt all nervous and jumpy inside— just waiting for him to say or do something that would upset her, that was the reason. The worst part was, she couldn't figure out if the jumpiness made her want to run away from him or hold him tightly in her arms and press her body against his to still the tingling.

If she could just figure out some way to get away from him as soon as possible.

"Hello, gentlemen," Dorothy said in a voice that was barely a breath.

She dropped Miranda's arm like a hot potato and maneuvered herself to stand directly beside Del. Miranda was stuck next to Will. She could think of worse places to be—but she could also think of a lot better.

"Hello, Dorothy, Miranda," Will replied.

"Miss Halstead," Max said, nodding to her. "Miss Hamilton, I'll bet you didn't think we'd see each other again so soon."

"No, I really didn't," she had to admit.

Del just nodded to Dorothy from over the top of his glass of lemonade. Miranda smiled with satisfaction. But then, Del just nodded to her, too, from over the top of his glass and turned back to the rest of the folks in the circle. No, she was *not* disappointed!

Maybe he believed, since he'd already welcomed her back to town at the train station, and told her in no uncertain terms that he'd never sell her the house of her dreams, he didn't have anything else to say to her. He was probably right.

If Widow Crenshaw and Miss Barber had invited people here today for her to talk to, they'd sure made a big mistake in inviting Del.

Dorothy laid her hand on Del's arm. She looked up at him with her big blue eyes and pleaded, "Oh, Del, we were so hoping you could tell us some of the exciting things you've been doing in Texas."

What do you mean "we"?

"I'm just dying to hear all about the cattle roundups," Dorothy continued.

Lassos and cow plop? I don't think so.

Miranda watched the girl with narrowing eyes. She was beginning to doubt Widow Crenshaw's and Miss Barber's wisdom in inviting Dorothy, too.

"It's not very exciting," Del admitted.

"I'm sure you're just being modest," Dorothy told him. "Such a sterling quality in a gentleman."

Since when did you become a gentleman, Del? Since Henry Richardson left you a manure cart full of money! That's when.

Del shook his head. "Not really. I was just a ranch hand—a pretty boring job."

"Oh, you could never be boring, Del," Dorothy enthused.

Miranda vowed that if Dorothy made one more remark like that to Del, she'd pull every naturally curly hair out of her friend's little head. Then Miranda cringed with remorse. How could she be so jealous and vindictive? That wasn't like her at all.

"Ah, now, if you want excitement, ladies and gentlemen," Widow Crenshaw interjected as she insinuated herself into the circle, "you've got to talk to Max."

"Yes, indeed, talk to Max," Miss Barber parroted as she followed her friend.

The two elderly ladies squeezed themselves into the circle between Del and Dorothy.

Miranda breathed a little prayer of thanksgiving for the two nosy little old ladies.

She was sorry this wasn't a ball. She felt just like dancing.

For that one act of selfless kindness alone, you are both completely forgiven all former transgressions!

"What about Max?" Dorothy asked with ill-concealed sullenness.

Somehow, Miranda noted, the glimmer had gone out of her conversation.

"Max is the one with the truly exciting job," Miss Barber said.

"He's just the sheriff," Dorothy remarked with a sneer.

"But weren't you surprised when he ran for sheriff after Amos Duncan retired?" Widow Crenshaw asked.

"No."

"I certainly was surprised to find that out," Miranda chimed in. "Never in a million years would I have expected to return home to find Max had been elected sheriff."

She figured she owed Widow Crenshaw and Miss Barber any favor. She also figured she owed this one to herself.

Slowly she moved across the center of the circle to stand directly beside Max. Of course, if Del happened to be standing on the other side of Max, and she just happened to wiggle herself between them, well, that was just a strange coincidence, wasn't it? But she was *here*—and Dorothy was way over *there*.

"I was pretty surprised myself when he told me," Del said. "Max was always such a rotten kid."

Del, you were such a Mr. Goody Two-shoes, you made me want to gag. I can't imagine why I ever thought I was in love with you.

"You never did tell us, and I've been wondering. Why did you decide to run for sheriff, Max?" Miranda asked.

"I guess I got tired of hanging around the saloons, cleaning up after my brother," he explained.

"Yes, I can see where that wouldn't be the most pleasant of pastimes," Miranda agreed.

"When I got out of the Army, I started reading law with Mr. Martin."

She blinked with surprise. "With him? Why would you want to do that? Were all the other lawyers dead or something?"

"I wondered that myself," Del said. "Funny how we keep wondering about the same sort of things, isn't it, Miranda?"

"Not really, since we've both been away for several years and have the same amount of catching up to do on the same things," she told him. Then she turned to Max again. "So you actually wanted to be a lawyer?"

"I thought I did."

"What made you change your mind? Not that it probably wasn't a bad decision," she quickly added.

"I thought being a lawyer was about defending the right from the wrong."

"It's not?" She blinked with surprise. That was what she'd always believed, too.

"No, it's not. I found out it's about winning."

"Winning can be good," Del offered.

"You ought to know," Miranda grumbled.

Max shook his head. "No, not the way Martin goes about it."

"You know, Max," Del ventured, "with those specifications for a job, you could've become a preacher, too."

"Me? Yeah. You've obviously mistaken me for somebody else. Del, I swear to God, that's got to be the silliest thing you've ever said!"

Max and Del laughed.

"What I'm doing now is about doing right and stopping wrong." Max nodded with certainty.

"Max has such an exciting job," Widow Crenshaw said.

"What do you like best about being sheriff, Max?" Del asked. "Breaking up fights at the Last Chance Saloon or throwing rowdies out of Miss Sadie's?"

What did Del know about Miss Sadie's House? Miranda wondered with alarm. Why should she care?

"Nope, nope." Max was shaking his head vigorously. "My favorite part of the job is hanging up the wanted posters."

Everyone in the circle laughed, even pouting Dorothy.

"I'll bet a lot of people don't know how dangerous it is tacking those things up," Del interjected with a chuckle. "You could nail your thumb, or get a really bad paper cut."

"Oh, those wanted posters are so unbelievably interesting!" Miss Barber exclaimed.

"They are?" Miranda asked.

"Have you ever read one?" Miss Barber demanded.

"No. They're just bad drawings and lists of crimes. Of course, the reward offered is usually pretty interesting to most people."

"No, no, no," Miss Barber protested. "There's so much more that most people miss."

"Have you read one?"

"Occasionally," Widow Crenshaw said noncommittally.

"Oh, I read each and every one of them," Miss Barber asserted.

Max nodded. "That's right. She's in my office every time a new batch comes in with the mail."

"Why?" Miranda asked. She didn't even bother to try to hide her surprise.

"Why not?" Widow Crenshaw quickly countered. "There's not much else to do in this town."

"Did MacKenzie's Bookstore close?" Miranda asked.

"No. Oh, no," Miss Barber answered slowly. She shot Widow Crenshaw a cautious glance, then continued, "There are so many interesting characters on those posters. They've all done such exciting things. Burglary! Robbery! Stagecoaches, mail coaches, trains!"

"Oh, do calm down, Catherine," Widow Crenshaw scolded.

"They're murderers, cutthroats, and thieves."

Miranda could hardly believe the gentle old lady found them so interesting. Didn't old ladies used to just sit around tatting and reading Bible verses? Maybe an odd interest in violence was part of becoming senile.

"You sound like you've been reading too many of Captain Jackson Armistead's books," Del said.

"Who?" Widow Crenshaw and Miss Barber asked at the same time. Both of them had their lips rounded and their eyes wide and innocent. They looked like two little owls caught in daylight.

"He writes . . . well, I guess you could call them adventure novels," Del explained.

"Indeed, is that what you call them?" Miss Barber asked.

"Hush, Catherine," Widow Crenshaw grumbled.

"But, seriously, Miss Barber, have you ever considered developing other interests?" Miranda suggested. She found herself more than a little concerned for the aging spinster and her widowed companion.

"Other . . . interests?" the elderly lady stammered.

"Oh, my goodness, no," Widow Crenshaw answered for her. "We have so many . . ."

"So very many," Miss Barber repeated.

"Interesting things that we do," Widow Crenshaw finished.

"Such as?" Miranda prompted.

Quickly Widow Crenshaw returned her attention to Max. "What else do you do, Max, besides hang up posters and keep the drunks until they sober up?"

Max shrugged without much enthusiasm. "Sweep up glass."

"Shame on you for being too darned modest!" Widow Crenshaw scolded. "Tell us more about something that has . . . mystery. Gun fights and shootouts, cattle rustlers and runaway stagecoaches!"

"Hush, Catherine." Widow Crenshaw glared at her friend.

"Mystery? Danger?" Del and Miranda repeated at the same time.

She glanced toward him. He was actually grinning at her. Now *that* was the biggest mystery she'd come across in quite a while. How dangerous, she wondered, would Del smiling at her turn out to be?

She *wouldn't* look at him again, she determined. She wouldn't want him to think she'd actually expected, actually hoped, that they might do something together once more.

"It's quite a mystery, finding out who's been masterminding all these darn robberies. How many men do they all figure are robbing these trains?" Widow Crenshaw asked.

"Two. Maybe three or even four."

"Such a difference?" Miss Barber said.

"Why do they think the number varies?" Widow Crenshaw asked.

Miranda listened as Max tried to explain. She understood about eyewitness accounts and horses' hoofprints. But Max began talking about more complicated means of trailing and tracking and identifying criminals.

She doubted that Max had learned these things reading the law with Mr. Martin. More than likely, he'd learned these dirty tricks by his own experience. He might be sheriff now, but she still didn't give a dang about Max or his experiences.

She found her mind wandering, and her glance scanning the crowd milling about the lawn. She'd leave now in search of Charles, or even of Mrs. Lowell, but she wasn't about to abandon Del to the predations of Dorothy Halstead.

All right, she didn't want Del—not now. She was quite satisfied with Charles and very proud of him. Dorothy was welcome to Del—*after* she was married and had left town.

She didn't mind the thought of Dorothy having Del, she kept telling herself. But she couldn't bear to think of Dorothy in *her* mansion! Hanging new drapes and wallpaper, rearranging the tables, the sofas, the beds. With Del. No! She wouldn't think of that. Not at all, she kept telling herself.

Suddenly she felt a little tug on her sleeve at the elbow.

"Miranda," Del whispered in her ear. "Is all this sheriff talk making you thirsty?"

She was so surprised that Del was actually talking pleasantly to her, was actually asking her if she was thirsty, all she could do was nod her assent.

"Come on. Let's go see what there is to eat,"

Why was he talking to her? Why was she actually listening to him? she wondered as she found herself following Del's lead. He backed slowly out of the circle. She backed up a little, too. As the circle widened, Widow Crenshaw drew closer to Max.

Both of the elderly ladies were still plaguing the new sheriff with questions as Del and Miranda finally made their escape to the punch bowl.

"It was nice of them to have a party for you," Del said.

"Yes, it was."

He handed her a glass, then refilled his own.

They couldn't just stand there, silently drinking punch. She ought to say something.

"I suppose your family will be having some kind of party for you, too, soon."

Del just laughed. "Not if Sally has anything to say about it."

Miranda gazed into the contents of her glass. Sally was his sister, and her best friend. She couldn't say anything bad about Sally.

Del took a step nearer to her. He leaned his head down until his mouth was close to her ear. She could feel her skin tingle and the muscles of her stomach tighten. She gripped the cut-glass cup. Maybe if she held on to it tightly enough, she could keep her hand from shaking.

"Can I ask you a question, Miranda?"

7

*M*IRANDA COULDN'T SPEAK, but she managed to nod her head without spilling her punch down the front of her.

Del gave her a sheepish grin, then bent his head again to study the contents of his own cup. What kind of a question was it, that he couldn't even look her in the eye to ask it?

"It's kind of a personal, girl-type question."

"That's all right," she managed to choke out.

She waited. She was still astounded that Del would be asking her any kind of question, much less a personal one. And a girl-type question, at that.

What in the world was a girl-type question, anyway? Were there boy-type questions, too? How did they differ? After Del asked her his question, could she ask him hers?

Shut up, Miranda. You're babbling because Del's making you nervous. You mustn't let him make you so nervous. There's absolutely no reason for him to make you nervous. Stop babbling.

Del cleared his throat and asked, "What's the matter with Sally?"

"Sally?" she repeated, and tried again not to choke on her words.

Well, Sally was definitely a girl, so she supposed that could be classified as a girl-type question. But it wasn't quite as personal as Miranda had expected. She eased her grip on the cup. At least he hadn't asked her about Dorothy.

"What about Sally?" she managed to ask in a much more normal voice.

He shrugged. "I was hoping you could tell me."

"She's . . . she's my best friend—at least, she used to be. But I've been gone—"

"So have I. But you sent each other letters—"

"So did you. Didn't you?"

"Yes."

Then why didn't she tell you I'd gone off to Boston? Why didn't she tell you I was getting married? Why didn't you ever ask about me? Why couldn't you ever care for me as much as I cared for you?

"Did she mention anything in any of her letters? Or maybe while you two were visiting?"

"We haven't really been able to spend much time together this visit. When I was here last summer, we had lots of time. But this year, with . . . with engagement parties and all . . ."

Why was she so hesitant to bring up her engagement to Del?

"I . . . I know she was busy planning the party for me. And I've been busy, too, since then. I'd kind of hoped we could do something together, just the two of us, later, like old times, but . . ."

She shrugged and left her sentence unfinished. She really didn't know what other excuses to give Del for knowing so little about Sally and her problem.

"I just thought maybe she'd confided something—"

"No, not a word."

Del made some sort of grunted reply. Either that, or Miss Barber's cooking disagreed with him.

"I'm sorry I can't help you more, Del." She really was,

and she tried to sound as sincere as she could. "I can't tell you anything because I don't know anything."

She really did feel bad about this. But it wasn't all her fault.

"Gosh, Del, you're her brother. You live in the same house with her. Hasn't she said anything to you?"

He looked up and gave her a sad little grin. "She yells at me a lot to do stuff I didn't do while I was away."

She shot him a wry look. "I can't say as I blame her."

He just ignored her jibe. He looked around to the people gathered in little groups on the lawn. He didn't seem to be looking for anyone in particular, she noted with relief. He really looked too distracted to be concentrating on anything in particular. He really seemed a lot more concerned about this than he had about anything since that winter his mother took sick with pneumonia and passed away.

"I mean, Sally used to have a temper—still does—but . . . well, so does everyone, at one time or another."

"Some more than others."

She waited for him to make some reference to her own temper. But he didn't. He must really be worried if he passed up an opportunity like that.

"She just seems so . . . so unhappy."

Miranda nodded.

"And I figured, you being friends, and you and Sally both being girls—"

"You noticed," she shot out as just a light quip. She couldn't stand seeing him so upset about his family. There had to be something she could say to cheer him up.

"Yeah," he answered. He just stood there, watching her with very serious eyes. "I noticed, Miranda. I notice more than you think I do." Before she could recover and make any kind of reply, he turned back to studying the leaves on the trees and quickly continued. "I thought maybe she'd said something to you about why she's so . . ."

Miranda spotted Sally, all alone, trudging across the lawn, heading for the punch bowl. Del was right. She did have an awful scowl on her face. She seemed more intent on studying the grass she was treading down than on where she was going, or who was there, or who she passed getting there.

She might not notice they were there, but she'd certainly be able to hear Del when she got close enough.

"Shh! Shh!" Miranda quickly jabbed her elbow in Del's ribs to shut him up.

Oblivious to her warning, Del continued, "So . . . gol-dang nit-picking about everything. Why she's . . ."

"Shh!"

Too late.

"Heck, Sally's turned into such a darn old grouch!"

Sally came and stood beside Miranda. She shot Del a withering glare.

She scooped up a cup of punch but didn't drink any of it. She just stood there, squeezing the cup tightly in her hands until Miranda was afraid the thing would shatter under the pressure.

She leaned against the table and released a disgruntled sound that was halfway between a sigh and a snort.

"Honestly," Sally muttered, "if that isn't disgusting."

"What?" Del and Miranda asked, again simultaneously.

This has got to stop. We can't keep thinking alike. Suppose he actually starts thinking about me some of the things I've been thinking about him?

Sally nodded toward the group still congregated under the elm. "Just look at that brazen display!"

"Brazen?" Del asked.

Miranda didn't like it one bit that, at the mere mention of the word, Del's gaze immediately focused on Dorothy. She had to admit, lately, that adjective did seem to suit Dorothy to a T. However, since Del had left the group, Dorothy was actually behaving herself quite nicely and could be forgiven for the time being.

"Just look at those two old biddies," Sally complained, "hanging around Max like they were looking for him to ask one of them to marry him."

Widow Crenshaw and Miss Barber? Old biddies? Maybe. Brazen? Never!

Miranda giggled "What on earth are you talking about? They're old enough to be his . . . his grand-mothers!"

Sally shook her head. "They think that just because someone, a long time ago, left them a lot of money . . . And Max, now that he's such an important pillar of the community, thinks he's too good . . . Everything's *Mister* Quinn this and *Miss* Pickett that. . . ."

Sally left her sentence unfinished as she downed her punch in one gulp. Miranda watched her friend with surprise. Where had Sally learned to belt back a drink like that?

Sally stared into the glass, a mixed expression of disbelief and disappointment on her face.

"Blah! It's fruit punch." She looked around for a place to set down her empty glass.

"What did you expect?" Miranda asked.

"Claret? Madeira?" Sally suggested hopefully. "Bour-bon? Scotch?"

"You know better than that," Del said. "Jackson Barber was a Temperance man. Medicinal purposes only. Why, he'd roll over in his grave if he knew his daughter allowed the Demon Rum at any of her social affairs. Didn't Pa ever tell you the story of Jackson Barber's infamous Independence Day oration?"

Miranda waited for Sally to ask, since Del was obviously talking to her. When she didn't say a word, Miranda felt obliged to break the awkward silence. Maybe telling a funny story would help to cheer Del.

"What was that?" she prompted.

"It seems as if Mr. Barber was not only a Temperance man, but he had a strong streak of Puritan "waste not, want not" philosophy in him. After he made an impas-sioned speech, convincing everyone to give up their brew, he collected it and, rather than seeing it go to waste, and being a loyal employee of the Bureau of

Indian Affairs, turned right around and sold it to the Indians."

"What a charming fellow," Miranda said.

Sally said nothing.

"You can understand how he and Armistead Crenshaw could get along so famously. Janet's late husband made his substantial fortune selling beef—well, they think it was beef—of uncertain age and dubious wholesomeness to the Union Army during the War between the States."

"Two enterprising gentlemen if ever there were," Miranda said with a little laugh.

Sally still said nothing. She just stood there, her fingers clenched around the cut glass, staring at Max.

A body would have to be dense as a brick not to see that Max was at the core of her discontent, although Miranda couldn't imagine why. She'd never liked him, and Sally had always laughed when Miranda made fun of him. She hadn't laughed real hard, but . . . well, Miranda'd always just attributed it to Sally's natural reserve. Obviously, she'd missed something important.

"Ah, Del, my boy," Mr. Hamilton called as he approached them across the lawn. "I've been looking for you."

"Hi, Mr. Hamilton. Nice party," Del replied.

"Miss Pickett . . . Well, you'll always be Sally with the pigtails to me. But I figure I ought to call you Miss now, since you're all grown up and so pretty," Mr. Hamilton said with a laugh.

Sally just grinned politely.

Del was right. Sally had turned into a real grouch!

"Are you having fun, Miranda?" her father asked.

"It was very kind of Widow Crenshaw and Miss Barber to do this for us," she replied.

That was the best she could do. The food was good, but she hadn't yet made up her mind about whether she was having a good time or not as long as Del was there.

"Del, why don't you and I leave the ladies to their punch and go see who's winning at horseshoes?" Mr. Hamilton suggested, pointing to the two groups of men gathered farther out in the field.

"Yeah, I think Sally's had about all she can handle of the punch," Del remarked, setting his empty glass on the table.

Sally slammed her glass down on the table and stomped off.

"Yes, indeed, she has."

Del, you are an incredibly insensitive oaf!

"Enjoy yourself," Mr. Hamilton told her as he and Del headed toward the game.

Apparently, her father figured she was very trusting. Del, if he considered her at all, probably thought she was very gullible, or very stupid. They were still a good distance from the horseshoe game when they stopped.

What did they think they were doing? Miranda wondered. They couldn't possibly see the game from there. Obviously, her father had something to say to Del that he didn't want her to hear.

Her daddy had underestimated her. She might be trusting, but she was also extremely curious.

She had a sneaking suspicion she was going to find what her father had to say to Del a whole lot more interesting than anything anyone else could be chatting with her about. This definitely warranted further investigation.

She didn't want to attract attention to herself and have someone drag her off in the opposite direction. So she strolled casually along until she was close enough behind them. Bales of hay weren't the only things good to hide behind. Fortunately, many years ago, Jackson Barber had had the foresight to plant these trees in his backyard. Out of their sight, she leaned against the bark of the elm and listened.

"Del," she heard her father say. "I think you know what I want to talk to you about."

Yep, she'd been right. Oh, she knew if she could count on anyone in the world, she could count on her daddy!

"Yes, sir, I'm afraid I do. And I think you know what my answer is, too."

Yeah, she knew she could count on Del, too, to give her a hard time.

"Yeah, I think I do. But I want you to consider real hard now before you give me a final answer, son," Mr. Hamilton advised. "Are you sure you're not just being cantankerous and contrary, not selling the house just because it's some back-East fellow you don't know from Adam looking to buy it?"

"No, sir."

"I guess, considering it was you, I should have known it all along."

"Thank you, sir."

Yes, sir. No, sir, Miranda silently mimicked. What a little toad he was being, she thought angrily.

"I mean, you understand it'd be me—not him— buying the house for Miranda as a wedding present."

"I know that. I'm not trying to be disrespectful, sir. You know, before my ma married Tom Pickett, I always sort of looked up to you as a father."

"I appreciate your saying that, son."

"I know you've always been a good father to Miranda."

"I appreciate that, too."

"I'm not trying to make things difficult for you or Miranda or that Boston fellow. You know I like that house—always have. I know it looks like nothing but a big pile of rubbish now, but I think it could be fixed up, and I intend to see to it. I really do intend to live in that house."

Yeah, right.

"I know that now. And, of course, you're not just being stubborn because it's for Miranda."

"Of course not."

No, you're never stubborn where I'm concerned, Del.

"I mean, I guess it came as a bit of a surprise to find the little girl who'd followed you around like a puppy had grown into a lovely young lady."

"Yes, indeed it did."

You don't have to sound so dang surprised.

"The way she always hung around you, I guess you were also pretty surprised to find she intended to marry someone else."

"Yes, it did just a bit."

You were surprised anyone would want to marry me, you stinking polecat! Don't you lie to my father!

"Of course, there's lots of other nice girls in town that you might marry."

"Yes, sir."

Oh, yeah? Name one!

"You're not a bad fellow, with lots of good qualities—"

Not to mention lots of money.

"I'm sure, now that you've come back to town, all the girls will be setting their caps for you."

Not Dorothy. She couldn't get a hat down on that mop of hers! Miranda clapped her hand over her mouth so she wouldn't giggle at her own joke and give her presence away.

"I'm surprised they haven't dragged you to the altar already." Mr. Hamilton chuckled again.

Miranda saw very little funny about it.

"So, you're figuring on fixing up that house?"

"Yes, sir."

"And setting up a family there, huh?"

She heard Del hesitate a bit before he answered.

"I might."

"Well, you can't say I didn't try for my little girl," Mr. Hamilton said. Miranda could hear her father clapping Del heartily on the back.

"No, sir. I can't."

"Good luck with the house, then—and any lady you might choose to share it with."

You're going to need it, you rotten sidewinder.

"Mr. Hamilton, I . . . I hope you're not mad at me for refusing your generous offer."

"No, no, not at all." Mr. Hamilton chuckled as he

walked away. "But then, I'm not the one you've got to worry about, Del."

You're dad-gummed right about that!

He was going to put Dorothy Halstead in her house, she just knew it. Then they'd fill it with a bunch of fluffy-headed kids. She pursed her lips and swallowed hard to keep her throat from tightening too much. Then she wouldn't be able to talk and laugh with all the other guests and make them believe she was really having one swell time.

Del didn't even care that she'd changed her mind about marrying him. He couldn't even be just a tad bit jealous, the unfeeling lout!

She felt her nose starting to itch. She needed to sniff really bad, but she couldn't. Then she'd give herself away.

It was bad enough she'd admitted she'd been eavesdropping on his conversation that time in the barn. She couldn't admit she was making a habit of it. She couldn't admit she still cared one stinking bit about Del Williams.

But the house was lost—completely lost to her. Not Charles, not even her daddy, could buy the place for her. She'd never have it now, and she didn't know quite what to do next.

Del had just bought all the nails in Quinn's General Store, and half the lye soap. He had a brand-new bucket and mop, and a new broom. He'd stopped by Melvin Hooper's lumber store and bought a few planks that would shore up the rickety stairs until he could get around to hiring a real carpenter to repair the fancy stuff.

He didn't care what Mrs. Cartwright had said about him not knowing how to take care of a house. He was ready to clean!

The first thing he needed was a lot more light and air in the place. He opened the front door wide. Then he made his way through the dining room, down the corridor, across the kitchen, and opened the back door.

He reached up to open the draperies. But what started

as simply opening a window turned into a full scale pulling down of every curtain on the ground floor. No sooner than he tried to open a curtain, the old fabric shredded off the rods and tumbled into a heap at his feet.

He looked at the stairs with anticipation and ultimate regret. He figured he had enough work on his hands right now. He'd have to wait before he went to work on that second floor, so the stairs could wait for a while, too.

As he pulled down the curtain in the front window of the parlor, he noticed three people advancing on the house.

"Who in tarnation are they?"

The last person coming up the walk, at a leisurely stroll, was easy enough to identify. Max. It was good to see a familiar face again. But what was he doing with these other people? And who were they anyway?

The two strangers were rushing, huffing and puffing, toward the house. The first one was definitely a man. The person behind him was probably just a dang ugly woman, judging from the skirt and the monstrous cleavage. On the other hand, judging from the mustache, it might be a weird little man. This person kept pushing the other person along with little jabs to the back.

Del ran through every memory he had of any person he'd ever encountered in Grasonville. Nope, he had no idea who either of these people might be.

"I guess there's only one way to find out."

Tossing the dusty fabric into a corner, he headed for the door. He got there just as the strange man set foot on the bottom step.

Del had never thought of himself as the guardian type, but a man had every right and duty to protect his own property. He stopped in the doorway. Taking a wide stance for balance, he folded his arms across his chest. He frowned and looked down his nose at the people.

"Can I help you?" he asked in a very deep voice.

The woman behind him—now that she was closer, Del could tell it really was a woman—gave the man another little push.

"Who are you?" the man demanded. "What are you doing here?"

"I'm Del Williams. Who are you and what are *you* doing here?"

"I'm Jasper Richardson." He jerked his thumb at the woman. "This is my wife Daisy."

She glared at Del and gave him a quick nod.

Del wasn't about to say "pleased to meet you" until he could actually tell whether he was or not. But he had a sneaking suspicion he wasn't going to be. He waited, silently examining them, until Jasper Richardson or his wife answered his second question.

Richardson. Oh, no. They didn't need to say another word. He knew close enough who they were, and he knew exactly why they were here. They meant trouble.

He decided he'd wait anyway—let them do most of the talking first, to see what they had in mind. That way, he could try to form some sort of plan of defense. He had a bad feeling in the pit of his gut that he was going to need some kind of defense.

Mrs. Richardson gave Jasper another shove. He marched across the few feet of porch until he stood face to face with Del.

"I'm here to claim my rightful inheritance. What are you doing in my house?" he demanded.

"I'm not in your house. I'm in my house."

Dag-nabbit! Did he have to go through this nonsense all over again? Did he have to argue about the house with almost everyone he met?

What was it about this house? Was it sitting on the secret entrance to some kind of gold mine? Did it house a treasure trove of Confederate gold? Why did everybody seem to want it?

"Your house? Balderdash!" Jasper exclaimed.

"Poppycock!" Mrs. Richardson chimed in.

"Horsefeathers!" Jasper declared again. "Now step aside, varmint. I waited long enough for the old skinflint to die and leave me my money. I came all the way from

Poughkeepsie on the most uncomfortable train ever built. Now I'm going to live in this house in style!"

"Go get him, Jasper!" Mrs. Richardson cried. "Throw the little skunk out. I can't wait to get into my new house."

Jasper tried to shoulder his way past, but Del stood his ground. He pushed a little harder, but Del still didn't budge.

Puffing, Jasper stepped back. "Sheriff! Do your duty," he ordered, pointing at Del.

"My duty?" Max replied slowly. "Well, as near as I can see my duty from here, it looks to me like I'd better stop the violent assault by an intruder on one of the law-abiding citizens of Grasonville in his very own home."

"What?"

"I tried to tell you, Jasper," Max said, shaking his head. "Lester Martin tried to tell you. But, no, you wouldn't listen to either one of us."

"Why should I?"

Max reached up and pushed his hat a little farther back on his head. "Now me, I'm just the sheriff. I don't make the laws. I just enforce them. However, since Mr. Martin was your uncle's attorney, I suppose that he ought to know what he's talking about."

Jasper stood there, sullen-faced. Del was just watching Max do his job.

"Your uncle left the house and everything else to me, fair and square, and very legal-like," Del explained. "My name is on the bank account and the deed to the house."

Jasper's scowl grew darker. "That miserable, egg-sucking sidewinder! That bilge-swilling, muck-licking polecat!"

"Who? Mr. Martin?" Del asked, grinning. "You certainly can't be talking about me."

"No! I should've known Uncle Henry'd do something like this!"

"Golly, hearing you talk about him like that, I'm really surprised he didn't leave everything to you!" Del said.

"Not a stock, not a bond, not a penny," Jasper continued to rant. "The bone-headed old skinflint never did like me."

"I can't imagine why not."

Jasper stopped his raving and glared at Del.

"Who are you, anyway, Williams? I don't recall seeing you at any family reunions."

"Nope. Near as I can tell, nobody ever saw your uncle there, either. Maybe that's why he left everything to a total stranger—me."

Del couldn't help himself. He had to chuckle.

"This is ridiculous! He just can't do this!"

"I tried to tell them even before we came here," Max said to Del as if the two Richardsons weren't even there. He shook his head with the futility of his job. "Darn, hardheaded varmints wouldn't listen to anybody."

"How come I'm not surprised?"

"But they had to go dragging me out here, insisting they needed the law to help them evict the intruder in what they claimed is Jasper's house. By Jiminy, I ought to arrest him for disturbing the peace."

"I don't see any crowd gathered round, so I'm not disturbing the peace," Jasper protested, flinging his arm around to indicate the vacant lawn. "I'm on private property, so I can't be judged a public nuisance. And the house is mine. It should be mine. It's *got* to be mine!"

"Yeah, and I should be king of England," Max said.

"It *will* be mine!" Jasper vowed.

"How many times do we have to tell you?" Del demanded. "Legally, you don't have a leg to stand on."

"Ha! That's just one man's opinion," Mrs. Richardson grunted. She elbowed her husband's side.

"Henry Richardson was my father's older brother. I'm a blood relative. I've got every right to this house— certainly more right to it than you do. I don't intend to stop until it's mine. Do you understand?" He raised his shaking fist in the air. "I'll get what's coming to me."

Del nodded. "Maybe someday you will. But right now, you're trespassing." He turned to Max. "Sheriff, isn't there some law in this town about setting foot uninvited on private property?"

"Sure there is. Are these people becoming a nuisance to you, Del? Do you want me to arrest them? A few days in jail ought to cool him down."

"No, no. That won't be necessary, Sheriff. Just get them off my property."

"Go ahead and try, Sheriff," Jasper declared. He took a wide stance, raised both fists, and shook them in front of him. "But I'm not going without a fight. You'll have to drag me out of here. You'll have to carry me out."

Max slowly began to reach for his gun. "Suit yourself. I can always shoot you for resisting arrest."

"Stop!" Mrs. Richardson held her substantial arm out in front of Max. She seized her husband's arm and practically pulled him down the steps. "Don't make more of a fool of yourself than you already are, Jasper," she hissed loudly in his ear.

Max let his arm relax. Sometimes that was all that was needed to scare some folks into behaving themselves.

"*No one* has ever thrown *me* out of any place!" Mrs. Richardson declared proudly. "I leave when I choose. And right now, Jasper, I believe we have pressing business elsewhere."

"We do?"

"Indeed we do." She hauled him down the walk. "Mr. Martin can't be the only attorney in town. I'm sure, for the right amount of money, someone will see things our way."

"But we don't have any money for a lawyer."

"We will," she assured him. "We will."

Jasper turned back and called over his shoulder, "Enjoy yourself now, Williams, while you can. That's going to be my house real soon. So don't you mess it up!"

Mrs. Richardson turned back, too. "Make sure you've scrubbed the floors and washed all the windows by the time we get back. I like to live in a nice, clean mansion."

Del waved at their retreating figures and called, "I hope you two bought round-trip tickets."

He turned and headed back to the parlor. He looked at the grimy windows, filthy gas jets, and dusty covers that still hadn't been removed from the furniture.

"Yeah, I'd sure like to live in a clean mansion, too," he muttered under his breath.

He continued pulling down the tattered curtains more vigorously than before. Amid the sound of shredding fabric, he heard a knock on the front door.

Oh, thunderation! Who wants the house now?

8

"*HEY! HEY, DEL!*" Will called. "Hey, are you in there?"

Del shoved everything aside and hurried to meet his brother.

"Yeah. Come on in!" he invited. "Did you come to help me clean?"

"Heck, no. I got enough on my hands with the farm and stuff Sally wants me to do." Will grinned. "You know she's looking to hang your hide on the shed if you don't mend that smokehouse roof soon."

"Yeah, I know. I'll do it, too. I just need to get a little start on this place."

"You sure got your work cut out for you." Will looked up at the high ceiling. "What in tarnation did Richardson want with a house this size anyway? It wasn't as if he had a wife and twelve kids. It wasn't as if he had any friends he wanted to impress."

He gave a short laugh, as if only paying lip service to his joke. Then he peered at Del intently.

"What the heck does *any* single guy want with a house this big?"

Del shrugged.

Will started walking around. Del followed.

"Wow! This place looks even bigger from the inside," he said as he moved from the vestibule into the parlor. He lifted up some of the dust covers on the furniture and peeked under.

"What are you looking for?" Del asked. "The ghost of Gertie Richardson?"

"Hey, don't laugh," Will admonished. "I've heard some pretty wild tales about weird stuff that happened in here."

"Geez, Will! What are you talking about? No kid over twelve years old believes that balderdash."

"Nice stuff," Will commented, dropping the edge of the sheet. "You know, behind every weird tale is a grain of truth."

"Yeah, and maybe behind your face is the grain of a brain."

Will just laughed and pointed up at the animal head trophies.

"Hey, why don't you move them into the dining room?" he suggested. "Make the place real appetizing."

He moved into the dining room.

"Wow! He left all this stuff?"

"Yep."

"It looks real expensive. What the heck are you going to do with all this china and glass—"

"I think it's crystal," Del corrected.

"Yeah? And silver, too? Hey, did you ever wonder if any of this silver came from Mr. Hamilton's mine?"

"No."

"So what're you going to do with all this fancy stuff?"

"Beats me. All I ever needed in Texas was a bowl for my beans and a mug for my coffee."

All the while he was admiring the woodwork and the ceilings, and all the wonderful things in the house, Will kept scraping the toe of his boot along the damaged carpet, tugging at falling wallpaper.

"Kind of makes you wonder what it's all for, though, doesn't it?"

"What are you talking about?" Del demanded.

"Kind of makes you wonder why people work so hard to get big houses and fine things when there's no one to leave it to but total strangers. Doesn't it?"

"No," Del answered sharply.

Will stopped to examine an oil painting, dark with grime and age. "I mean, what good did it do Henry Richardson to accumulate all this wealth?"

"Apparently you're ignoring my complete disinterest in this subject. That could be the only reason you're still talking."

"You're darn right." Will moved on to admire another painting. "Nobody else ever saw any of it, except maybe Mrs. Cartwright, and I really don't think she's got the right frame of mind to appreciate things like this."

"Oh, and you do?"

"Maybe. But Richardson never did anybody a lick of good with his money while he was alive and—no offense, Del—he's only done you good now that he's dead."

"Is there a point to any of this, Will?" Del asked impatiently. "If not, I got a lot of work to get back to. If so, I wish you'd make it."

"No. Oh, no. No point. Not from me."

He held up his hand and waved it back and forth, as if waving away the notion that he had any goal other than chitchat.

"I'm just rambling on, enjoying looking at all this fine stuff. Yep, I'll just bet this is the first time anybody but Mr. Richardson and Mrs. Cartwright has seen this stuff for . . . well, for *years!*" He continued to wander around. "What are you going to do with this big house, Del?"

"Live here. Why? Do you want to come stay here, too? Is that what all this talk about doing people good while you're still alive is leading to?"

"No! Thunderation, no. Why, I'd get lost on my way to the outhouse in a big place like this."

"He's got indoor plumbing."

Will gave Del a wide-eyed stare. "You don't say. For

just him? I mean, it's not as if he'd find a line waiting to get in."

Then he started to wander around again.

"Nope, I'm real happy at home—when Sally stops complaining. And if I get too unhappy, I'll just go off and make my own way, like you did. Of course, I don't think any stranger'll be leaving me a wagonload of money, but, well . . ." He shrugged. "That's life."

"So, what's your point, Will?"

"No point," he said, heading for the door. "It's just, well, you're my big brother and I love you. You might not have known it, but I always looked up to you. So I don't want to see you end up like Henry Richardson—all alone here, nobody but you rattling around in this big old house like a marble in a rain barrel, your girl gone off and married to someone else."

"What the hell are you talking about? My girl?"

As soon as he'd said it, Del knew he'd said it way too loud, and had way too much reaction in his reply. Why, Will might think he'd actually struck a sore spot with him or something.

"Nothing," Will replied.

Del was hot on his heels to the door. "You mean Miranda, don't you?"

"Do I?"

"She's not my girl."

"I know. You've said it enough times."

"She's going to marry that sissy little dude from Boston," Del continued to insist.

"Guess so. Hey, good luck cleaning this place," he said as he continued out the door. "I got to get back to work or Sally'll have my guts for garters. See ya'!"

Will bounded down the steps and jogged off down the walk. Del stared after him long after he'd rounded the corner onto Main Street.

"What the dickens was that all about?" Del muttered as he returned to his work.

He shook his head. There must be something in the

water around here, he decided, making Sally so grouchy and Will just plumb loco.

Miranda, his girl? *She* might have thought she'd been. *He* never had. What would make anyone else think so now? She'd been ignoring him—mostly. He'd been trying to avoid her—sort of. It wasn't like he was one bit jealous of that rich guy.

Why should he be jealous? What did Charlie have that he didn't? A bigger bank account? A bigger house? Maybe. His own company? Well, Del could do something about that if he could figure what kind of business to go into.

What was it Miranda saw in Charlie that she didn't see in him? Obviously, there were plenty of other girls in town who might set their cap for him.

Why, there was Dorothy Halstead. She hadn't stopped eyeing him since he'd arrived. But Dorothy was so . . . so . . . He couldn't think of the right word. She was smart, pretty, lively. She just wasn't what he was looking for. Oh, well, there were plenty of others.

Yeah, now that he was rich, he thought with a laugh, they'd be all over him like hens on a june bug. But Miranda had wanted him from the very start, when he was still poor.

As much as he hated to admit it, Miranda had been right all along. When he actually gave some thought to settling down, to a wife, a home, a family, Miranda was the only woman who really fit into his picture. Miranda was the woman he wanted for his wife.

Now if he could just convince her of that.

But what had made her change her mind so completely about him? And how could he get her to change it back again?

He shook his head. She was doing her best to ignore him. Shucks, he couldn't even get a straight answer out of her when he tried to talk to her about his sister.

How could he ever figure Miranda? The answer was, he never could.

She seemed awful skittish around him lately, edgy and

prickly when she'd never acted that way before. As if she couldn't stand to be near him. As if his very presence made her tingle inside, sort of like the way he felt, too, when he was around her.

Nope. Three years ago they hadn't felt that way about each other.

But three years ago, she was just a kid who claimed she wanted to marry him, he argued with himself. Now she was a woman, with decidedly womanly assets. And she was engaged to someone else.

Nothing could ever come of it, he told himself, so he might just as well get back to work.

To clean a house just for him to rattle around in—like a marble in a rain barrel, his brother's words came back to him. Like the reclusive and ultimately lonesome and alone Henry Richardson.

Del grabbed up an armload of old curtains and hauled them out back for the bonfire he'd have tonight. It had rained a couple of days ago. There weren't any trees overhead. The grass wasn't too dry yet, and he'd rake it all back to form a clear spot anyway. It would be safe.

He'd made several more trips before the downstairs rooms were clear.

He took up his broom and started making swipes at the shattered glass on the dusty carpet. He bent down and picked up one of the rocks lying around on the carpet that someone had obviously used to break that window. He tossed it up and caught it several times. He wondered if these were the same kids who'd broken Liz Englemeyer's windows and taken Mr. Quinn's hammer and Mr. Nichols's sixty bucks.

He stopped tossing the rock and looked around. Had they taken anything from here? This place was such a mess, how would he ever know? Checking everything against the inventory Mr. Martin had given him would take the rest of his life. He figured he had better things to do.

He tossed the rock out the open window and went back to work.

He was making pretty good progress, he noted with satisfaction. There were safe paths where he could walk through the rooms. He could actually see now that the parlor carpet had once been red, with some kind of green and brown design running through it. At least, it looked green and brown. It was going to be impossible to tell what the colors had originally been.

Creak, creak.

Just the tiniest little sound. He stopped, lifted his head, and listened.

"Hey, Will, you big coward. Did you change your mind and decide to come back and help me after all?"

No answer. The house was so silent, it was as if he hadn't heard anything at all. It was probably just his imagination. He turned back to sweeping.

Creak, creak.

He stopped and listened again. Yeah, he'd definitely heard something. It wasn't only his imagination. But it was probably just the sound of his broom, echoing around the rooms as it brushed along the carpet. He went back to work.

Creak, creak. Creak, creak. Creak, creak.

He listened harder. It was louder this time, but it still sounded just like the other two times. Yes, then there could be no doubt. He'd definitely heard something besides himself moving around in this house.

Creak, creak. Creak, creak.

There they went again—like footsteps.

Creak, creak.

Those darn Richardsons were back again, he thought angrily. Some people just didn't know when to stop. He leaned the broom in a corner and stomped off toward the front door.

"I'm not going to have the sheriff arrest you two this time," he called. "I'll shoot you both myself if you don't get off my property immediately!"

No one was there.

He stuck his head out the door and looked around outside. It was for certain that no one was heading down the walk. He might not have been able to see anyone hiding in the bushes, but if they'd tried to run around the side of the house real quick, he certainly would have heard them crashing through the tall grass.

He stepped back into the house and turned around to survey the vestibule and both the parlor and dining room that opened from both sides.

A little earlier and he might have been able to track the intruders through the house by the marks they made in the dusty carpet. But he'd cleaned up some dirt and disarranged the rest so much while working that he wouldn't be able to spot a thing now.

Creak, creak.

The noise came from farther in the back of the house.

Creak, creak.

He'd only been working in the parlor, with a clear view of the vestibule. How could anyone have made it past without him spotting them?

Creak, creak.

The noise was too light to be both of the Richardsons. He doubted those two could be that quiet for this long, anyway. It couldn't be them.

Creak, creak.

Maybe Mrs. Cartwright was the one who couldn't take no for an answer. She was a lot more familiar with the house than the Richardsons ever could be. It would have been easy for her to sneak by him, even if she was a little too heavy to make such a light tread. Maybe she'd made her way back to the kitchen, her old domain.

Del didn't care. She still had no right to be here. He'd be polite about it, but he'd still throw her out, too.

Very quietly he made his way down the corridor. Maybe he'd made a mistake in calling out a warning to them the first time. He'd be quiet this time. The element of surprise was always good to have on one's side.

Very slowly, so they wouldn't squeak, he pushed the swinging doors inward. Boldly he stepped into the kitchen.

Empty.

He looked from side to side. He looked on the other side of the icebox, and of the big cast-iron stove. No one was there.

For just a moment the fleeting suspicion arose in his brain that maybe the kids and Will had been right. Maybe Gertie Richardson's ghost did haunt her house. Mr. Richardson might have willed him this place, but maybe Gertie wasn't too happy about having him here when she hadn't invited him.

He shook his head.

"Wendell Monroe Williams!" He hadn't called himself by his full name in years! He must really be nervous. Maybe he ought to stop drinking the water around here. It was doing strange things to his head, too. "You are going plumb loco!"

He pulled at the pantry door. The wood had swollen, making it hard to open. Finally it gave way. It still scraped along the floor, leaving a semicircular track in the dust. There was a little worn spot along the floor. This door had been sticking for a long time. He'd have to get a plane and even it up.

There was nothing in the pantry but dust and mouse debris. He left the door open. No sense letting the little critters think he was inviting them to stay. Anyway, it was too darn hard to close.

Mice. It had been mice, he told himself. It was silly, he knew, but he even allowed himself to feel a little relief. But they sure were some gol-darn loud mice. Maybe left alone here for a while, they'd grown into some awfully big mice.

First thing tomorrow, he decided as he made his way back to the parlor to finish his work, he'd go back to Quinn's and buy every mousetrap in the place. Maybe even some rat traps.

"Hello, Del."

"Miranda!"

She stood on the porch, peeking in the doorway.

"Hi, Del." She raised her hand and waved shyly.

"How long . . . ? When did you . . . ?"

He was stammering like a fool, partly because he was still a little puzzled by the strange noise, and partly because he was so surprised to see Miranda.

No, he told himself, he shouldn't be surprised to see her here. She'd always wanted to be here.

He wouldn't admit he was surprised at how glad he was to see her. It wasn't just that he was glad to have a little human company after the mystery of the strange sounds. She looked awful pretty with the sunlight behind her, shining gold on her hair, silhouetting her slender figure. She'd been right. She really looked terrific with bosoms!

"I . . . I hope you haven't been waiting long."

Maybe she hadn't been waiting. He wouldn't put it past Miranda to do a little snooping, a little trespassing, a little breaking and entering. But then, how in the world had she managed to be standing there at the front door? The house was too big for her to have run out the back door, around the house, and back to the front. She wasn't breathing hard at all, either, so she couldn't have been running.

"I just got here."

She smiled so shyly, he could hardly believe it was really Miranda. By golly, you know, she really did have sort of a sweet smile—when she tried.

He hadn't seen Sally smile much while he was here. Mrs. Hamilton was always smiling. Mrs. Lowell looked as if she kept hers in a box and only pasted it on for special occasions. Dorothy smiled a lot, too, when he was around. But it was a slick smile, one he didn't think he could trust.

He could trust Miranda, he'd decided that long ago. Oh, she might do sneaky things once in a while, but at least she was always very open and honest about it.

"May I come in, Del?"

"You're asking permission?"

"Of course." She looked at him and blinked in surprise. "I know you think I'm still the rotten spoiled rich little girl you once knew—"

"No, now I think you're a rotten spoiled rich young lady," he replied.

She didn't laugh at his joke. But she didn't get angry and tell him to go to blazes, either. Miranda really had changed.

"I hope you're teasing, Del," she said very seriously.

"Of course I am."

Since when had Miranda ever worried about his teasing her?

"Look, Del, I'm not here to make trouble," she said.

"That's a change."

Miranda made no retort to his jibe. That really was a change.

"I realize the house is legally yours, Del. I've also resigned myself to the fact that there is absolutely nothing I can do about it." She threw both hands up in the air. "So I give up. You win."

He frowned at her in disbelief. "Excuse me, miss. I don't know who you are. I mistook you for Miranda Hamilton. But Miranda Hamilton never gave up a fight."

"It was merely a difference of opinion. I should hope we wouldn't really fight."

Del just blinked and waited. Miranda was never this pleasant about losing. The next thing he knew, she'd be sprouting wings and taking off for Boston without waiting for the train.

"I came here to ask a very small favor of you."

Del nodded to himself. He should have known Miranda wouldn't have come here without having in mind something she wanted.

"What's that?" he asked.

She drew in a deep breath and began. "I've always loved this house—"

"Wait! Stop!" Del exclaimed, holding his hand in front of her. "I've heard all this before. Your fiancé tried. Your father tried. Don't think you're going to come here, wailing and sobbing, and I'll give in."

"No, no, you pudding-face addle-brained slug! Let me finish."

"Ah, now, that's the Miranda Hamilton I know. All right, what were you starting to say?"

"In the first place, I don't wail and sob."

"Yeah. Well, at least you didn't used to."

"In the second place, as I was trying to say," she said very slowly and deliberately—he could tell she was trying very hard to regain her polite voice, "I have always loved this house from a distance, from the outside. Just once I'd like to see the inside."

"You want . . . ?"

"I've never seen what this house looks like inside. Before I return to Boston, I'd like to see it."

"Oh, you would?"

"Please, Del. It . . . it won't cost you anything but a little time. I'd say, all things considered, you had plenty of free time on your hands now."

"Oh, really?"

"Look, if you don't want to be around me, would you at least let me kind of wander around and look? I promise not to touch a thing. If you tell me so, I promise not to say a single word the whole time I'm here."

"Golly, that's an offer that's hard to refuse."

"Please, Del."

Well, what the hey! What did he have to lose? He had the money. He had the house. She was going to marry someone else and move away. He could afford to be magnanimous.

"Please?"

She was looking at him with a world of pleading in those big blue eyes. If he lived to be a hundred, he didn't think he'd ever see Miranda this subservient ever again!

He wanted to savor the moment. What if he made her grovel and beg on her knees? He had some perverse vision of Miranda kneeling before him, hands raised in supplication, like some captive before her pirate abductor, pleading for her life—or her virtue.

Stop it, Del!

"Come on in."

He stepped back and motioned for her to enter. He

tried to sound very devil-may-care, as if having her here didn't phase him in the least.

"Really?"

"Yeah, sure, come on in. I . . . I'm sorry I was so rude at first."

"No, no, you weren't being rude," she said as she walked in. "You're just being Del. I'm used to you by now."

She eyed him warily, as if she was afraid he'd suddenly grab her and throw her out. Then she laughed.

"Of course, the Del I'm used to was a lot cleaner."

"Oh, oh, yeah," he said, brushing at his shirt and trousers. "I've been trying to clean this place."

"So you can live here?"

He shrugged. "Probably."

She looked around and gave a little laugh.

"It looks like you've got a lot more to do before you're through. Of course, it really looks more like you've been trying to tear the place apart."

Del reached up for the corner of a sagging piece of wallpaper and gave a tug. It slithered down the wall, raising a cloud of dust as it landed on the floor.

"I got a bad feeling it's going to come to that in some places."

Miranda peeked into the parlor. She pointed up at the dusty animal head trophies, with cobwebs strung across their horns, antlers, and exposed fangs. "I think you should start tearing those things down first."

"Why does everybody hate those things?"

"Who else has been in here to see them?" she countered.

"Will," he replied. She already knew about Mrs. Cartwright, the little snoop. If she was such a good little spy, let her find out on her own about that delightful couple, Jasper and Daisy Richardson.

"Badlands Bighorn Sheep. Arizona jaguar. New Mexican wolf. Dawson's Caribou." She moved along the line of hunting trophies, naming the animals one by one. "I can't believe he traveled this much just to shoot these animals."

"How do you know them?"

"Mrs. Bigelow's zoology class."

"Oh."

"'If a lady is to lead herself, her home, and one day the world, she needs to know what's in it.' That's a direct quote from Mrs. Bigelow," she added.

"Oh."

"There's not many of these left."

"Oh. I didn't know that."

"Of course not. You didn't take Mrs. Bigelow's zoology class."

Miranda continued looking around the place with an expression of awe and wonder.

"I think it'll be worth it, though, once you're through. This was a beautiful house once. It could be again. It's just such a shame Mr. Richardson let the place go to ruin. Is the rest of the house this bad?"

"I don't know. I haven't been through the whole house yet."

"Not yet?"

"I mean, I've been all around the first floor. But the second floor's in a lot worse shape—and a little harder to get to."

"Del, there's a big staircase right there," she pointed out to him. "What have you been trying to do? Get there by scaling a ladder outside?"

He laughed.

"No. But apparently during the last couple of months of his life, Mr. Richardson had trouble going up stairs," Del explained. "So he had the back parlor downstairs made up into a bedroom. The staircase must've been in pretty bad shape even before that. When you step on them, some of the stairs creak like you're going to be going straight on through to the basement. So I've only gone up there once, and I've never gone up to the attic."

He looked around. He gestured to the peeling paper on the walls and the corner of the ceiling that was sagging.

He pointed out the piles of dusty, dry-rotted fabric in the corners.

"I guess this place isn't exactly what you expected it to be, is it?" he asked.

"I don't know," she repeated his own words back to him. "I haven't been through the whole house yet."

Del supposed that was intended to be some sort of cue or something. Well, what the heck? She might as well see the whole thing while she was here.

"Would you like a tour?" he offered.

She gave a little gasp. "A what?"

"Would you like to see the house—the whole house?" he offered, laughing. "We could kind of do the grand tour together."

"Would you? Could we? Really?" she stuttered in her excitement. She gave a little jump.

"I wouldn't do that if I were you," he warned. "In this house, who knows when the floors might cave in and you'd get a grand tour starting in the cellar."

"Oh, really?"

Any ordinary girl probably would have drawn slightly closer to him, as if for support and protection from the unpredictable flooring. Not Miranda. She merely gave one more little bounce.

"You always were hardheaded." He shook his head in frustration. "Come on. Why don't we start there anyway?"

The corner of Miranda's lip curled upward. "What? The basement? Why? Are you trying to lure me down there to bury me alive?"

"Don't be silly. You make too darn much noise to keep you in my house alive."

"So you'll make sure I'm dead first. How considerate of you!"

"Oh, anything for you, Miranda."

How strange! Why did he feel like he really meant it?

"So, what do you say to checking the cellar?"

"It would sure be different. Very unlike you, Del."

"Now if I can just figure out how to get to it. Mr.

Martin gave me the keys to this place, and a list of what's in it, but apparently nobody saw fit to draw me a map."

He headed for the door he'd seen under the broad sweeping staircase in the vestibule. He paused with his hand on the doorknob.

"Do you think this might be it?"

"You've been here longer than I have. Remember, you've got squatter's rights."

"This is the usual place for cellar doors."

"I don't think Mr. Richardson had enough imagination to put anything out of the ordinary into his house."

Del pulled the door open. His scream rent the dust-laden air.

"What is it? What is it?"

Miranda rushed over to him. Leaning on his back, she peered over his shoulder into the darkness below. He could feel her soft breasts pressing into his shoulder blade. Oh, he couldn't politely refer to them as bosoms anymore, not when they were this close. Not when they felt that good.

"What is it?" she cried.

"A basement, by golly." He laughed. "Gotcha!"

"Oh, you!" She slapped at him, but laughed, too. "I thought you'd found a dead body, or the ghost of Gertie Richardson, or something really interesting."

"Well, who knows? We might find something really interesting down here."

He reached out and turned up the gas jet at the top of the stairwell. The yellow light tumbled down the steps.

"They look pretty steep. I'll go first." He held out his hand to her at the top of the steps. "Let me help you."

"To a fast trip to the bottom?" she asked.

But she placed her hand trustingly in his palm. He closed his fingers around hers. They were small and warm. He'd never figured Miranda could ever be helpless.

No, not helpless. Never helpless. Just more willing to let him take the lead once in a while. Maybe that school in Boston had done her more good than he'd imagined.

She was trying hard not to touch the handrail. It was covered with dust and spiderwebs. It was rough, too.

"You'd think with such a fancy house upstairs, Richardson would have at least put in a better handrail to the basement," Del said.

"Do you actually believe Mr. Richardson ever went in the basement?"

"Guess not."

"I don't even know why I'm letting you take me down here."

Her voice was just a little shaky. Her hand trembled in his just a little. He tightened his grip on her fingers and moved closer to her as they descended the rickety stairs. Just in case she tripped, he'd be there to steady her. Just in case she fell, he'd be there to land on.

"You wanted the grand tour of this place," he reminded her. "You got it."

He paused in the middle of the staircase, turned, and gave her a wicked glance. "How do you feel about mice?"

"Dead or alive?"

"Alive, I'm afraid."

Her lip curled up just a little farther. "They're cute in little cages. A friend in Boston's little brother had two for pets."

"Couldn't they afford anything better?"

"No, she could only get just the one little brother."

"I was talking about the mice!"

"Oh, I was talking about other rodents."

"Speaking of pests, come on, Miranda."

They stopped at the bottom of the stairs. Miranda remained on the last step. He walked back and forth in front of her. She could hear the sounds even more clearly now of the mice scratching in the dark corners and in the space between the ceiling overhead and the floor above that.

"Come on, Miranda." He ran his hand over the rough brick walls and stamped his heel on the brick floor. "You don't have to worry about this floor caving in. But then, when did that ever stop you?"

"No, thanks. I think I'll stay right here." She tapped her toe on the last wooden step.

Del peered into the darkness on either side of the steps. She ducked her head and looked, too.

"It's not as big as I thought it would be," she remarked.

"I thought it'd be bigger, too. I guess it's just a half basement. Probably there's just a little crawl space under the back of house."

"It's not even as full of junk as the upstairs."

"Disappointed?"

"Not really. I mean, I really hadn't expected to find any dead bodies or hidden treasures down here."

"It looks as if Red Wilkins—"

"Who?"

"Mr. Richardson's handyman. He must've used this area to store tools and things he used to do repairs in the house."

"He didn't use them often, did he?"

"Mr. Martin told me he died a couple of years ago. I guess I was away when it happened."

"Oh, I'm sorry, but I guess I wasn't paying too much attention at the time." Miranda glanced around again. "From the looks of this place, he died many years ago, and left it to all the mice."

She kept looking down and holding her skirt up with her free hand.

"Do you think mice can't jump up that one step?"

"Shut up, Del," she grumbled. "I think it's time to get on with the other highlights of this tour."

Her grip on his hand tightened.

He stepped closer to her. "You're not afraid of mice, are you?"

"Shut up, Del. I'm not afraid of anything," she declared boldly.

With his free hand, he reached up to stroke his chin thoughtfully. "I seem to recall you are."

"Your memory's as bad as Miss Barber's."

"No, it's not. If you're afraid of mice, then why the devil did you come down here?"

"Because . . . I wanted to see the place. The whole place. Now, let's get on with this grand tour."

"You might be safe on that step—for a while," he teased. "I think I also remember you declaring that I'd protect you."

"I seem to recall that was in reference to farm equipment, not mice. I also recall quite clearly that I was a very little child at the time."

"And now you're all grown up, aren't you?"

"Yes."

"And you have your fiancé to protect you."

"Um, yeah."

"You don't sound so sure of him, Miranda."

"Shut up, Del," she snapped. "I'm sure enough of him to know he'll marry me in two weeks and won't go running off to Texas without me."

"Can Charles protect you from nasty old mice like this?" he asked. He tried to keep smiling, so she wouldn't yell at him. But his eyes searched her face, looking for some kind of vulnerability.

"What? Well, um . . . yes, of course. Yes."

"No, he doesn't."

"Yes . . . yes . . ."

"No, he doesn't. He tries to buy them."

She laughed, but it wasn't very loud, and it was awfully short-lived. Standing on the step, she was almost eye to eye with him. Her eyes were watching him, too. He wanted to lose himself in the blue depths.

"When he tries to protect you, does he hold you, Miranda? Does he hold you like this?"

9

"*C*AN HE HOLD you like I do, Miranda?" Del asked.

He moved his hand to entwine his fingers with hers. She didn't pull back.

She kept watching him cautiously, but her smooth fingers willingly and readily laced through his like they'd always been made to fit together.

"He's . . . my fiancé. Of course he does," she replied.

"Does he hold you like *this*, Miranda?" he whispered.

His other hand rested on her waist. She still had made no attempt to move away from him.

He could feel the subtle bending of her body toward his. She tensed, like a strung bow, but softened as if she were just waiting to press against him, to mold herself to his body. He felt his own body tense in anticipation.

"Yes."

He leaned closer to her to speak softly in her ear. "Does he hold you like *this*, Miranda?"

One hand slid around to hold her back while his other hand moved along her arm to rest behind her shoulder. He leaned just slightly, to cradle her in his embrace.

"That's none of your business, Del," she told him with a nervous little laugh.

He could feel her body tensing more, and his own body tuning to match her.

"How could I ever have imagined I didn't want to be around you? That I didn't want you, Miranda?" he whispered. "The way you laugh, the crazy things you laugh at, the wisecracks you're always making, the trouble you're always getting yourself into and dragging me along with you. I never realized until I had to live without you. Do you have any idea how dull Texas was without you? You were what made my life fun, interesting. I see you again, and I can't believe it's only now that I realize all this."

"Horse puckies, Del!" Her body tensed more. But this time it wasn't in response to his nearness. "You just want me now that you know you can't have me. When you think I'm not interested in you anymore—"

"You just said when I think you're not interested in me. Does that mean I'm wrong? Does that mean you *are* still interested in me, Miranda?"

"Don't be ridiculous."

She was trying to use that same haughty expression she had before, he noted. Probably something they'd taught her at that fancy boarding school. She didn't sound as haughty as she probably wanted to. Did that mean she wasn't sure of herself anymore? Did that mean she was having second thoughts about marrying that other fellow now that she'd seen him again?

"You know he's not the man for you, Miranda. You know he could never make you feel like this."

Boldly he began to lower his lips to hers.

"That's definitely none of your business!" She tried to push him away with both hands. "I can't do this. You shouldn't. I shouldn't."

"When did that ever stop you, Miranda?"

She pushed harder. He couldn't force her. He couldn't make her stay. Del reluctantly let her go.

As she turned to run up the steps, she tripped over the hem of her dress. She caught herself with both hands flat on the grimy step.

"Oh, crap!"

"That sounds more like my old Miranda."

"I'm not your old Miranda," she protested as she pushed herself upright. She dusted her hands off against each other and tried to continue up the stairs with more grace. "You didn't want the old Miranda. Don't think you can have the new one."

"But you . . . but I thought you—"

"Yeah, so did I, once, but I was mistaken."

She didn't stop until she'd reached the top of the stairs.

"Thank you for that very interesting tour," she called down to him as she brushed the dust and wrinkles from her skirt. Her voice was tight and strained. "I don't believe it's wise for me to be staying for the remainder."

"I'm sorry, Miranda. I just thought—"

"It's all right, Del. I . . . I was a bit . . . mistaken myself."

She reached up to wipe at the corner of her eye.

"It's so very dusty in here," she remarked, wiping at her eye again.

She pulled open her little bag and dug around inside. At last she drew out a lacy handkerchief and began dabbing at her eyes.

"I can't believe the incredible dust in here."

She wiped her eyes once more, then blew her nose very hard.

"We can still be friends, can't we, Del?" she asked as she replaced the hankie.

"Yeah, of course."

"And nary a word of this from either of us to anyone—ever?"

"Yeah, sure."

He looked around. Each long window and each doorway seemed to glow blue in the twilight.

"It's starting to get dark. That's not much of a problem here."

He reached over and turned the key on the bottom of one of the gas jets. The yellow glow spread across the floor, turning the dust-laden air to gold.

She looked more beautiful now than ever—a softer gold than the brilliance of the sunlight she'd been standing in when she'd first arrived.

"But are you sure you can make it home safely in the dark?"

"I think so."

"You thought you could run up those steps, too."

"Shut up, Del."

"They still haven't caught the guys who are holding up the trains. Or the idiots who are breaking into the stores in town. Are you sure you'll be all right?"

"As long as I don't stand still long enough to look like a building or move fast enough to be mistaken for a train."

Del laughed, but he was still concerned for her.

"I borrowed a wagon from Simpson's Livery to use for hauling stuff from Quinn's today. It's still around back. If you don't mind sitting with a couple of buckets of paint, I can offer you a ride home."

"No, thank you."

"I'll just drop you off at your front gate. Charles doesn't even have to see me."

"Charles is the least of my worries," she muttered. She spoke as if she wanted him to hear what she was saying, but didn't want to actually come right out and say it. A bit more loudly she added, "I still don't think that's a good idea."

She turned to go. She took a step toward the door, but stumbled over a doubled-up rug.

"Will you at least let me help you to the door?" He held his hand out to her again.

She barely placed her fingertips on his arm.

"Sure, Del. After all, you're just my old childhood friend, Del."

"Yeah, that's me," he grumbled.

That's quite a change from what you used to think of me. And I sure as hell just botched any other feelings you might have had for me.

"Ah, so there you are, my dear!"

Without the softening effect of the draperies, it was amazing how loudly Charles's voice could ring through the house.

Miranda's hand flew back from Del's arm as if it had been a firebrand.

"We were very concerned for you, my dear," Mrs. Lowell said.

Miranda cringed, hoping she was safe from having her expression of utter disgust seen in flickering shadows rendered by the gaslight.

Why? If you'd found us, half naked, emerging from the bedroom, I'd say you had cause for concern. But the basement?

"I was very, very concerned for you," Charles repeated with more insistence.

She shouldn't be embarrassed. She hadn't done anything wrong. Really, she hadn't. Then why was she blushing? She hoped the gaslight disguised the embarrassed flush she could feel flooding her cheeks with warmth. On the other hand, she felt so warm, she believed she must be glowing like a beacon. How could they miss her?

She didn't mind being found by Charles, but did he have to bring his mother along *everywhere*?

"I wish you'd let me know you'd be coming here for a visit, Miranda. Mother and I would have come with you," he said with just a hint of a threat in his voice—or was she just feeling guilty? Miranda wondered. "We'd certainly be very interested in seeing the challenge Mr. Williams has set up for himself."

"I'd be happy to give you all a tour, too—someday," Del offered.

Charles didn't even acknowledge Del's remark.

"It's very dangerous coming to dilapidated houses alone, Miranda," Charles continued.

"But I wasn't alone. Del was . . ." Miranda stopped with a little gasp she hoped no one else heard. Del *was* there—and that was what was *really* making Charles sore.

"One never knows when a roof or staircase will collapse. I believe it would be a good idea if you never came here again without me."

"I'm sorry I worried you, Charles."

She couldn't tell him she was sorry she'd come—because she wasn't. She wouldn't promise him she'd never come here again, either, because she knew darn good and well she would.

"I can't imagine why you'd want to come to such a wretched mess in the first place!" Mrs. Lowell declared, glancing around.

"If nobody'd cleaned you up in two or three months, you might not look so great, either," Del pointed out to her.

Miranda had a hard time not laughing.

Mrs. Lowell harrumphed. "I can overlook that, but what an abysmal piece of architecture."

"What?" Miranda demanded with disbelief. "This place is beautiful."

Mrs. Lowell was such a narrow-minded, shortsighted old biddy. Of course she wouldn't be able to see the forest for the trees. She wouldn't be able to look beyond the superficial covering of dirt to the true beauty that was the soul of this house.

"Don't be silly, my dear." Mrs. Lowell gave her a withering glance. "What do you know of architecture?"

What do you know? Your husband's business is shipping, not building.

"I mean, just look at this place." Mrs. Lowell gestured disdainfully at everything around her. "The moldings are all wrong for this size room. And who decorated this place?"

"I guess Mr. Richardson did," Miranda ventured.

Mrs. Lowell clucked her tongue.

"No taste, no discernment. I haven't seen anyone use a carpet of this style since I was a small child. And how could they ever have supposed that wallpaper would complement this carpet?"

Mrs. Lowell was wandering about as she criticized everything she saw.

Miranda found herself cringing as she allowed herself a brief fantasy that the old harridan would trip over something. Where in the world was that bunched-up rug she'd tripped over when she needed it? Of course, she wouldn't fall and hurt herself, she quickly amended. Just enough to take some of the wind out of her critical sails.

"Aha! Now, there's one thing of which I do approve," she declared looking upward. "Such an impressive collection of hunting trophies. Why, it's almost as extensive as Bernard Wiggenbottom's."

She returned to the vestibule and studied the empty space in the curve of the staircase.

"The only thing missing is a huge grizzly bear—right here!" she commanded. "That might be the only thing that would truly improve this place."

"What about a stuffed rattlesnake by the door?" Miranda suggested. "With a big, hollow elephant's foot, with a maroon fringe around the top, to serve as the umbrella holder?"

Mrs. Lowell looked at her in surprise.

Oh, now I've done it. I've really made her mad.

But Mrs. Lowell said, "Why, Miranda, my dear. Perhaps there is hope for you after all."

Then the lady heaved a huge sigh and looked around again.

Nope. Right on by her. It's just as I suspected all along. No sense of humor.

"No, I don't care how anyone might try to decorate this place," Mrs. Lowell pronounced. "It's perfectly abysmal!"

"Well, then, it's a good thing you don't have to live here, isn't it?" Del declared.

"I beg your pardon."

"You're very lucky, you know," Del told her. "You can go back to Boston, to that really big, fine, architecturally perfect house, and you never have to come back here ever again."

Del strode with purposeful steps toward the front door. He held out his arm, clearly indicating the exit.

"In fact, you don't even have to wait until you get back to Boston. You can leave here now and never come back."

He remained in the doorway, arm outstretched. There was no way on earth Mrs. Lowell could mistake Del's invitation to be gone.

Mrs. Lowell harrumphed again. "I believe I shall. Come, Charles. And don't forget to take your fiancé."

Charles turned and took Miranda's hand. "Come along."

Miranda wanted to pull away from his grasp. She'd had to swallow a large dose of pride to work up enough nerve to get into this house, and now she wanted to stay here.

Of course, after that awfully embarrassing incident with Del in the basement, she didn't believe he'd ever let her in again, either. And after Mrs. Lowell and Charles found them alone together, she doubted either of them would let her out of their sight long enough to give her the chance to come here again. If they were on better terms with Max, they might ask to borrow a pair of shackles and chain her to her bed. Gosh, she hoped they didn't ask. Knowing they were for her, Max just might give them to them.

"Thanks for the tour, Del," she called to him as she had no other choice but to follow Charles.

She wished Del could see her expression now. She wished he could see how proud she was of him for telling Mrs. Lowell off. She wished he could see that she really had enjoyed being in his arms for those few moments.

If only she weren't already engaged.

If only he'd held her because he really loved her, not just because he was trying to outdo Charles.

"Well, I certainly hope you've satisfied your curiosity about that house," Charles said as he led Miranda to the carriage waiting in the street.

She gave a noncommittal shrug. She'd been longing to

get inside that house for years—and she'd spent less than an hour there, and she'd only seen those morbid animal heads and the lousy basement. Of course she hadn't satisfied her curiosity.

"I hope you've seen what a wretched ruin the place is."

"Yes, I have." She could freely admit that.

"I hope you've realized what an exercise in futility trying to fix that place up is."

"I suppose so," she replied.

"And I certainly hope you've gotten your desire to own that place out of your system."

"I . . . I suppose so."

"You really wouldn't want to own any house that he'd lived in anyway, would you, my dear? I mean, those sort of people just don't know how to care for their homes properly."

Those sort?

"No matter how much he tried to repair the roof and replace the wallpaper, the place would be a shambles again within a year."

Those sort of people? Did those sort of people not worry their pretty little heads about anything? she wanted to ask him. No, not now. She'd caused enough trouble already. If she didn't want to really stir things up, she'd better just keep her big mouth shut, as Mrs. Bigelow had tried very hard to teach her.

As they drove home, Charles and his mother continued their discussion.

"He'll spend all that money, renovating that wretched house," Mrs. Lowell predicted ominously. "Then he won't have anything left for the upkeep."

Charles shook his head as he jiggled the reins over the horse's back. "That's the way all these yokels do, Mother. I'm just surprised he's spending his money on the house, instead of just running out and buying new clothes, and lots of whiskey, and spending it on fancy women."

"Oh, Charles!" Mrs. Lowell exclaimed, clapping her hands over her ears.

"Forgive my plain speech in front of a lady, Mother."

What about me? Aren't I a lady? Didn't my parents spend loads of money to have me made into a lady?

"It just infuriates me so to see how the lower classes waste their resources. Is there any wonder they continue to stay in their wretched existence without hope of betterment?"

"No, I suppose you're right. I mean, can you imagine those two silly old women serving a fruit punch?"

"I understand they're Temperance people." He chuckled.

Mrs. Lowell's laugh was more of a snort. "I suppose, as with most of the lower classes, they can't handle their money or their liquor."

"Do you mean 'those people'?" Miranda mimicked.

Charles nodded emphatically. "Precisely. I'm so glad to see you're learning, my darling."

Oh, I'm learning all right. But I don't think it's quite the lesson you might expect.

She looked at Charles as they rode along. She was seeing him now in a completely different light—one that she wasn't sure was very flattering.

She'd never heard him talk about anyone that way before. He'd always seemed so . . . so democratic. Was there something in the water around here that hadn't been in Boston? Or was there something in Boston that he wasn't getting out here that was making him act like this?

Whatever it was, she knew she didn't like it at all. Not at all.

He was jealous. That was it, she decided in a sudden flash of insight. He was jealous of Del. That was what accounted for his boorish behavior.

She breathed a sigh of relief and settled back against the seat. Once they returned to Boston, he'd be his old congenial self again.

She hoped.

Del slammed the door shut.

"What a pair of doggone, gol-darn, conceited snobs!"

he muttered to himself as he trudged back into the parlor. "How in the world did Miranda get mixed up with those two in the first place? Back here, she'd have laughed a couple of snots like that out of the room! Now she's agreeing with them."

He slid his back down the wall to rest in a corner.

"How in heaven's name did she ever become engaged to that Charles fellow in the first place?"

He shook his head.

"She's so different when she's around them. With me, she laughs, she jokes, she makes horrible remarks about other people who really deserve them. But around him all she ever says is 'Yes, Charles. No, Charles.'"

He waggled his head from side to side.

"'Whatever you say, Charles. You're the boss, Charles.'"

He slammed his fist on the floor.

"Whatever happened to my old Miranda? 'Drop dead, Charles. Go soak your head, Charles. Go play on the railroad tracks, Charles.'"

The hammering of his fist grew louder as he grew increasingly angry.

"It's as if the real Miranda were trapped inside this cage they've put her in. I've got to rescue her! I've got to break her out of that cage so she can be the real Miranda again. The Miranda I love."

Del slammed his fist down one more time to indicate his determination. Then he sprang to his feet and started working on his house again. His house, Miranda's house. How about *their* house?

"Hey, Sally, I need a favor."

Del stood in the doorway to the kitchen, grinning at her. She turned from stirring the kettle of soup on the stove and laughed at him.

"No, really. Seriously, Sally. I need a favor."

"Yeah? I need a serious favor, too." She turned back to the soup.

"I need your help for a party."

"A party? For who? Miranda?" Del watched her heave her shoulders in a shrug. "Miranda's already got plenty of parties, and holding a 'Welcome back, Del' party for yourself is a little conceited, don't you think?"

"No. It's not for me—or Miranda," he quickly added. "It's for . . . for everyone."

"Not everyone will fit in our barn."

"No, just some really good friends."

She turned to him, her eyes wide with exaggerated surprise. "You have friends?"

"Yeah, lots of them."

"We can't afford to feed lots of—"

"I can."

"Oh, sure, rub that in, thank you very much, Del."

"Look, Sally, I'd just like to have a party, but I'm going to need your help."

"How do you figure that?"

Sally wasn't too eager to help him with much of anything right now. Telling her he wanted to impress the Lowells wouldn't help one bit.

But it wasn't to impress the Lowells that he wanted to have the party. He wanted to prove to those snobs that he wasn't just a dumb country bumpkin. He was a man who knew how to work with wood and plaster. He was a man who could appreciate the beautiful silver, paintings, and statues that Henry Richardson had collected, and knew how to show them off. He was a man who could take care of his home as well as any well-bred, yacht-sailing, polo-playing stuffed shirt.

How would he explain this to Sally?

"I've been fixing up the Richardson—no, *my* house."

"No, no, oh, no!" she declared emphatically. She banged the wooden spoon on the side of the kettle to shake the noodles back into the pot, but the hammering matched her protests. "I've got enough work around here—that not a blessed soul will help me with—to keep me plenty busy. I'll be darned if I'm going to go doing someone else's work for them."

"I don't need your help for that."

"Good. Because you know darn good and well you're not getting it."

"Although I might need your help to pick out some new draperies and stuff."

"Shopping?"

Did Del detect just a slight brightening of Sally's eyes?

"At Quinn's? Or Englemeyer's?" she asked.

"Geez, Sally, I don't know anything about that kind of stuff. I guess whichever place you like best."

Sally just nodded and stirred the soup. That was going to be the most thoroughly stirred soup in the history of the world before this conversation was done.

"When I get the downstairs all done, I want to have a party at the house. Just to kind of show off how really good-looking the place can be. That's what I'm really going to need your help for."

"Yeah," she answered. She placed both hands on her hips and watched him, chuckling. "I guess you will."

"And I'd appreciate it if you wouldn't mention any of this to anybody—especially Miranda—until it's all done."

"Especially not Miranda, huh?"

Del nodded. "So, will you do me this favor?"

"Nope." She turned back to the soup.

"No?" He tried not to sound too angry. If he made her mad, he knew she'd only refuse even more adamantly to help him.

"Not yet. See, I need that smokehouse roof fixed a lot more than I need to help you with some silly party."

"Oh. Oh, all right." A job for a job. It seemed only fair.

Pulling a pair of work gloves from the shelf in the laundry room, Del headed out the door.

He returned a little while later.

"Now, will you help me?"

"Did you stretch that new wire around the chicken run?"

Without a single remark Del turned right around and headed out the door.

"Then there's some shutters on the barn that need to be tightened before the rain sets in.

"This party better darn side impress the living daylights out of those uppity Lowells," Del grumbled as he made his way to the chicken coop, "to make this worth all the trouble."

Miranda stood in the doorway of the Picketts' house. She held several of her dresses draped over her arm.

She knocked on the wooden frame of the screen door.

"Miranda!" Sally sprang up from her seat by the fireside where she'd been doing her mending and rushed to the door.

Miranda was glad to see her friend finally smiling.

"Come in, come in! It's so good to see you."

She held the door open wide, but Miranda and her burden still had to squeeze to get through.

Once through the doorway she looked around. "Where's . . . everybody?"

"Alice went over to help Mrs. Swenson with the twins. The men are all out cultivating the north field."

"All?"

"Yes, Del, too—for a change he's actually doing some work about here. But no, he won't be back to the house until dinnertime."

Miranda nodded, but she still glanced around one more time, making sure they were completely alone. She swallowed hard, then laid her hand on her friend's arm. Very seriously she peered into her eyes.

"Sally, I need a favor."

Miranda never expected Sally to laugh.

"Don't tell me. You're having a party."

"What? No, no. What are you talking about?"

Sally shook her head and tried her best to stop laughing. "Nothing, nothing." She reached out for the bundle of fabric Miranda held. "What on earth do you have there?"

"A few dresses."

"New ones?"

"No."

"Do they need repairs? Hemming? Certainly not letting out. Maybe taking in?" Sally frowned. "What did you bring them here for anyway? Why didn't your mother help you?"

"No, there's nothing wrong with them."

Sally's frown deepened. "Then why are you carrying them around?"

"I had to tell Charles and Mrs. Lowell something, Sally. I . . . I just used these . . . as an excuse," Miranda said as she tossed the unwanted dresses over the back of one of the other chairs.

"Excuse?" Sally eyed her warily. "You're young, rich, beautiful. You're engaged to a rich man. All right, his mother's a bit of a harpy, but . . . well, what the heck do you need with excuses anyway?"

She took Miranda's arm and led her toward one of the chairs arranged in front of the fireplace.

"I told them my mother was too busy, and that I had to get you to help me," Miranda said as she settled into the chair opposite Sally. "Even then, it couldn't be easy. Mrs. Lowell tried to convince me to take everything to the 'professional' dressmaker in town."

Sally laughed and raised her hands in front of her. "Oh, heaven forbid a lady should do anything for herself!"

"Even worry her pretty little head," Miranda mumbled.

"What?"

"Nothing, nothing," Miranda said. "It was just something silly Charles told me."

That was certainly the truth. It was one of the silliest things she'd ever heard him say.

"I finally managed to convince Mrs. Lowell that we'd been helping each other for years, and that you'd be able to make the adjustments so much faster. I know it was tricky, but it was the only way I could come over here alone."

"Miranda," Sally said, fixing her with a sharp stare.

"Are you sure you want to marry this man? I mean, you know they always say you don't just marry the man, you marry the family. And brother! What a family!"

Miranda heaved a deep sigh. "I feel like I've just paid a visit to the Spanish Inquisition. I had to tell them . . . I had to *swear* to them that I'd seen Del riding by earlier on his way into town. That was the only way I was able to convince them to let me come over here alone."

"Why are they doing this to you, Miranda?" Sally demanded.

"I went to Mr. Richardson's—oh, all right—Del's house the other day," she admitted. "To see the house."

"You mean to see Del." Sally started laughing again.

Miranda grimaced. "Gee, Sally, do you think you could be a little more blunt?"

"I could," she answered, still chuckling. But then, much to Miranda's relief, she didn't say anything else. She looked at Miranda, her eyebrows raised expectantly. "And?"

"And Charles and his mother found us there."

"Good heavens, Miranda! What were you and Del doing?"

"Nothing, nothing," she answered quickly. She hoped Sally didn't notice that she answered a little too quickly. "Of course we weren't doing anything."

"Of course." One last giggle managed to escape from Sally.

"I mean, I'm engaged, and Del's . . . Del's an honorable man."

Sally shrugged. "He's just my brother. Yeah, I guess he is."

"Oh, Sally." Miranda felt just enough relief joking with her old friend to laugh a little. "But I need to go back there again."

"So? Go," she replied with another laugh.

Sally was clearly not giving this situation the serious consideration it warranted. On the other hand, maybe she was being too secretive.

"I sure as the devil can't get Charles or Mrs. Lowell to take me there."

"Your parents?" Sally suggested.

Miranda grimaced. "No. Right about now I don't think they'd understand."

Sally pursed her lips as if that would help her think.

"So you see, Sally, you're the only person I can come to for help. You've *got* to help me."

"What makes you think I'll help?"

"Because you've always been my friend."

"What do you think I can do?"

"I've got to go back to the house, Sally."

"You mean you want to see Del."

"It's not just that, Sally. Really. I just want to look at all the interesting things in that house," Miranda insisted. "I never had any idea how many nice things Mr. Richardson had collected. You ought to go see it, too."

"Oh, I might."

"Del's off to a great start fixing up the place. I'd really like to—"

"See Del." Sally pursed her lips and glanced at her out of the corner of her eye.

"No. I . . . oh, thunderation, Sally! You know I've always liked Del, but . . . I've outgrown that childishness. Del and I can still be friends."

"Sure. That's why Charles wasn't too happy to find you there the other day and forbade you to go there ever again."

"How did you know?"

Sally shook her head. "I might be an old maid, but I'm not stupid, and I have friends."

That was the problem. Sally wasn't stupid. She seemed to know what Miranda was thinking—almost. Miranda wasn't even sure herself of exactly what she was feeling, or what she should do about it. She wanted to be near Del again, but she knew she had an obligation to Charles, and to her parents not to hurt or embarrass them.

She wasn't sure what to do.

Maybe if she spent a little more time with Del, she'd

remember what a weasel he'd been to her for so many years. Maybe she'd realize what she was feeling was just a stubborn remnant of her girlish infatuation. Maybe she'd finally get rid of it completely.

Sally reached over and patted her hand. "This is going to be tough, Miranda. You might've been a sneaky little kid, but you never were a liar."

"Thanks, I think."

Miranda hesitated. How could she explain what she wanted, even to her best friend? What would Sally think of her? On the other hand, she did sort of seem to understand. There was only one way to find out.

"I think I need to do a little sneaking again, Sally. That's where I need your help."

Sally grinned at her. "What do you want me to do?"

"I want you to pretend we're going into town to see some friends, maybe Liz Englemeyer or someone. What we'll really be doing is . . . well, I want to go to Del's house."

Sally laughed and laughed.

10

*T*HE LITTLE BELLS attached to the inside of the door of Quinn's General Store jingled as Del entered. He drew in a deep breath. The place still smelled the same as always—coffee, cinnamon, kerosene. The place was full of wonderful things to buy.

He looked toward the potbellied stove in the middle of the store, surrounded by barrels of crackers and pickles. That was the only place in the whole crowded store that really looked empty.

When he was little, he could remember the two old men who sat there, day after day, arguing about who had beaten whom the most games. After Reuben Taylor died, Pops Canfield never could find a checkers partner he could argue with half as well. When Pops passed away a few years later, no one in town had the heart to take their places.

Maybe someday, when he was an old, old man, with nothing else to do except go to his big lonely house and rattle around in it like a marble in a rain barrel, he'd come down here, open up his checkerboard, and see who else wanted to play.

"So, what can I help you with today, Del?" Mr. Quinn asked, rushing over to him.

Del could almost see the man greedily rubbing his pudgy hands together over his sagging paunch.

"I need a few more mousetraps," Del answered.

"Golly, Del, you nigh onto bought me out the other day," Mr. Quinn said with a laugh. He reached around behind him to take a few more mousetraps off the shelf, anyway.

"It probably wouldn't hurt to throw in a few rat traps, too," Del added.

"The place that bad, huh?" Mr. Quinn headed for the rat traps on the shelf beneath.

Del shrugged. "Oh, it's a little worse than I'd expected, but nothing I can't handle."

"Good for you."

Mr. Quinn placed all the traps in a paper sack on the counter, then stood there waiting for Del to add more things to his order.

"You know, I just got some new rat poison in," Mr. Quinn suggested. "Good white arsenic. Real effective."

"I reckon so."

"Seeing as you don't have any kids yet that might get into the stuff, and I don't suppose you have any pets, you might want to consider using it."

"Yeah, thanks. If the traps don't work, I'll be back for it."

"If you think you might want a cat, my daughter's cat just had a litter. If they're anything like their mother, they'll be pretty good mousers."

"I'll keep that in mind."

"You know, if you got mice and rats in the cellar, you might want to check to make sure there aren't any bats nesting in your attic, too," Mr. Quinn warned. "It's funny, but it seems like one kind of critter sort of draws other critters. You know what I mean?"

"Yeah, I think I do."

"Bats can do a lot of damage. Stink like the devil, too."

"I haven't noticed much of an odor," Del replied. "So I guess I can wait awhile for that. After all, it's not as if you're closing up the store or I'm taking my house anywhere."

"Yeah, I guess not." Mr. Quinn laughed.

Del had the feeling the man would laugh at almost anything he said if he thought he could sell him something else. He was amazed at the attentive service he was receiving from all the shopkeepers in town lately. It was absolutely amazing the difference a little money could make. He liked it. A lot.

"Oh, I almost forgot. I need a jack plane."

"One of your doors sticking?"

"Yeah."

"I'm surprised all of them aren't sticking," Mr. Quinn said as he added the plane to the bag.

"I haven't checked them all yet."

The front door slammed loudly against the wall behind it. The bells jingled wildly. The windows rattled and a couple of rakes fell off their hooks on the wall.

"Hey, Del, my good buddy!" Jimmy called from the doorway.

Allen followed him in with an unsteady gate.

"I thought I saw you comin' in here," Jimmy said as he rushed toward Del. "Allen said no. But I recognize my best ol' buddy. Dang it, don't ever listen to Allen. You know why he wears boots?"

Del knew he was going to hate himself for asking, and encouraging these two idiots. "No, why?"

"'Cause he's too gol-danged stupid to lace up his shoes!"

Jimmy broke out in loud guffaws.

"Don't listen to him, Del. He's drunk," Allen grumbled as he leaned against the counter for support.

"Hey, Del, out again spendin' some more of all that money of yours?" Jimmy demanded. "I can think of a hell of a lot of better places to spend it than the general store."

"Whatcha buyin' anyway?" Allen asked.

"Mousetraps."

"Mousetraps!" Allen exclaimed in disbelief. "Criminy,

man! Can't you think of somethin' better to buy than mousetraps? How 'bout a big bottle of good ol' redeye?"

"How 'bout the company of a pretty gal to share it with?" Jimmy suggested.

"How 'bout treatin' your two best buddies to a bottle of that good ol' redeye, too?"

"Mousetraps are all I need right now," Del said quietly. Maybe if he kept his voice low, these two idiots wouldn't get too excitable and out of control. Then they'd just go away and leave him alone.

"We been lookin' all over town for you for days. Where you been, good buddy?"

"Working." He could have been right under their very noses and they'd have been too drunk to notice him.

"Naw! You're a rich man," Allen protested. "You don't have to work."

"Sure I do," Del replied. "It's just that, now, I get to choose what I work on."

"Hey, you know, you're real smart, ol' buddy!" Jimmy declared. He tried to lean on Del's shoulder, but missed and stumbled into a shelf, sending several boxes of oatmeal rolling across the floor.

Jimmy started chasing the elusive oatmeal. He tried to set the boxes on the shelf again, but kept knocking off what he'd just put up.

Del wondered exactly how much they'd had to drink last night to stay drunk this long, or how early this morning they'd started on their second round.

Jimmy's stack of boxes fell over again.

"Just leave it! I'll get it myself when I finish serving Del. Now go on, you loud-mouthed troublemakers," Mr. Quinn yelled. Brandishing a crowbar, he gestured angrily toward the door. "Get out of here before I call the sheriff."

"What? Why? We ain't done nothin' to you, old man," Allen declared with a loud belch.

"I tried to pick it up," Jimmy blubbered.

"Well, nothing. Nothing yet," Mr. Quinn admitted.

"But I know you two. You're just dying to pick a fight anywhere you go."

"Tarnation, no. The only people in here now is me and Allen and Del and you," Jimmy said, glancing around the store. "Now, I know for sure I ain't goin' to be fightin' with my two best buddies in all the world. And you're just an ol' man, so I ain't gonna fight you. Ain't no sport in that. And my ma, she taught me to respect my elders. So there."

Bleary-eyed, Jimmy stuck his tongue out at Mr. Quinn.

"You're still troublemakers, the pair of you," Mr. Quinn said, slowly replacing the crowbar under the counter. "Just do your business, say your piece, then get out."

Jimmy threw his arm around Del's shoulder and leaned on him. Yeah, Del could definitely smell the whiskey on him now. That confirmed his original suspicions. But then, there never really had been much question about that in the first place.

"Dang it, Del. It just ain't fair," Jimmy complained. "Just 'cause a fellow ain't got a steady job, and likes to down a little likker and visit the ladies from time to time, don't mean he's some kind of law-breakin' varmint. Does it, Del?"

"Not necessarily."

"There, see, Quinn. My ol' buddy Del, one of the richest men in the whole dang town, thinks we're innocent."

"Yeah, well, Del's no Judge Roy Bean."

"Yeah, and this ain't no royal court, neither."

"Del's been gone for three years," Mr. Quinn replied. "He doesn't know the half of it."

Jimmy and Allen laughed. Jimmy tried to tug Del closer to him. Del tried to be subtle as he pulled away, but he didn't want to linger. He couldn't hold his breath that long.

"Del, ol' buddy, would ya like to find out the half of it? Huh? Huh?"

"To tell the truth, Jimmy, I'm not all that curious."

"Oh, we lead real interestin' lives."

"I guess starting bar fights, then cleaning up the mess, could be interesting," Del commented. If you have a brain the size of a dried pea, he finished to himself.

"We like it," Jimmy declared emphatically. "When Miss Sadie throws us out, we just go on over to Miss Rosie's 'til she throws us out. Then there's this new place—Miss Blue's. You oughtta see some o' the gals she's got! She never throws nobody out."

"I think I'll pass on that one. Thanks anyway."

"No, no. You gotta come with us. Your treat, of course, ol' buddy," Allen declared. "Cripes, we ain't got no money."

"No, I guess not." Del shook his head. "But I can't go, fellows. I got work to do."

"What? No! It ain't 'cause you don't want to go spendin' your money on us, is it?"

"No, no."

"Just 'cause you're livin' in that fancy house now don't mean you're turnin' into a tight-fisted, graspin' ol' miser like Richardson, are you?"

"Me? You're kidding. Not me," Del claimed, with a grin he hoped eased Allen's and Jimmy's tempers.

"Yeah, well, all right for now," Jimmy said. "But someday you gotta come with us."

"Maybe someday I will. Maybe."

"We'll visit all them places."

"We'll start at one end of the street and not stop till we reach the other end—or keel over dead drunk."

"Whichever comes first," Del added with a laugh.

"Course, when we're done, if we're still walkin', we'll need to find a place to sleep it off till the next round. Hey, you got lots of room in that house of yours, Del! Can we stay there?"

"Well, fellows, it's been lots of fun visiting with you, but I've got a lot of work to do."

"Work? Oh, criminy, Del. You still workin' on that ol' house?"

Del nodded. Hadn't they been listening? Or couldn't they hear through the liquor that soaked their brains?

"Doggone it, Del. That dust'll still be there when you're dust. Why do you want to spend your time pushin' it around when you could be havin' fun with us?"

"I got my reasons."

Jimmy jabbed Allen in the side. "I'll bet one of them reasons is Miranda Hamilton."

"Yep, yep, that's one," Allen agreed, holding up one finger, as if he needed that to help him keep count. "That's a big one. That's what keeps him outta Miss Blue's. Y'know," he confided, leaning a little closer to Jimmy, "she'd be enough to keep me outta all them places, too. Yes, siree."

"Leave Miranda out of this," Del said.

Calm, stay calm, he tried to tell himself. But the thought of them using their whiskey-sogged brains to think about Miranda set his teeth on edge.

"Course she's done gone off and got herself a new beau," Allen said. "Maybe she wasn't too happy with you, Del."

"Shut up, Allen," Del said, with more than the hint of a threat in his voice.

"Now you gotta come to Miss Sadie's—or someplace like that—with us," Jimmy insisted. "Maybe they'll teach you a thing or two that you can use to keep Miranda happy with you, and she won't want to go off to Boston no more to find some sissy-pants little miss nancy guy to marry."

"Shut up, Allen," Del repeated.

He didn't want to have to beat the tar out of them again, but he would, if they made one more remark about Miranda. The best way to avoid that was to just get out of there. Even if they followed him, at least he wouldn't wreck Mr. Quinn's store.

"I'm leaving now."

"You goin' back to work in your house?"

"I want to clean it up so I can live in it."

"Live in it!" Allen exclaimed. "You're serious? No-body could live in that rat pile!"

Del lifted one of the traps out of the bag. "That's why I've got these. Now, you fellows go on and play nice. I've got work to do."

"Oh, criminy, Del," Allen grumbled as he and Jimmy made their way out the door. "When're you goin' to learn to have fun?"

The bell jingled again as they slammed the door behind them.

"Oh, gracious! I thought they'd never leave!" Mr. Quinn exclaimed with a gasp of relief. Then he turned a beaming smile on Del. "Want me to put those things on your tab, Del?"

"I don't have a tab, here or anywhere else," he reminded the man of something he already knew very well.

"Want me to start one for you?" Mr. Quinn offered.

"No, no," he protested, pulling a bill out of his pocket and laying it on the counter. "I always pay cash."

He scooped up the sack and his change, then headed toward the door.

"Good luck with those mice."

"Thanks, Mr. Quinn."

Del stuck his head out of the door and looked up and down the sidewalk before he left the store. He wasn't a coward. He just didn't want Jimmy and Allen to get a hold of him and drag him into their wild carousing.

The coast looked pretty clear. He stepped out and almost collided with Miranda and Sally.

"Miranda!" he exclaimed. "Sally? What are you doing here?"

"Don't look so surprised, Del," Sally told him. "I do have some sort of a life aside from cooking and cleaning for you all."

"Yeah, sure, good. But what are you doing here?"

"Looking for you," Sally answered.

"Why? What chore did I forget to do for you this time?" he asked with a wry grin.

"Nothing."

"Then what happened? Is something wrong? Is it Pa? Tommy?"

"No, no. Calm down," Sally told him. "If it was, I'd be heading for the Doc, not you. What good can you do?"

Del looked pointedly at Miranda. "I think you might be surprised if you knew."

Miranda could still feel her face warming. What did she have to feel embarrassed about? They hadn't done a thing—not a thing—to be ashamed of.

Sally grimaced and shook her head. "Not me. Nope. Nothing surprises me anymore. I don't want to have anything to do with anything. If you need me—which I seriously doubt—I'll be over talking to Liz, helping her get her store back in shape again. We old maids, we've got to stick together."

Del sort of figured this meant the new draperies would be coming from Englemeyer's.

"Don't worry about me," she said airily. "I'll be by your place to pick Miranda up on my way home, so no one's the wiser—I hope."

"Thanks, Sally," Miranda said, grasping her friend's hand. "Really."

"Sure. Why shouldn't at least somebody be happy around here?" Sally moved along down the sidewalk, muttering to herself, "Yeah, there's nothing like having an old maid friend you can depend on. Thunderation, do you think I'll turn out like Miss Barber, with my nose in everybody else's business, talking to myself?"

Miranda turned to Del. She figured she owed him more of an explanation. "We stopped at your house—" she said.

"My house?"

"Shut up, Del," she said. "We ended that discussion, a long time ago."

She frowned, as she usually did, but this time she added a little laugh. She was relieved to see him laugh, too. She'd been so afraid she'd ruined everything the last time she went to his house. The first time she was faced with actually kissing him—the one thing she'd looked forward to ever since she was a little girl—and she'd panicked. She'd bolted like a scared colt.

Mrs. Lowell had acted like a raging old harridan, but then again, that was normal for her. Charles had gone and acted like such a complete, pompous ass. Miranda was beginning to have a nasty suspicion that that kind of behavior was normal for him, too.

No, it couldn't be, she tried to tell herself. He'd been so charming in Boston, gracious and attentive.

But what if Charles really was like this all the time? What was she going to do about it? At this point, with the wedding only two weeks away, how could she refuse to marry him? What excuse could she give? She didn't like his attitude?

"Sally and I stopped by your house, but you weren't there," Miranda tried to continue.

Grinning back at her, Del lifted the bag. "I had some shopping to do for a certain lady I know who isn't too fond of mice." He rattled the bag. The clattering of wood and metal should have been her clue to the contents. "Mousetraps."

She laughed.

"If I get rid of the mice, maybe she'll come visit me again, I hope." He gave her a bold wink. "Maybe she'll stay a little longer this time."

"Is that an invitation?"

Del nodded. "I know it's one that'll be hard to accept."

"Don't be so sure of that."

He looked at her very seriously. "Are you sure, Miranda? I don't want to make any more trouble for you than I already have."

"Excuse me, Del, but I'm a big girl now. I make my own trouble for myself."

He laughed. "You're really good at it, too. You've had so much practice with other people."

"Practice makes perfect."

"Yes, it does."

Del was watching her, his eyes glowing in the morning

light. Her heart grew lighter. He wasn't angry with her after all.

Suddenly his head shot up. He looked over her shoulder, past her.

She turned to see what had so riveted his attention. If it was Dorothy Halstead, she swore she'd push her in front of an oncoming stagecoach.

A strange couple stood behind her on the sidewalk. The woman had her arm laced through the man's so tightly, neither one of them could move. She held him so close, he couldn't even stand up straight, but leaned in toward her at an angle. They looked very nervous at encountering Del.

"Hello, Mrs. Richardson. Jasper!" Del declared, nodding to each person.

They nodded their heads at him like two automatons. She could see them frantically glancing right and left as if they couldn't wait to get away from him.

Trying very hard not to move her lips, Miranda whispered to Del, "Who are they?"

Much more loudly than Miranda had expected, Del declared, "You haven't made the acquaintance of these charming people. Come on."

Taking her by her elbow, Del urged her along the sidewalk toward them. They backed up just a bit at his direct advance. They looked as if they wanted to turn around and run away.

They might be able to run, Miranda decided, but she didn't think either of them could run very far for very long, especially if the woman didn't release her death grip on her companion's arm.

"Miss Hamilton, may I introduce you to Mr. Jasper Richardson and his charming wife, Daisy."

"How do you do?" Miranda responded.

Daisy glanced nervously from Del to Miranda, then around the sidewalk, then back to Del again. Was she looking for a way of escape? Or was she trying to decide which of them to kill first, and making sure there were no witnesses?

"Mr. Richardson is the late lamented nephew of Henry Richardson."

"Don't you mean the nephew of the late lamented Henry Richardson?" Miranda corrected.

Del just shrugged.

Miranda stopped herself from a burst of laughter. Instead she just nodded and responded again, "How very nice to meet you both."

"Yeah, yeah, nice meeting you, too," Mrs. Richardson said quickly. "Come on, Jasper. We've got business to attend to."

What was making the pair of them so nervous? Miranda wondered. Del was pretty harmless and they didn't even know her. But they were itching to run away.

"Still looking for a lawyer so you can sue me?" Del asked. He shook his head and made sympathetic clucking noises with his tongue.

Jasper frowned. "That's my business," he declared grumpily.

"Nope. My house. That makes it my business."

"Good-bye, Williams," Jasper grumbled.

"Are you leaving town?"

"No. But I'll bet you wish we were."

"Well, you said good-bye, which usually means we won't be seeing each other for a while, maybe never."

"No. I mean, not yet. No," Jasper stammered. Mrs. Richardson started giving him definite tugs on his arm, pulling him away before he was done with his speech. "No, we still have some business in town. I'll see you with my lawyer, in court. Good-bye."

Jasper and Daisy hurried away down the sidewalk.

"What a weird couple! Who in the world are they?" Miranda asked.

"I told you, Henry Richardson's nephew and his wife."

"You said that, and I really was listening to you that time. But I never heard of them before."

"Neither had I. Neither had a lot of people. For a while there, I was wondering if Mr. Richardson had even heard of them. Or maybe he'd pretended he never had."

"Where did they come from?"

"Crawled out of the woodwork?"

"No, really."

"Poughkeepsie."

"What are they doing here?"

"He claims the house is his inheritance."

"My house?"

"His house, if you listen to him. I'm surprised they haven't pitched a tent on the front lawn."

"That's preposterous!"

"The last time I talked to them, they claimed they couldn't afford a lawyer." He turned to look at her, mischief dancing in his eyes. "Are you sure you don't want to run after them, give them some financial help so they can take the property, and then you can buy the place from them? Isn't that what you said you were looking for?"

"Will you shut up about that!" she declared. "I wouldn't touch those two slimy-looking characters with a ten-foot pole!"

Del laughed. "I just wanted to make sure."

Miranda nodded at his bag and gave him a wry smile. "Go set your mousetraps, Del. And catch your nose in one while you're at it."

"Does this mean you don't want to see the house again?"

"No, no!" Her eyes widened with eagerness. She'd better be nice to him if she wanted to get into that house again. "I'd really like to."

"After all, you never did get your grand tour. Why don't you come back with me now?"

She hesitated.

"Isn't that why you and Sally came into town anyway?"

"Well, of course. But . . ." Was she so painfully transparent?

"Who knows how long Sally and Liz'll be chatting?"

Miranda nodded. "I just don't think it's a good idea if everyone in town sees me riding off with you."

"Am I that awful? Can't two childhood friends ride together?"

"I . . . I guess so."

"I took the cans of paint out of the wagon."

She laughed. "In that case, how can I refuse?"

As they approached his wagon, Miranda noticed Widow Crenshaw and Miss Barber hurrying over to them.

"My goodness," Widow Crenshaw said, "did you notice how many lawmen are in town this morning?"

"No, ma'am, I hadn't," Del replied. "What happened? Did someone break into the Last Chance? The Lonesome Whistle? Not Miss Sadie's!"

"No, no. Something much worse. There was another train robbery last night," Miss Barber announced.

"What did they steal?"

"The mail! That's horrible!" Miss Barber continued. "Now no one will get their letters. No one will find out that Aunt Maude died and Cousin Ruthie had a baby girl."

"Catherine! Have you been reading the neighbors' mail again?"

"Yes," she boldly admitted. "And you have, too, otherwise how would you know Aunt Maude died?"

"Hush, Catherine!" Widow Crenshaw mumbled.

"Was anyone hurt in the train robbery?" Miranda asked.

"I think one of the conductors dropped a box on his toe and broke it trying to hand the bandit a bag of mail," Widow Crenshaw answered.

"Did he break the box or his toe?" Del asked.

"That's still terrible," Miranda said, giving him a jab in the ribs.

"Oh, we agree," Miss Barber said.

"Isn't it strange how, with all that liquor and money laying around, nobody's robbed any of the saloons yet," Del observed.

"Or the whorehouses," Miss Barber eagerly added.

"Catherine!" Widow Crenshaw exclaimed. "I declare, she scandalizes me everywhere she goes."

"Our biggest problem is Max," Miss Barber continued as if Widow Crenshaw hadn't said a word.

"Why Max?" Miranda asked.

"Well, he's so busy now with all those other lawmen in town that he doesn't have time for us anymore." She gave an injured sniff.

"Hush, Catherine."

"Miss Barber, Mrs. Crenshaw," Miranda asked, "if you don't mind my being so inquisitive, why are you two so . . . so interested in Max?"

"He's . . . he's just a nice young man, but rather inexperienced, trying to do a very difficult job," Widow Crenshaw replied quickly. "We . . . we thought perhaps he could benefit from our years of experience in observing human nature."

"And he's always so helpful," Miss Barber added.

"Hush, Catherine."

"How does he help you?" Miranda asked.

"He's always so ready to answer any questions we might have, no matter how foolish—"

"Hush, Catherine."

"We really appreciate that now that Sheriff Duncan's gone."

"Hush, Catherine." Widow Crenshaw turned her glare from her companion, and smiled at Miranda and Del. "We really need to be moving along about our business now."

"We might as well. We can't get anymore done without Max anyway," Miss Barber lamented as Widow Crenshaw grabbed her by the hand and practically dragged her down the street.

Del turned and gave Miranda a puzzled glance. "What in the world was that all about?"

"I don't know. The older those two get, the stranger they get."

"I thought little old ladies planted lavender and took in stray cats. That's what my grandmother did."

"Not these two. These two interrogate the sheriff and have a morbid fascination with breaking and entry."

"What if they're the two who've been breaking into—"

"Del, you're crazy as a loon!"

"No, no, really. No one's been hurt. Nothing really valuable has been taken. What if they're just doing this because they're . . . you know?" He twisted his finger around at his temple.

"Balderdash! Why would they take men's hats?"

"The same reason Gus Masterson likes his wife's dresses?" he suggested.

"Why would they wreck Liz's store?"

"She overcharged them?"

"I think *you're* the one who's . . . you know." She mimicked his finger motion at the side of his head.

"I wonder what their illustrious relatives would say if they knew—"

"You mean the illustrious Jackson Barber and the highly notable Armistead Crenshaw?"

Del laughed. "What a pair they must've been!"

"Jackson, Armistead."

"Yeah. I guess you could definitely tell Mr. Barber's parents' political leanings, couldn't you?"

"Jackson, Armistead," she repeated. She tugged on his sleeve, just to make sure he was paying attention. "Don't you get it?"

"Jackson, Armistead." He shrugged. "Sure. Unusual names, but . . . big deal."

"Big deal is right! Captain Jackson Armistead."

"Who? The man who writes those penny dreadfuls?"

Miranda couldn't stop grinning. She raised her eyebrows knowingly at him. "I don't think it's a man anymore, Del."

She looked around, but Widow Crenshaw and Miss Barber had disappeared.

"I can't wait to talk to those two again!"

11

"YOU'VE BEEN WORKING hard since the last time I was here," Miranda said as she surveyed the parlor. "But, my goodness, what did you do with your furniture?"

"It's in the other rooms, for the time being."

She looked up. "You still haven't gotten rid of those awful trophies."

"I've been too busy working my way from the ground up."

"Couldn't you at least dust them?"

"I'll get to them, as soon as I can find the ladder around here," he promised. He laid the bag of mousetraps on a side table. "I'll get to these later, too."

"You know, I seem to recall there's lots of room in the cellar," Miranda suggested.

"Later, Come on. You've got such a morbid fascination with them, you didn't notice what good I've been up to."

He pointed down.

"The carpet!" she exclaimed. "My goodness, it actually looks like a real carpet, not a dust blanket."

"It really was red and green."

She surveyed the room with approval. "I don't care

what Mrs. Lowell said. I think it matches the wallpaper very nicely."

"Hey, they're both green. What more could she want?"

"Me, out of here," Miranda muttered.

On the other hand, after what happened last time, she didn't think Mrs. Lowell wanted her at all. She wouldn't be surprised if Mrs. Lowell wasn't trying to talk Charles into calling off his engagement to her this very minute. The only thing that was saving her was probably Mrs. Lowell's horror of any kind of scandal—except what happened to someone else that she could gossip about.

"Now that the carpet's pretty clean, I need to roll it up, take it outside on a nice day, and give it a really good beating."

"Oh, you horrid man!" she teased.

"Then I'll scrub the floor, wash down the wallpaper, paint the woodwork, go through the whole process again in the dining and room, and I'll be—"

He suddenly stopped.

"You'll be what?"

He didn't answer immediately.

"You'll be what, Del?" she repeated insistently.

"Oh, I'll be done. Yeah, that's it. I'll be done."

You'll be done so you can bring Dorothy here. That's what you don't want to tell me. That's why you don't want to talk about it.

She was just about ready to double up her fists and pound on the walls in frustration.

Shut up, Miranda, she scolded herself. You're the one who's here with him. Not Dorothy. Ha, as if Dorothy would help him clean any of this!

And if you help him, she told herself, no matter who comes into this house ever after, whenever he looks at anything, he'll always have to think of you.

Small consolation. But not bad advice.

"Is there anything I can do to help?" she offered.

"You? Work?" He grinned. His eyes were bright with amusement.

"Yes."

"But I thought you just wanted a tour."

"At first, yes. But . . . well, can't I do something besides just watch? You know I never was the kind of person to just stand idly by while other people were doing really interesting things."

Del reached up and stroked his chin thoughtfully. "That's the truth." He glanced over to the paper sack sitting on the table.

"Something besides putting out mousetraps," she quickly qualified her offer.

"I can't think of anything."

"Del Williams, there's lots of work to be done around here. I'm not some delicate blossom, some fading flower."

"You could've fooled me lately."

"Shut up, Del. There's lots of things I can do."

She looked around for something. No, she didn't think she wanted to climb a ladder and dust off the hunting trophies. She didn't want to get any closer to those things than she absolutely had to.

"I can help you roll up that carpet," she declared, pointing at it, excited that she'd finally been able to think of something."

"No, you can't." He crossed his arms over his chest.

"Yes, I can." She mimicked his gesture, trying to look just as stubborn as he.

He still wasn't ready to admit it.

"You're afraid I'll work better than you."

"Don't be silly."

"Come on."

"You can't work in that outfit."

"Fiddlesticks! I'm so good, I'm even willing to give you a handicap."

She tossed her purse into the corner. Then she knelt at one corner of the carpet.

"Well, go on," she ordered, gesturing toward the corner beside her. "You know what you're supposed to be doing."

Dumbfounded, Del knelt beside her. Together they

lifted the edge of the carpet. Carefully tucking in the fringe, they folded the edge over.

Over and over, they continued to roll it. The darn thing didn't look that big when it was laid out on the floor. The closer they got to the middle, the carpet was getting heavier and heavier to push. Miranda was beginning to worry that she'd been wrong. How was she ever going to keep pushing this roll? But she'd never stop. She'd rather die than stop. She'd never admit to Del that she'd overestimated herself!

Putting her shoulder to it, she gave it her best push. The carpet took her with it!

"Stop! Stop!"

Del gave it two more pushes before he'd realized she was yelling and he should stop.

By then, Miranda had tumbled over the top of the roll and lay sprawled on the other side.

"Miranda! What happened?"

She looked up, dazed by the sudden flip. Del's face peered down over top of her.

"What happened?" he repeated.

"I'm caught."

"Caught?"

"Don't you dare laugh," she warned, frowning ominously. "I'm caught."

She reached out and tugged at her skirt. The long length of fabric had gotten caught in the carpet somehow, and twisted around as they rolled it. She was stuck.

Del broke out laughing.

"Stop laughing and get me out of here."

He couldn't stop. "I . . . I thought you were so good at this."

"I am," she told him with a proud sniff. "I'm just not good at it in a skirt."

She gave the offending piece of clothing a little tug.

"My skirt's rolled up in the carpet. I have no idea how it got caught, but it did, and it's stuck in here really good."

She tugged at the fabric again—this time a sharp little yank. She heard a rip and stopped immediately.

"Oh, no. I can't see how bad it is. I can't go home with a torn dress. How in the world will I ever explain *that* to Mrs. Lowell?"

"That's a good question," he managed to agree through his laughter.

"You know, when you're laughing that hard, you don't sound real sympathetic. Now, stop laughing, unroll this darn thing, and get me out of here!" she ordered.

She could tell Del really was trying to stop laughing. He was drawing in big gulps of air. He wasn't laughing quite as hard. But he'd managed to lay himself down on the carpet beside her, and was still clutching his sides.

Every time she thought he'd finish and help her up, he started laughing again.

She didn't think it was funny, not one bit. But with Del laughing his fool head off, it was hard not to join in.

"Come on, get up, you big lazy oaf." She reached over and, between bursts of laughter, gave him several hard pushes. "Get me out of here."

"Why? What's your hurry?"

"Oh, gee, nothing. Silly me, to think I might want to get off the floor."

"You know," he said, settling himself in beside her, "it's pretty comfortable down here." He'd managed to control his laughter to the point of a few deep chuckles.

She wasn't just dizzy from the tumble. The nearness of him sent the blood rushing to her head. She wanted to hold on to him to keep from getting dizzy.

"You're crazy. Get me loose."

"No, no. Feel how soft this carpet is," he insisted.

He reached his hand out and began jabbing his fingers into the deep pile. His hand got closer and closer to her head.

She crossed her arms firmly over her breasts. "I prefer to have the carpet feel soft on my feet, not my head, you puddle-brained ninny."

She watched his hand coming closer to her face.

"Get me up!"

"Relax. You know I've cleaned the place."

She pressed her lips tightly together. "Don't lie to me, you conniving little polecat. I've seen the rest of the place."

"No, you haven't. You chickened out when you saw the mice."

Miranda tried not to cringe. She couldn't let Del see her reaction to the mere mention of mice. Who knew what diabolical deviltry he'd come up with while she was stuck down here?

His hand continued to creep closer to her.

"Are you afraid the mice'll get you while you're stuck down here on the floor?"

"No!" The weasel-nosed sneak *had* read her mind! "Now help me up."

His hand crept closer. She'd roll over and slap at him, but she was stuck on her back, and that was as far as she could reach. He was stubborn and continued to inch his hand closer.

"Will the little micies creep up close to you?" he asked in a squeaky voice.

One finger touched her cheek. She pulled back as much as she could, but she didn't hit at him.

"Will the little micies touch you?" His voice remained high.

"Shut up, Del." By contrast, she hoped her voice was low and very threatening. "Get me up."

"Will the little micies climb up on your neck?" His voice resumed its normal pitch. In fact, if Miranda was any judge—and of course she was because she'd spent the first sixteen years of her life mooning over him—his voice was getting deeper, huskier.

"Will the little micies touch you here?"

He ran his finger up her throat until he reached her chin.

"Or here?"

He leaped his fingers from her throat to the tip of her chin.

"Or here?"

He smoothed his finger across her chin, around her lips, and up onto the tip of her nose, then back around again until he lingered at the edge of her mouth.

She didn't like the talk about the mice. But she didn't mind Del talking to her like this and touching her, not at all.

"Will you shut up about those stupid mice?"

He chuckled again, but he didn't say anything else. He didn't move his fingers any farther.

Miranda held her breath and waited for him to pull his hand away. But his fingertips stayed, resting gently at the corner of her mouth. She could feel her pulse pounding, waiting. She could feel her lips tingling in anticipation of what was sure to come.

He propped himself up on one elbow beside her. He began to move his fingers again, gently stroking up and down her cheek, along her jaw, then back again.

"Do I bother you as much as the mice, Miranda?"

"No."

"No?"

He sounded so disappointed. She could see his broad shoulders sagging.

"No," she repeated quickly before he could pull his hand away in defeat. "You bother me a whole lot more than those mice ever could."

"I do?" A big grin was spreading over his face.

"Yeah. I don't have a cage big enough to put you in."

She tried to laugh, but her throat felt too tight with nervousness. She could feel the heat of his body radiating to warm her as he remained poised above her. That must be why she was feeling so warm herself. Warm and cozy, like she wanted to cuddle into the crook of his arm as they lay there on the carpet together. She'd do it, too, if she weren't stuck to the darn thing!

"Is that the only way you'll feel safe with me, Miranda?"

"No."

His fingertip trailed gently over her lips again.

"I don't want you to feel safe with me, Miranda. I want you to feel nervous and excited. I want you to feel all warm and tingling inside."

"I do, Del. I already do."

She lifted her hand to touch his cheek. He was smooth and tough all at the same time. His tanned skin felt so soft beneath the stubble of his beard.

"I . . . I want to make you feel that way every time you're near me."

"I do, Del."

When are you going to shut up and kiss me, you coward?

She trailed her hand over his cheek, around to the back of his neck. She was so tempted to just pull him down to her and kiss him first. No, she didn't think he'd mind her being a little bold. But she'd been too bold her whole life with Del. Maybe this time, she needed to be the one who laid there, the one who gave in, the one who let him take command.

Patience, Miranda. Patience.

Del slowly leaned closer to her. His lips brushed gently over hers. She savored the flavor of his lips, the soft aroma of his gentle breath. She swallowed hard as her throat constricted. She couldn't believe he was touching her, still coming closer to her.

His lips pressed firmly against hers, warm, passionate, insistent.

She reached up to twine her fingers through his hair, drawing him ever closer to her.

He lifted his kiss from her lips, then descended briefly for a tiny, extra kiss.

He pulled back and gazed at her with eyes glowing with love and passion.

"Are you happy, my love?"

"If I died right here tonight, if I never got loose from this darn carpet and had to lay here looking up at those stupid dead animal heads, I'd still be a happy woman."

"I want you always to be happy, Miranda."

He moved closer to her again. She closed her eyes, awaiting another kiss.

Creak, creak.

Del froze above her.

Creak, creak.

"Did you hear that?" she whispered against his lips.

"Yeah," he murmured, drawing back. He looked around the room.

She tried to look, too, but when she tried to glance at the doorway, everything was upside down.

Creak, creak.

"Then it wasn't just my imagination that it sounds like footsteps?" she asked.

"Nope."

"You've heard it before?"

"Yep."

"What is it?"

"I don't know. I haven't been able to figure it out yet."

"Yet?" She looked at him, startled. "Get me loose, Del."

He leaned back, away from her.

Creak, creak.

"What if it's those rotten kids who broke into the stores? What if they've taken to breaking into private homes now?"

And there she was, stuck in a carpet on the floor. She was trying very hard not to get hysterical.

"Get me out of this. Now!"

Del sprang to his feet and gave the carpet a sharp kick. It rolled away until the last of it flapped down flat on the floor.

"That's it?" She stared after it in disbelief. "That's all we had to do?"

"Nope," he said, extending his hand to help her to her feet. "I had to kiss you."

He pulled her up easily, holding her close to him.

Creak, creak.

"It sounds like they're in the dining room."

"Stay here," he told her.

"I will not. If someone's broken in, I'm staying with you for protection."

"Why do you have to be so stubborn?"

Creak, creak.

Del, with Miranda following closely behind, slowly made his way to the vestibule and peeked around at the staircase. The door was closed. No one was there.

"Could they have gone upstairs?" she asked.

"No."

"Are you sure?"

"Believe me, those stairs creak very badly, with a very distinctive sound all their own. We'd have heard them loud and clear."

They made their way into the dining room.

Creak, creak.

"Where's the sound coming from?" she asked. "I feel stupid, but I can't tell."

"I can't tell, either. Right now, it sounds like it's coming from the kitchen. But you can be in the kitchen and they'll sound like they're coming from the parlor."

Miranda's grip on Del's arm tightened.

"Goodness gracious, Del! Who is it? What is it?"

"I've looked and looked. I can hear them, but I can never find anyone. If you're in the parlor, they sound like they're in the cellar."

"The only thing wooden in the cellar are the steps. Is someone coming up the steps?"

"I guess I'll have to find out."

Del moved toward the cellar door. Slowly he reached out. Quietly he turned the latch. He yanked the door open.

No one was there. Miranda sagged against him with relief. Immediately she tensed again. They still hadn't found whoever—or whatever—was making these noises.

Creak, creak.

She could feel his body tense again.

"Now they're in the kitchen."

She followed him into the kitchen. Except for a few scattering mice, the room was empty.

"Do you know what I think?" she asked in a tight whisper. "I think the kids have all been right about this place being haunted. I think we're being led on a wild goose chase by the ghost of Gertie Richardson."

"A ghost? Oh, come on, Miranda. You don't believe in ghosts, do you?"

"I think Henry Richardson has joined her in the afterlife, and the two of them will spend eternity bickering in this house. I just hope you have the good sense not to spend the rest of your natural life chasing them from parlor to kitchen to cellar."

"Oh, I'm going to keep chasing them, all right. But I'm going to find them," he vowed. "I don't for one minute believe these noises are made by ghosts."

She perked up and listened. "I don't hear them anymore."

"We've probably chased them away—for the time being. See, kids haven't changed that much since I was a boy."

"All right, Methuselah," she remarked. She leaned her back against the wall and crossed her arms over her chest, challenging him. "Give us the benefit of your sage wisdom."

"I think some kids broke into this house while it stood vacant and kind of made it their summer clubhouse. As long as they didn't damage the place—outside of a few broken windows—that was no real problem. But now, apparently, they think they can still get away with sneaking in here. Well, no, they can't. Not anymore. Not while I'm living here. Let them make their own clubhouse behind a barn or up in a tree like other kids have to do. I intend to find them and make them change their tune."

"How do you intend to do that? I don't think Mr. Quinn sells children traps."

"I'll tear this place apart and put it all back together again, if I have to."

"I think you're already off to a good start on tearing it apart."

"I'll find them," he promised.

"I think you might need a little help for that."

"Is that a warning or an offer?"

"Probably an offer."

His gaze swept her figure. She felt as if someone had just tightened her corset a little too much. She'd always felt giddy and silly around Del. Now she felt warm and breathless. She had a feeling it was going to get much more intense, too.

He was surveying her figure appraisingly.

"You shouldn't be doing any work in that outfit."

She'd especially picked this outfit to wear that morning, expecting him to tell her how wonderful she looked, how beautiful, how tempting. Now it was dusty from the floor and the back seam was just a little bit torn.

"If you're going to help me around here, we can't risk having you get your skirt all tangled up again."

"But I didn't bring anything else," she complained. "I'll have to go home and change."

"Then you'll have to figure another way to get out here again. I don't think Charlie and his mommy are going to believe the story too many times that you and Sally have gone visiting without them."

"You're right."

She looked up at him. For once, she wasn't exactly sure what she was going to do. She'd always bossed him around. It seemed strange to look to Del for advice. It seemed even stranger to be believing he could actually help her.

"I have an old pair of jeans you could try on," Del suggested.

"You've got to be kidding!"

"With a good belt, or a strong length of rope, we might be able to keep them from slipping off you."

"And what about a shirt?"

"I've got a couple of old ones I wore in Texas. You can use one of them—if you promise not to mess it up too much."

She lifted her chin proudly. "I'll have you know I'm a paragon of neatness."

Del spared just a glance at her breasts. "Oh, you've definitely got a nice paragon."

She could feel the color rising already. It was bad enough when she'd blushed in front of her mother, or Charles, or Sally. But did the darn man have to make her blush even when the two of them were alone?

"Where's the shirt, you big dummy?" she asked.

"Back here."

Del motioned for her to follow him out of the kitchen, down the corridor, through the large main parlor and into a smaller room in the back. She felt as if she were following him through a labyrinth, or a rabbit warren.

Instead of sofas, chairs, ottomans, and tables with long cloths and lamps and other bric-a-brac on them, the room was sparsely furnished with only a bed, a chair, and a dresser with a small mirror over it.

"This was supposed to be more of a family parlor, I guess," Del said.

"Probably," Miranda agreed. "Most of the larger homes I've been in have two, or even three—one just for the ladies." She raised her eyebrows to a haughty angle.

Del struck a heroic pose in front of the fireplace, pretending he was holding a pipe, and raising one eyebrow to a haughty angle.

"I suppose the gentlemen spent their time in the billiard room."

"Indeed."

"Mr. Richardson used this for a bedroom, so I figured it was probably the cleanest room in the house, after the kitchen."

"You've got to be joking!"

"Yeah, well, after I saw the kitchen, yes, I figured I'd been really mistaken. But it's a darn-sight easier to get to than anything upstairs—"

"Yikes!" Miranda jumped back with alarm. "You mean you've been sleeping in the bed Henry Richardson died in! Ye gads, Del! That's morbid, and disgusting, and—"

"It is not. He didn't die in here."

"He didn't?"

"No. I found out he keeled over into his fried eggs and grits one morning seated right at the dining room table."

"Oh, that's even more disgusting. No wonder the poor man haunts this place."

"At least the bed's safe to sleep in. I restuffed the mattress and made sure I changed the sheets."

"Changing sheets, rolling up rugs. My, I'm certainly impressed with all your accomplishments, Del."

"I can hog-tie and brand a calf, too," he said as he came up behind her. He whispered in her ear, "Someday I'll have to show you how."

"You're horrible!"

She pushed him away before he could see the horrible blush that she could feel rising even more strongly in her cheeks.

"Where are those jeans?"

He reached into the dresser, pulled out a pair, and tossed them on the bed.

"Get out." She gave him a shove toward the door.

He turned and gave her a wink. "Just let me know if you need any help."

"Get out of here before I slam the door on your nose."

He closed the door behind him.

She rushed to the door and called, "No fair peeking through the keyhole."

"Now I'm really ready to tackle that carpet," Miranda announced as she stepped from the bedroom in her new attire.

"No, you're not," Del declared. He was laughing again.

"What's wrong now?"

"You're just as apt to get tangled up again," he said, pointing to her feet.

Miranda looked down.

"Well, you're a good head taller than me. What did you expect?"

"I expect," he said, kneeling in front of her, "that you would have enough sense to roll up your pants."

"Excuse me for not being aware of all the refinements of cowboy attire, but I'm not in the habit of donning men's clothing."

He reached out and grabbed the hem of one leg.

"Like this."

He began doubling the fabric in small hems until her ankle was exposed. She could feel his fingers running along the top of her boot. She wished there was something to hold on to. She felt weak in the knees at his touch. Just how far up would he roll the hem? she wondered. She reached out to hold his broad shoulders.

They were strong and muscular. They'd support her, come what may. She could count on Del to be strong. She could count on Del to be—could she? Could she count on him to be there? Or the first time something went wrong, would he take off for Texas again, just like he did when his mother died? But it felt so good to have him touch her while he was still around.

The loud rapping startled her.

"Who's that?" Del demanded. Springing to his feet, he headed down the corridor.

"Oh, good!" Miranda exclaimed as she followed him.

She was laughing. It was the only thing she could think of to ease the tension she still felt from Del's caress.

"Now Henry and Gertie have taken to rappings. Maybe we should alert the Fox sisters. Or send a telegram to Sir William Crookes so he can investigate. Maybe we could do a tour with P. T. Barnum, too."

"Shut up, Miranda," Del said. "Everyone knows they were just fakes."

"They were not."

"That's a matter of opinion. But there's a very substantial, physical reason for these noises, most specifically, the person who is knocking at the door."

"Oh, my gosh!" She clapped her hand tightly over her mouth. Through silently spread fingers, she murmured, "Suppose it's Charles and his mother again!"

She grabbed at the front of Del's big shirt, pulling the fold of fabric together as if they could shield her from Mrs. Lowell's wrath.

"Go back in the kitchen," Del ordered. "Maybe they haven't seen you yet. Although with the window wide open, and you raving loudly—"

"I do *not* rave."

"About spirits, I doubt it," he finished his sentence. "I'll tell them you're not here. You're out with Sally. I haven't seen you all day. I'll say 'Miranda who?'"

"But . . . but I can't . . . you can't lie for me."

"Yes, I can," he insisted, waving her back toward the kitchen. "Now, be quiet."

Instead of hiding all the way back in the kitchen, where she'd miss all the interesting happenings, Miranda ducked around the corner into the parlor and flattened herself against the wall.

Del pulled the door open.

"Good afternoon, Mr. Williams," Mrs. Cartwright declared.

The woman was still smiling like a sunbeam. But Del knew from their last encounter that it only took a few seconds and a negative answer to bring on the thunder-heads.

"Have you changed your mind yet?"

"No, Mrs. Cartwright. I have not. As a matter of fact, it was never my intention to leave you with the belief that there might ever be any chance that I'd change my mind."

"But . . . ain't you seen by now, a young feller like yourself can't handle this place alone?" Yes, the clouds were gathering with the frown that grew in intensity on her forehead.

"Nope." He shook his head emphatically. "I haven't found that to be the case at all."

Miranda peeked out from the parlor, curious to get a

look at this woman who insisted she have a job. As soon as she saw the squared woman, she recognized her. She might not have paid much attention to the name, but she knew her by sight immediately. Mrs. Cartwright was the one who was always begging for handouts at church to give to the poor, pathetic, needy Indian children, but everybody had the sneaking suspicion most of the stuff went to her. Trouble was, nobody had ever been able to prove it.

Mrs. Cartwright spotted Miranda peeking around the corner and threw her a venomous glance. "No, I can see you ain't changed your mind about me one bit. Even though I can see plain as day you've changed your mind about hirin' *somebody* to help you."

"No, no, I haven't—"

She didn't give Del time to continue. She pointed accusingly at Miranda. "Same fancy little blond that was spyin' on me the other day."

Miranda stepped boldly into the vestibule. She drew herself up proudly and gave the housekeeper her most haughty glare.

"I was not! How dare you have the audacity to assume that because I was perusing an edifice that you, by mere happenstance, were standing in front of, that I was in any manner interested in you. What presumption! What effrontery! What makes you think you're so interesting to look at anyway?"

Mrs. Cartwright stared at her. Miranda knew that words of more than two syllables usually confounded hired help like Mrs. Cartwright. Mrs. Bigelow would be proud of how well her student handled the household help, or even the would-be household help.

Mrs. Cartwright turned back to Del. Miranda couldn't blame her. At least he was someone she could under-stand.

"A skinny little thing like her ain't gonna do you one bit o' good, Mr. Williams. Look at them puny arms. Why, she couldn't do a lick o' decent work."

"No, she couldn't." Del shook his head.

At first Mrs. Cartwright could only stare at him in amazement. Then, apparently satisfied that Del had decided to trust her judgment, she started nodding her head vigorously.

"She probably couldn't climb a ladder to dust the ceiling without falling off," Del continued.

Mrs. Cartwright continued nodding her agreement with Del's assessment of Miranda's working skills. She was probably glad to be hearing someone else saying all the things she knew to be true about Miranda.

"She probably couldn't even roll up a carpet without getting herself caught in it."

Suddenly she frowned. "What?"

"Now that I've really got your attention, Mrs. Cartwright," Del said. "I want to make it perfectly clear to you that this is not my housekeeper nor my cleaning lady. She is a visitor. Do you understand? Visitor," he repeated very slowly, pronouncing each syllable distinctly.

"Not in that outfit she ain't," she grumbled.

"Yes, she is." He held out his index finger to keep her attention. "And you are in no position to argue with me."

Mrs. Cartwright gave a loud harrumph—one that would certainly give Mrs. Lowell some stiff competition.

"I do not now, nor will I never need, a housekeeper," Del continued. "Do you understand that, too?"

"You'll regret this, you stingy old miser," she grumbled.

She spun around on her heel and stomped off down the walk. Miranda fully expected to see the bricks cracking and crumbling under her angry, forceful tread.

"You'll be sorry you couldn't give a poor old workin' woman a job."

12

"*I*SN'T THAT BETTER?" Del asked.

"Isn't what better?"

"Wearing those clothes?"

"Better than what?"

"Stop being ornery," he scolded. "Aren't the work clothes easier to—"

"To work in?" She laughed. "Yeah. Gee! Maybe that's why they call them work clothes."

"Shut up and roll, Miranda," he ordered from his side of the carpet. "At least this time you won't get rolled up in your own carpet."

At last the carpet was rolled back. There was a frame of dust around the clean spot on the hardwood floor beneath.

"At least you can see Mrs. Cartwright didn't sweep anything under the rug."

Del gave a little snort. "She just wasn't too good with the rest of the place."

Miranda stood up and brushed the dust off her hands on her back pockets.

"Hey, take it easy on my good pants."

"Golly, can't I do anything to please you?"

"Yes," he replied, coming to step closer to her. He

wrapped his hand around her waist and pulled her to him. He placed a kiss on her lips.

She reached up and wrapped her arms around his neck.

Dell pulled back. "If we start this again, I'll never get this place finished."

"Finished for what?" She stepped back, too. "Or should I ask finished for whom?"

"I . . . I . . ." Del paced up and down. At last he gestured to the carpet. "Just leave it pushed up against the wall there."

"What for?"

"So I can be ready for work tomorrow."

"No, I mean, why are you in such a rush? It there something—or someone—special you need to be doing this for?"

"Yes, but I wish you wouldn't ask."

"Well, I am asking. I don't like thinking I'm doing all this work for . . . for someone else."

"Who else?"

"Your . . ." She shrugged. "Wife?"

"I don't have a wife."

"Not yet."

"You're right, not yet. But the woman I want . . . is promised to someone else."

Miranda's mouth hung open with surprise. "Why, the closed-mouthed little minx! She never said a word to me about a fiancé."

"What are you talking about? *Who* are you talking about?"

"Dorothy."

"Dorothy?"

"Well, she does have her sights set for you. You did seem to be watching back."

"Miranda, I'm a red-blooded American man. I'm not blind. Dorothy's a pretty girl. I'm going to be watching until they nail down the coffin lid. They doesn't mean I'm really interested in her—or anyone else—as a prospective wife."

"It doesn't?"

"Of course not. I . . . I don't want to say anything. I can't—I shouldn't say anything now. For so long I acted like I didn't want you. I was stupid. I was a boy, and didn't know what I wanted. Now I'm a man and I know what I want. I won't ask you to marry me while you're engaged to Charles. It's not fair. It's not right. You know what I want, Miranda. But I have to let you make up your own mind about what—and who—you want."

She'd been so bossy with him for so long. Now he was telling her to make up her own mind. To choose between him and Charles. The bug-brained moron! She'd done that a while ago.

But it wasn't that simple. Nothing ever was. There was more involved in this than just three people. There was a lot more thinking that she had to do.

Del glanced out the window. The dining room was bathed gold in the light of the setting sun.

"It's getting late. Sally will be here soon to take you home, and you still have to get out of those work clothes."

"Will you save them for me? For later?"

"For later," he promised.

"We forgot these," she said, holding up the bag of mousetraps. "I can't go home and leave you defenseless, at the mercy of those little rodents."

"How thoughtful of you to think of me and dead mice together."

"I . . . I need to come up with some kind of excuse . . . not to go home."

He stepped toward her to take the bag from her hands. He wrapped his other arm around her waist and drew her close to him. He kissed her hard, to show her he really meant it. To show her he wanted to keep her here.

She wanted to stay. But what was she going to do with Charles? Until she'd figured that out, she wasn't sure what she was going to do.

She swallowed hard and moved back a step.

"I . . . I still need to . . . I can't worry . . . or shame my parents."

"Yeah, I know," he said, loosening his hold on her but not letting her go completely.

Even if he let her go, she knew Del would always have a part of her heart.

"Come on, let's get this done."

While Miranda tied small pieces of cheese to the latches, Del placed the traps in as many corners as he could find.

"I haven't seen any rats. I don't really think there are any in here," he said.

"That's a relief."

"I'll still put some out, just in case, but I'll put them in the cellar. I'll do them tomorrow, when the light's better." He set the bag of rat traps in front of the cellar door. "Now, is there any place we've forgotten?"

"The kitchen."

He smacked the side of his head. "How could I forget the one place most likely to attract mice?"

Miranda set a trap in the corner. Del set one under the empty icebox.

She turned to the pantry.

"Now here's a place that definitely needs two or three," he told her. "It was a mess the first day I got here."

"I'll bet it hasn't improved any."

"Hey. I've been busy with what shows."

She reached out to open the door.

"No, wait." He grabbed her wrist before she touched the small knob. He gave the door a frown. "There's something odd."

"It's a door, Del. What's so odd about that?"

"I could've sworn I left that door open."

"Are you sure?"

"Positive," he stated emphatically. "There was such a mess inside. I didn't want to leave it closed up and give the little critters any more privacy for their dirty deeds. I know I left it open."

"If they closed it, those are some pretty big mice," Miranda said. "Do you think you ought to take those mousetraps back and see if you can't get something bigger, like an elephant gun?"

"I *know* I left it open," he insisted.

"The wind probably blew it shut."

"No. It couldn't happen." He pointed to the floor. "That door sticks. A person would have to push pretty hard to close it. I got a plane at Quinn's today, but I haven't gotten around to fixing it yet."

"Oh, you probably closed it yourself, you big dummy, and forgot you did it. You're getting as bad as Miss Barber."

"No, I'm not! I know I left it open!"

"Well, for goodness' sake, Del. It's nothing to get yourself into a state about," she told him. "I'll just open the door again."

She shook off his grasp.

"Suit yourself," he said, walking off to set another mousetrap at the far corner of the kitchen. "You always were too stubborn for your own good."

She reached out and pulled the door open. She stood there, frozen, with her mouth wide open, unable to utter a single sound.

She stared at the large rattlesnake in the pantry, coiled and ready to strike. At last, very softly, she was able to whisper, "Del."

"What?" he called from across the room.

She knew the slightest movement might send the rattlesnake striking for her throat. He was a big one and could probably jump pretty far. The distance between them was only the width of the pantry door—two feet at best.

She drew in a deep, slow breath. She knew movement would agitate the rattler. She wasn't sure about sound.

Just a little more loudly she called, "Del."

"What do you want?"

"Del." She was afraid to say anymore. The snake might take it into his head that he just didn't like the way her lips were moving.

Finally, out of the corner of her eye, she could see Del

glance in her direction. He had to notice her frozen posture and terrified expression.

"All right, Miranda," he said. "Turn about's fair play. I got you at the cellar door, but you're not going to fool me into thinking there's something really horrible in the pantry, and then it's nothing."

"Del!" It was very difficult to scream with her mouth closed. Couldn't the chowder-brained oaf detect the hint of near panic in her voice?

"Del, if you don't get over here very slowly but immediately, I'm going to kill you with my dying breath."

"Dying breath? What in thunderation are you talking about?" he demanded. "You know, you really are carrying this joke too far."

He strode toward her.

"Slow down, slow down, or he'll strike."

"What the—!"

As he looked into the pantry, the snake began to sway and emit his telltale rattle.

Del stopped in his tracks behind Miranda.

"Don't scream," he warned.

"Oh, I passed screaming a long time ago. And I'm really sorry about the jeans. I'll have them washed for you. But now what should I do? I don't think a mousetrap is going to work on this one."

"I don't think so, either."

"I wish you'd said something different. I really haven't had a whole lot of experience with snakes, Del, especially not rattlesnakes. You've been to Texas and know all about them, don't you? Please tell me you do."

Instead, he asked, "How did it get there?"

"Slithered?"

"Good guess."

"How the devil should I know? The correct question is, how do we get it out of there?"

"Where did it come from?"

"Visiting from St. Louis? I don't really care. The

question is, how do we get rid of it?" she repeated with more emphasis.

"I don't recall too many rattlesnakes in these parts anymore, not since the railroad came through."

"Me, neither."

"Especially none that size."

"That's so comforting, Del. How did it get into your house?"

"Oh, now that there's a snake in it, it's *my* house, huh?"

"Your house, your snake. You get rid of it."

"It's my fault, I guess," he admitted. "I left the pantry door open."

"No, no, no," she insisted. "That might explain how the snake got in, but how did he close the door behind him?"

Del shrugged.

"No hands, remember," she reminded him. She'd have lifted her arms to gesture, but she was still too frightened to move anything but her mouth.

"I noticed."

"I don't think he grabbed the knob with his tail and pulled it shut behind him."

"I don't think so, either."

"Somebody had to put it there. Who?"

"I don't think it was the ghost of Gertie Richardson."

"Me, neither."

"I don't think it was a couple of kids pulling pranks, either. It's too big to be something they'd play with."

"Me, neither."

"It's too big and dangerous to be just a prank."

"This thing could kill somebody, Del, so I'm going to ask this question one more time, and I really want an answer this time. A really good answer. How are we going to get it out of here?"

"Wait here while I get my gun," he told her.

"Wait? Here?" she repeated. She'd have run away with him, but she still couldn't move. Desperately she called after him, "No, no, Del. You don't understand. Waiting here with the snake is not a good thing for me to do. I have to get away from it. Far, far away. Do you understand?"

Hearing his voice behind her again was very comforting. Now, if only the rattlesnake weren't in front of her.

"Very slowly now," he told her, "back away."

"I can do that," she said, nodding.

But when she tried to move, her feet had turned to stone. She couldn't lift them from the floor, no matter how much she wanted to. The only thing she could still do was nod her head.

Had the snake already bitten her, she wondered, and she was already dying from the venom and didn't even know it? Would Del kiss her one last time before she died? Would the big dummy even notice when she collapsed at his feet?

"Miranda, I said move back."

"I'm trying."

She really was. The best she could manage was to scrape her feet a few inches backward. At least, she thought they were moving backward. The snake and the pantry shelves looked as if they were getting smaller and, seeing as how walls seldom moved, she must be the one moving back. But she couldn't even feel her feet to tell for sure.

"Good girl," Del encouraged her. "One more step. One more. You can do it."

He held his arms out in front of him, training the barrel of his gun on the snake. She had just stepped back enough to pass his shoulder. He took one step in front of her and fired several times. The rattler went limp on the shelf and tumbled to the floor.

Miranda was able to back up several steps now, and very quickly. Did she back up too quickly, or had her knees simply given way? Either way, she ended up sitting on the floor.

Del laid the empty gun on the table. He placed his hand on her shoulder. "Are you all right?"

She nodded. "Did you learn to shoot like that in Texas, too?"

"Yep. When I learned to lasso, too."

"I'm so glad you're a man of many talents." She nodded toward the snake. "Do you want to have that mounted and add it to Mr. Richardson's collection?"

"I don't think so. I haven't seen any really long, narrow empty places on the walls."

She laughed and leaned against his leg.

Del supposed she still wasn't thinking clearly after a shock like seeing that rattler. Otherwise, Miranda wouldn't ordinarily hold her cheek so close to his hip. She wouldn't wrap her arm around his leg and hold on. She certainly wouldn't be slowly moving her hand up and down the inside of his leg.

Geez, he was already riled enough because of the snake. He didn't need Miranda upsetting him in whole new ways.

"Come on, Miranda." Reluctantly he tugged his leg away a little. "I have to get rid of the snake. You have to change clothes. Sally'll be here soon."

"What? Yes, oh, yes."

He reached down to help her stand. She rose and cradled her head against his chest. He wrapped his arms around her.

"That has got to be the scariest thing that's ever happened to me."

"Me, too, I think."

He kissed her tenderly on the forehead. She snuggled closer to him, but he didn't kiss her again. She was still so scared, so vulnerable. She just might be liable to do anything he asked of her. He wouldn't take advantage of her that way.

"Go get your dress on," he said. He pushed her toward his bedroom door alone.

Mrs. Harriet Nichols was beaming like the sun.

"I'm so pleased you could come to my party," she told Miranda as she entered their home.

"How kind of you to invite me, Mrs. Nichols," Miranda responded automatically.

Mrs. Nichols also said the same thing to Charles as he followed Miranda through the doorway. And to Mrs. Lowell, and Mr. and Mrs. Hamilton.

"Harriet Nichols has been dying to be the society queen of Grasonville for years," her mother whispered in Miranda's ear. "At last she gets to show off tonight."

"It was very kind of her to invite us," Miranda replied with the same polish, and equal lack of enthusiasm.

She scanned the crowd for Del. He'd shown up at every other party, and not just because he'd been given an invitation by her mother. He was pretty much a celebrity in his own right now that Mr. Richardson had made him one of the richest men in town.

She hoped he was there this evening. Another part of her wished he'd stay home.

She had something very important to talk to Charles about—alone. She didn't want Del around muddying her thinking.

She hadn't been able to talk to Charles at her home. His mother was always hanging around. She didn't want to ask her own mother to get Mrs. Lowell out of her hair so she could talk to Charles. After all their preparations, she wasn't sure her mother would like what she had to say any more than Charles would.

She wasn't even sure she was going to bring up the subject yet. She was still so torn between her feelings for Del, and the duty she owed her parents, as well as the obligation she'd made to Charles.

She stayed close to Charles and his mother, something she didn't usually do at these parties. Maybe it was just being home among all the people she knew she'd see rarely—if ever again. That was what was confusing her. Maybe if she spent more time with Charles she'd realize she'd only been homesick, confused, and mistaken.

"I can't believe the number of people here," Mrs. Lowell leaned over and whispered into Charles's ear.

"Apparently, Mrs. Nichols is well regarded," Charles

remarked. "Although to be well regarded by these people is no true accomplishment."

"I understand Mr. Nichols is the local haberdasher."

"One of two, I believe," Charles replied.

"He . . . he owns the store," Miranda mentioned in his defense.

"Oh, indeed, that makes *all* the difference," Mrs. Lowell remarked sarcastically.

"But the late Mr. Lowell owned a shipping company."

"My dear," Mrs. Lowell said with a scornful laugh, "there's a world of difference between owning a shop and being an industrial magnate. She still has very little reason to take on airs as if she were Mrs. Cornelius Vanderbilt herself!"

Charles snickered.

"She's not taking on airs. It's a party—and a darn good one at that!" Miranda corrected. She was rapidly approaching the limits of her patience.

"Really, my dear," Mrs. Lowell remarked with a disdainful sniff. "After all the fine social affairs you've been to, for you to believe this is a . . . a good party . . ."

She said no more, as if the very words would shock her delicate sensibilities.

Miranda said nothing more, either. For the time being. If only she could manage to talk to Charles alone.

At last her mother managed to lure Mrs. Lowell off to the dining room, where refreshments were available. Mrs. Lowell made some protests about preferring to be served, but Mrs. Hamilton told her the gentlemen were all busy, and she'd have to make do herself.

At last they were almost alone in a sea of party guests. Slowly Miranda turned to Charles. Her knees were shaking almost as badly as they shook when she was around Del, but for a very different, and much more unpleasant, reason.

"Charles, I . . . I'd like to take a little walk with you," she said.

"Here? Now?" He glanced around the room.

"Yes, now. No, not here," she replied. "I think it would be . . . nice if we took a stroll outside."

Charles peeked out the window into the darkness.

"Outside? But it's getting dark."

"It does that just about this time every day. Let's go. It's very nice outside," she insisted.

He hesitated. In the distance an owl hooted.

"What in heaven's name is that?"

"An owl. It won't hurt you, Charles. It eats mice."

Should she try to shoo the owl over to Del's house? He'd find a feast there.

"What other creatures are out there?"

"Wolves, bears, lions." She hoped there weren't any more rattlesnakes.

"No. Oh, my dear, you've been teasing me."

Miranda just grinned.

"It's rather stifling in here," she said, fanning herself with her hand. "There's a cool breeze outside."

"Really, I find it rather comfortable right here"

"Mrs. Nichols's roses should be in bloom. Everyone in town says hers are—"

"You know I have hay fever and am allergic to the blasted things."

"Then we'll walk on the other side of the house."

"No. I really must put my foot down on this, my dear. We will *not* go outside."

"Can we at least stand by a window?" she suggested.

He was silent, considering for a moment. "Very well," he grudgingly agreed.

Miranda looked around, trying to find a secluded spot in the Nichols's house. She'd only visited them a few times. Any place she could recall that might be suitable for a private conversation was pretty crowded now due to the party.

At last she spotted a little corner, blocked with a potted palm that didn't look too healthy. Maybe what she had to say to Charles would kill it and put the poor thing out of its misery. If only she could put herself out of her misery.

"Charles," she said very quietly. "We've known each other such a short while."

Hooking his thumbs into his vest pockets, he rocked back and forth on his heels and stated, "I believe we met at the Independence Day party on the Whites' yacht."

No, they'd met at Rowena Crabtree's birthday party the previous April. But at this point Miranda didn't see much use in arguing with him about it. It didn't really matter much now at all.

"We've been engaged for several months now."

"Since this past Christmas."

No, he'd proposed to her at Delphine Markham's Twelfth Night Party. Well, that was close enough.

"So, actually, we really haven't known each other all that long a period of time, have we?"

Charles pondered again. "No, I suppose not."

"Most . . . most other couples have a lengthier courtship, don't they? A year? Two?"

"I've never really paid much attention. I could always ask Mother." He moved to go.

"No, no," Miranda insisted, reaching out to stop him. The last thing she needed now was Mrs. Lowell sticking her nose even further into her business. "It doesn't really matter, because . . . well, it doesn't really pertain to us anyway."

"My dear, I wish you would tell me what you want, and let's get back to the party—such as it is."

"Well, that's part of the problem, Charles," she began.

This is it, she told herself, drawing in a deep breath so she could say it all in one piece and get it over with more quickly.

I want to break our engagement. I don't want to marry you. I think you're a nice man, but— Over and over in her head she tried to decide exactly the best way to say this.

"The party is part of your problem? Well, of course it is." Leaning forward, he confided, "It's a bit of a problem for me, too."

He offered her his elbow.

"You've just been going to too many parties lately," he stated. "Parties every evening, and then going to visit your girlfriends in town every day. It's small wonder you're worn to a frazzle. Why don't we just take you home?"

Before she could speak a work of the truth, Charles had linked her arm with his and was leading her toward the door.

His grasp tightened on her arm as they approached Del, standing to the side of the front door, with Widow Crenshaw and Miss Barber stationed on either side of him.

"Miranda! Miranda!" he called, motioning for her to join them.

"Just keep walking, my dear," Charles ordered. "You're far too exhausted to be suitable company any longer."

"Especially not for 'those kind of people'?" she demanded.

"Oh, Miranda," Miss Barber called, squinting at her. "Is that you?"

"Miss Barber, Mrs. Crenshaw, I'm so glad to see you again," Miranda said with extra pleasantness. After all, they might just be the pair who could get her out of this situation.

Leaning a bit closer to Charles, she whispered, "I truly cannot leave without some sort of chat with these dear, elderly ladies. They've been such close friends of the family for so many, many years."

She hoped Reverend Knutson wasn't at this party. She wouldn't want to get condemned to perdition for lying like that!

"After all, *noblesse oblige, tu comprends?*" she added with a regal lift of her head.

"Oh, oh, yes, of course. Duty demands." He released her arm and bowed. "I shall be searching for Mother. I'm quite certain she, too, is ready to return home."

Once again, with an inward chuckle, Miranda gave thanks to Mrs. Bigelow for insisting she sit through all those boring French lessons. Apparently French phrases had the same effect on the upper classes as words of three syllables had on the housekeeper.

"Del has been quite a nuisance," Miss Barber complained.

"Del? A nuisance? No!" She shot him a grin.

"He tells me he's been reading these novels by a Captain Jackson Armistead. Although we've tried to change the subject several times, he just keeps rattling on and on and on about them."

"Well, Del can be very stubborn," Miranda said with a grin.

"We thought perhaps you'd like to tell us about your wedding gown."

"It's not a secret, is it?" Widow Crenshaw asked.

"No, although I believe you two are as good at keeping secrets as anyone I've ever known."

"Oh, we certainly are," Miss Barber confirmed.

"Hush, Catherine."

"As a matter of fact, if you stop by the house, I'll be happy to show it to you," Miranda invited. "Although it does look much better on me than it does on the mannequin."

She figured a modest giggle was in order.

"But, you know, I can hardly blame Del. I've read *all* of Captain Armistead's books."

"Oh, dear, now she's bringing up the blasted subject!" Miss Barber lamented.

"All of them?" Widow Crenshaw repeated.

"All seventy-three of them?" Miss Barber asked.

"Oh, I see you're a fan, too," Del interjected.

Widow Crenshaw stammered and stuttered and at last managed to mumble, "Sort of."

"I *love* his books!" Miranda exclaimed.

"You do?" the two elderly ladies demanded together.

"Of course. But do you know what I like best?"

"What?" Two sets of myopic blue eyes peered at her.

"His name."

"His name?"

"Yes, indeed. What an interesting name. Don't you think so, Del?"

"Definitely."

"Captain Jackson Armistead. I wonder what he was the captain of. Did he serve in the Army? The Navy? Which war? After all, no one is exactly sure how old the gentleman is."

"I'm sure he'd be very young and handsome!" Miss Barber asserted.

"Jackson—well, we can certainly tell who his mother or father admired, can't we?"

"I . . . I suppose so."

"Armistead. Now, I'm not very good at history, but wasn't he an admiral or something in the Second War for Independence?"

"I'm . . . not sure."

"But that was your late husband's name, wasn't it, Mrs. Crenshaw?"

"Oh, my, what a coincidence!" Widow Crenshaw threw up her hands before her in surprise.

"Wasn't Jackson your father's name, Miss Barber?"

"Oh, my, what a coincidence?" Miss Barber tried woodenly to imitate her friend's gesture and tone of voice.

Miranda linked her arm through Miss Barber's and began to lead her to the same secluded corner she'd just vacated with Charles. Del offered an arm to Widow Crenshaw that, for the protection and welfare of her scatterbrained partner, she could hardly refuse.

"It's also quite a coincidence that you two and Sheriff Duncan still correspond when I don't recall you having much to do with each other previously."

"As a matter of fact," Del said, "I seem to recall tales of him threatening to sell tickets while Mrs. Hamilton punched you in the nose."

"Oh!" Widow Crenshaw's hand flew up to protect her nose. "You horrid little boy, listening to gossip like that."

"It's also quite a coincidence that you two and Max,

who is now the sheriff, have a . . . a connection, one might say."

"Well, what is it then?" Miss Barber demanded. "Out with it!"

13

"*DO YOU WANT* to blackmail us?" Miss Barber wailed pathetically.

"I can't imagine why," Widow Crenshaw grumbled. "I mean, yes, certainly, Catherine and I inherited a bit of money, and we've set a little aside from our . . . our own enterprise. But you've both got enough money already to make any three people happy. Why should you need ours?"

"No, no. It's not that at all," Miranda hastily assured them.

"Do you just want to shame us?" With a flourish Miss Barber pulled a large handkerchief out of her sleeve, and began to sniff and dab at dry eyes.

"Are you trying to get even with us for that little unpleasantness so long ago when we suspected your mother of trying to murder your father?" Widow Crenshaw asked. "I really thought we'd completely cleared up that little misunderstanding."

"No!" Miranda protested earnestly. "No, no, no! That's the farthest thing from my mind."

"That's why we wanted to ask you this as privately as we could," Del added.

"So you confront us at Harriet's big party?" Miss

Barber demanded with a grimace. "That's really private."

"We didn't intend any harm," Miranda tried to assure them. "Honestly, we didn't."

"It just happened to work out this way," Del said.

"I just need to know." Miranda looked back and forth between the two elderly ladies. "Are you Captain Jackson Armistead?"

Widow Crenshaw fixed her with a sharp glare. "Miranda Hamilton, have you been drinking too much of Harriet's punch?"

"No. I just have a very strong suspicion that I need you to answer for me. Please. Are you Captain Jackson Armistead? I've just go to know!"

Widow Crenshaw was still trying to stare her down.

"You always were far too curious for your own—or anybody else's—good."

"Oh, fiddle-dee-dee! They've found us out, Janet," Miss Barber said with a sigh of resignation.

Widow Crenshaw just groaned.

"Why, they're almost as good at being detectives as we are."

Widow Crenshaw just groaned again.

"Oh, Janet, don't be an old curmudgeon. They've found us out, fair and square. We might as well let them join in on the fun."

Miss Barber eagerly leaned forward. She jerked her thumb at Widow Crenshaw. "She does most of the actual writing. *I* think up the plots," she declared proudly.

Miranda fairly bounced up and down. "Oh, my goodness. I can't believe it! I've read *all* your books."

"Does your mother know you read those things, my dear?" Widow Crenshaw asked. "I mean, they are rather . . . titillating."

"Blood, gore, murder, mayhem . . ." Miss Barber was too excited to go on and had to fan herself with her handkerchief.

"Mother loves them, too."

"She does?"

"Of course."

"So do Will and Harry," Del added. "I have a sneaking suspicion Tommy reads them, too, when Pa's not looking."

"Oh, your father doesn't approve?" Miss Barber wailed.

"No, he just doesn't like it when Tommy takes his copy when he's in the middle of an exciting scene." Del laughed.

"It all started because of your parents, you know," Widow Crenshaw told Miranda. "When someone hit your father over the head and tried to murder him, we sort of suspected your mother—although, of course, we all know now she didn't do it."

"That's all right, Miranda," Del tried to console her. "My mother tried to shoot my pa."

"We started doing a little investigating of the crime and found it so fascinating . . . well, one thing led to another, and we started writing it down," Miss Barber explained.

"Then Catherine started adding little incidents she'd made up," Widow Crenshaw continued. "The stories just started getting better and better until we decided to send them to a publisher and . . . well, they liked them, too. They bought them. Someone actually published them! And then, other people started buying them. And liking them. And asking for more!"

"So we wrote more," Miss Barber said, as if it were that simple.

"But you won't tell, will you?" Widow Crenshaw pleaded.

"Sheriff Duncan and Max have already sworn to carry our secret to the grave!" Miss Barber informed them in hushed tones. "Why, just suppose some of our friends—"

"If Reverend Knutson—"

"Harriet Nichols—"

"Isobel Baldwin—"

"Your future mother-in-law, dear," Miss Barber said, putting the cap on the horror of exposure.

"What if they all found out that we were Captain

Jackson Armistead?" Widow Crenshaw finished with a look of dismay and imminent doom.

This was the absolute first time Miranda could ever recall Widow Crenshaw looking truly worried.

"You must promise me, for the sake of all you hold dear," Widow Crenshaw commanded in sepulchral tones worthy of one of her own novels, "what we've confided in you because you found us out, you will never divulge to another living soul."

"Hey, did I hear someone mention Captain Armistead over here?" Will asked, sauntering over with a glass of punch.

"Does Pa know you've got that?" Del demanded, scowling darkly at Will's drink. "Mrs. Nichols's punch is almost ninety proof!"

Will just grinned and sauntered closer.

"I'll throw your no-good tail in the woodshed where you'll stay until you sober up," Del threatened, even though he knew darn good and well he'd only help his slightly cock-eyed brother get safely home to bed.

"Did I also happen to hear you two mention that you actually *are* Captain Armistead?"

"Nope." Widow Crenshaw snapped her lips shut tight and shook her head.

"No, no, dear boy," Miss Barber said. "We just write under that name."

"Oh, Catherine!" Widow Crenshaw hung her head.

Miranda could see the headlines tomorrow. "Writing partnership dissolved when Armistead murders Jackson."

She also wondered if Miss Barber's careless admission absolved her of all vows she'd made by all that she held dear.

"I think that's terrific!" Will exclaimed.

"Well, my goodness, I couldn't help overhearing," Carvel Marsh said, joining the little circle. "I've read all his books. Or maybe I should say *your* books," he added with a nervous chuckle.

Hal Danvers, Sophie Baldwin, and Mr. Nesbitt joined the circle of excitement and admiration.

"Oh, dear," Widow Crenshaw murmured as she looked around. "This is getting out of hand."

Isaac Stanley, Dorothy Halstead, Mr. Quinn, even Sally joined them. Max came up and stood behind her, grinning broadly.

"We couldn't have done it without Max," Widow Crenshaw declared modestly.

"Nope, nope. Not me. I'm just reference material." He shyly slipped away from the crowd.

Miranda knew Sally was as interested in Captain Armistead as she was, but Sally slipped away, too. Miranda smiled. No doubt she was going to discuss with him his part in the famous writing partnership.

Max had done a lot of growing up. He'd quietly helped two old ladies. He hadn't even once called anybody—not even her—"poopy-head." Maybe she ought to revise her opinion of Max now, too.

"Oh, I'm so glad to hear you like our books, but . . . please," Widow Crenshaw pleaded. "Please don't mention any of this to some of the more prominent—"

"And disapproving old sticklers," Miss Barber added.

The look of dismay on Widow Crenshaw's face deepened as Harriet Nichols approached. Miranda believed she could actually see new wrinkles forming and what was left of her dark hairs turning gray.

"Oh, we're done for now," Miss Barber murmured to Widow Crenshaw.

"What is this I hear?" Mrs. Nichols asked. "You two actually write penny dreadfuls as Captain Jackson Armistead?"

"Yes," the both answered cautiously.

"How wonderful! Of course, I've never actually read any of your books, but I think it's so absolutely thrilling to have you as my guests!"

"Thank you for inviting us," Widow Crenshaw replied politely.

"Even before you knew who we were," Miss Barber added.

"I've always thought I could write one of those silly little things," Mrs. Nichols declared.

Miss Barber gave Widow Crenshaw a telling glance.

"All about my life, you see. I've had such interesting experiences."

Widow Crenshaw pursed her lips and shook her head at Miss Barber. Miranda didn't think it was going to do any good. Miss Barber just sort of said whatever she had a mind to.

"Perhaps you could, Harriet," Widow Crenshaw answered noncommittally.

"I mean, it can't be too hard, can it?"

"Of course not!" Miss Barber declared.

"I mean, it's all the same story anyway, just change the names of the characters."

"I'll tell you what, Harriet. The very next time there's a robbery or a gun fight, you must come with us while we investigate," Widow Crenshaw invited. "Be sure to wear old shoes in case there are splinters of wood or shards of glass—"

"Or blood or body parts strewn in the street," Miss Barber finished.

"Maybe not, but thank you for that kind invitation. I think I'll see to my other guests and leave the books to you." Mrs. Nichols smiled and backed away.

Carvel squeezed through the crowd, back into the circle. He was breathing hard and his dark hair hung in long strings across his forehead as if he'd been running very fast. His arms were laden with well-worn, red-covered copies of the accumulated life works of Captain Jackson Armistead.

"Would you . . . I mean, would you both . . . sign my books?" His face was as red as the covers and split with a broad grin.

"Mine, too?" Marvin Platt asked. "If I bring 'em 'round to your house sometime next week?"

"Do you think you could sign the copies that are in my

store?" Ian MacKenzie asked. "Although it's really hard to keep them in stock, they sell so fast. As soon as I get one shipment in, I've got to order another."

"Well, I always supposed the books were selling well," Miss Barber said. "Especially in areas that don't yet have access to hygienic paper for the toilette."

"I never expected this," Widow Crenshaw said.

"Oh, my goodness!" Miss Barber exclaimed. "Janet, we're famous!"

Widow Crenshaw looked up from trying to scribble her name on a book balanced in the palm of her hand and gave Miranda and Del a broad smile. "I guess we should say thanks to you two."

"No, no. You wrote the books," Miranda said. "Your readers made you famous."

"Yes, but now, people in town actually *like* us!" Miss Barber cried.

"In that case," Del said, "I have a small favor to ask of you."

"Oh, anything for you, Del!" they both murmured simultaneously.

"I've been having a small problem with . . . with what might be intruders at my house. I'm having a party there in a few days, and I hope you'll come, not just as my guests, but as . . . well, as investigators as well."

"Oh, how exciting!" Miss Barber exclaimed. "An actual investigation! We won't have to rely on Max. We'll be able to see it all first hand."

"We'll be there. Indeed, we will," Widow Crenshaw vowed.

"A party?" Miranda asked Del. "At your house in a few days?"

He nodded.

"Is that what we've been cleaning for, not just so you could live there?"

"Well, of course I'm going to live there. But I want to show . . . certain people . . . that even out here in the country we know how to take care of a beautiful home—and how to treat a beautiful woman."

"Oh, Del."

Before she could say anything else, Miranda felt a slight tug on her sleeve at the elbow. Did someone want her place in the circle around Widow Crenshaw and Miss Barber—or should she call them collectively Captain Armistead? She'd had her turn. She could be generous to other eager fans.

She turned. Charles had shouldered his way through the crowd. Was he interested in Captain Armistead? Miranda highly doubted that.

"It's time to leave, my dear," he told her very seriously.

"Oh, no. Not yet."

"It is time to leave," he repeated even more sternly.

"Oh, just a few more minutes won't hurt," she pleaded. She should have known it wouldn't work on Charles.

"Mother is already in the carriage and the horse is waiting," Charles said insistently.

Del leaned over and whispered in her ear, "Don't keep the horse waiting, my dear."

Miranda stifled a laugh.

"Miranda. Now!" Charles commanded in a low whisper.

The party that Mrs. Nichols had anticipated for so long had turned into a raging success—one that people would undoubtedly be talking about for months to come. Mrs. Nichols would bask in the limelight of her social triumph. Future hostesses would only aspire to equal the great festivity. Widow Crenshaw and Miss Barber were truly smiling for the first time in a long time. Everyone else looked so excited at having actual celebrities living in Grasonville.

Miranda couldn't spoil this wonderful party by making a scene with Charles.

"Please excuse me," she said to Isaac Stanley, who was pressed closer behind her to get a better look.

He let her pass, then quickly slipped into her place.

Miranda was glad to see somebody was going someplace he'd be happy. She certainly was not.

Even before Miranda was completely settled into the carriage, Mrs. Lowell demanded, "Tell me, Miranda, is what I hear from Charles true?"

"I don't know. What did you hear from Charles?"

"I heard something quite scandalous."

"I suppose a person hears what she's listening for," Miranda commented.

"I hear those two deceptively frail old women in there are actually sensationalist peddlers of scintillating, perverse, pornographic smut!" Mrs. Lowell gave a haughty sniff.

"They write adventure novels, if that's what you mean."

"Scandalous!" Mrs. Lowell declared. "For women of their breeding and social standing, to indulge in such lascivious, prurient tales for the amusement of the lower classes. At their time of life they should be looking to the welfare of their immortal souls and reading uplifting sermons."

"Should they plant lavender and take in stray cats, too?" Miranda asked.

"What? What on earth are you talking about?" Mrs. Lowell sniffed.

"Miranda," Charles said ominously, "have you been drinking too much of that punch?"

"You read those silly books, too, don't you?" Mrs. Lowell accused.

"Yes." She saw no reason whatsoever to lie about it.

Mrs. Lowell heaved a great sigh. "Just as I feared. Rambling on. That just goes to show what happens to the brain when fed a steady diet of such trash. It turns to mush."

"Have you ever read any of their books?"

"What? I? Read that sort of drivel?" Mrs. Lowell's hand flew to her breast, as if she could protect herself from the horrid tales. "Why, I wouldn't stoop so low!"

Of course, the gossiping you've been doing isn't considered stopping low?

"Well, if you've never read any of the books, how do you know they're so terrible?" Miranda asked.

"I've heard." She pressed her lips tightly together and nodded her head knowingly, as if what she knew was too horrible to relate. "Oh, I've heard."

"What have you heard? Who have you heard it from? Other people who've never read the books, either?"

Mrs. Lowell sniffed loudly and turned her head from Miranda.

"Of course, my dear, once we return to Boston, we'll not be allowing any of *those kinds* of books in the house," Charles instructed.

"Oh, I suppose *those kinds* of books are only read by *those kinds* of people."

"Actually, yes."

"How do you know what *those kind* of people read if you don't stoop to associating with them? I'm surprised you've stooped to associating with me!"

"That's different, my dear. You've . . . you've managed to rise above the impediments of your birth and background."

"What?" Miranda could only sit there with her mouth hanging open in utter shock.

"Now, as far as your choice of reading material, only the classics will be allowed," Charles informed her. "They're the only truly proper matter for intelligent people to read."

"I've already read the English classics. I've read what some might consider classics of American literature. I've read the French classics in the original language—not just translations. Do I have to wait a hundred years until they come up with more classics to read something new or do I have to keep reading the same old stuff over and over?"

"Don't be flippant, Miranda," Mrs. Lowell cautioned. "It's unbecoming to a wife."

"I'm not sure I want to—"

"What you want is rather unimportant now," Mrs.

Lowell said. "Your parents have spoiled you terribly all your life."

"My parents are good to me," she insisted. She tried not to let her voice crack, but she could feel her throat tightening from the tears that were threatening to fall.

"I'm sure you think so, when they give you everything your little heart desires. Now, however, you must realize that you are *not* the center of the world. The earth does *not* revolve around you. You must put your own personal wishes and desires aside and look at the best advantage for society as a whole."

"What is the best advantage for society as a whole?" Miranda asked.

"In our home in Boston," Mrs. Lowell pronounced, "it's whatever I say it is."

Miranda had tried to tell Charles nicely tonight. She'd tried to tell him in a way that wouldn't hurt his feelings too badly. She'd tried to tell him in a way that wouldn't cause too much scandal. She'd tried to tell him in a way that wouldn't reveal how very much she detested his mother. She'd tried. She'd really tried.

She couldn't wait to break her engagement to Charles— the pompous little mama's boy, and his overbearing, opinionated mother. She wanted to tear the ring off her hand right now and give it back to him. *Throw* it back at him. Maybe it would bounce out of the carriage and he'd have to go searching for it on his hands and knees along the side of the road. A rather satisfying picture.

But she was too angry even to speak to him. In her current state of mind, if she managed to take off the ring, she might just shove the darn thing up the aristocratic nose he was always looking down on everybody over.

She tugged at the ring until it finally came off. Then she tucked it into her purse. She'd find just the right moment to give it back.

She choked back tears of anger, but not of regret. She'd *never* regret not marrying Charles.

But right now she didn't want to talk to him. She

didn't even want to look at him, or his mother. She stared out at the dark countryside.

She couldn't wait to get home.

"Doesn't this horse go any faster?"

Miranda stood beside Del in the vestibule of the big house, placed her hands on her hips, and surveyed their handiwork.

Del placed his hand around her shoulder and pulled her into the crook of his arm.

The hardwood floors visible at the edges of the carpets shone with polish. The carpets gave a soft cushioning underfoot. The woodwork gleamed with several coats of new paint. The wallpaper had cleaned up nicely, with outstanding paintings to hang over tears, holes and stains. The furniture had survived well under the dust covers. Even the hunting trophies had finally been dusted.

"It looks wonderful! You can really be proud of this place," she told him.

"I am."

"Does Sally have all the food prepared?"

"Just about."

"Then I suppose you're ready."

"Just about."

"Did you get all the mice out of the kitchen?"

"I hope."

"How about the cellar?"

"At this point, if the mice agree to stay away from the other floors, they can have the cellar."

"Generous of you."

Del chuckled.

"How about the upstairs?"

He shook his head. "I'm not worrying about that now."

"How about the staircase?"

"I still haven't gotten around to doing anything with it. I don't think I have time now to pull the stairs apart and put them back together again before the party. I don't think it would look real inviting if the first thing the guests see is a torn-down staircase."

"Maybe not," Miranda agreed.

But it was just a half-hearted agreement. The curving staircase with its carved balustrade and newel post was too pretty not to deserve special treatment.

If he hadn't wasted his time dusting those horrendous hunting trophies, and had just gotten rid of them, and spent the time fixing the stairs, it would all be done now, she thought with discontent.

"I'm going to put these dropclothes in the cellar for now," he told her.

She shrugged. "Out of sight, out of mind."

Del scooped up the material in his arms and made his way noisily down the cellar steps.

Meanwhile, Miranda was busy examining the stairs. There had to be something they could do with it. And once she figured out what it was, how could she convince Del that it absolutely, positively had to be done before the party?

"Hey, Miranda," Del called from the bottom of the cellar stairs.

"Don't tell me. Is it a rat? I'm *not* coming down if it's a rat."

"No."

"A mouse?"

"It's not a mouse."

"A rattlesnake?"

"No."

"The ghost of Gertie Richardson?"

"No, but Henry says to tell you 'hi.'"

"Ask him why he shot all those pretty animals and then let these beautiful stairs go to ruin."

"No, seriously, Miranda. Come on down. I need you to look at this."

"I'm coming."

This was the first time Miranda had been in the cellar since that disastrous first almost-kiss. It was much easier to descend the stairs in Del's rolled-up jeans than in her dress.

She bet it would probably be a lot easier to get up them again, too. She knew this time she wouldn't be running up them away from him like an addlepatted ninny.

"We've already determined there are no dead bodies or buried treasure down here," she said, coming to stand beside him in front of Red Wilkins's old workbench. "So, what's this amazing discovery I came all the way down here to see?"

Del pointed at a hammer lying on the table with the rest of the tools.

"Big deal." Miranda shrugged, then turned her back on him to go up the steps.

Quickly she turned back to him. "Unless you intend that to be the murder weapon when you kill me. Are you going to leave it as a clue for Widow Crenshaw and Miss Barber? It would make them so happy. Make sure it's really bloody so they can show it to Mrs. Nichols."

"No, Miranda, look at this," he insisted, still pointing at the hammer.

"It's a hammer, Del. Is there something special about this hammer? Does it jump up and do a buck and wing? Can it whistle 'Dixie'?"

"It was lying right here on this table with the rest of Red Wilkins's stools."

"Wow! A hammer in with other tools. That *is* unusual."

"Yes, it is."

"And it was just lying there, you say."

"Yes."

"Well, you're more familiar with tools than I am. I just can't see it." She placed her hands on her hips in frustration and impatience. "So let's stop playing games and just tell me what the devil you're so excited about."

"It's new."

"Big deal. I can go into Quinn's any day and get one . . . just like it. Oh, my goodness, Del!"

"That's right. That's just what somebody did, except they probably didn't bother to pay for it."

"What is it doing here?"

"It wasn't here the last time I was down here."

"Are you sure?"

"Yes. Positive," he declared emphatically.

"Who else has been here?"

"Just us. So it's got to have some connection with the footsteps we've been hearing."

"All right," she said, throwing her hands up in the air in resignation, "I take back everything I said about the ghost of Gertie Richardson."

"Apology accepted."

"Yep, if it had been something from Englemeyer's, I might still suspect her. But a hammer from Quinn's— nope, that's just not like our Gertie."

He hefted the hammer from one hand to another. "I'm taking this upstairs. I'll show it to Max tomorrow. See what he has to say about it."

"See what Widow Crenshaw and Miss Barber have to say about it, too," Miranda suggested.

"Sure. Why not?"

Miranda followed Del up the cellar stairs.

"I'm going to put this in the kitchen, so I don't forget it."

"And so it's out of the way for the party," Miranda added.

He chuckled as he made his way down the corridor.

Miranda stood there, waiting for him to return. She looked up at the wide curving stairs. She'd been up and down much bigger, much fancier staircases, curving double staircases, marble staircases with wrought-iron and gold-plated handrails.

But this was the one and only Richardson staircase.

She'd seen the cellar—twice was more than enough. She'd seen more of the ground floor of this house than she'd ever expected. But in all this time she still hadn't seen the upstairs.

She looked around. Del hadn't returned from the kitchen yet. Why did she feel she had to go sneaking up the stairs? It wasn't as if Del could stop her. She supposed old habits were hard to break.

Miranda placed her foot on the bottom step.

Nothing horrible happened.

She moved up several more steps. They started to creak badly. Yes, Del had been right. These stairs made their own peculiar sound, unlike anything else. This sound would definitely draw Del. She'd better get up those steps quickly.

"Miranda! Get down from those stairs!" Del called from the kitchen.

She sped up. She'd reach the top before he could stop her.

It was much easier to run up the stairs in Del's rolled-up trousers. She was almost at the top. *Squeak! Crackle! Crunch! Crash!*

"Miranda!"

14

"DEL! DEL! HELP me!"

She clung to what was left of the stair. Her fingers dug into the threadbare carpet. She hoped to find something more to cling to, if only a thread, to keep her from falling.

Her legs stung from the scratches made by the splintering wood. She could feel little trickles of blood running down her calves and shins. She could feel the remnants of the stairs digging into her ribs through Del's thin shirt. But she couldn't feel anything pressing on her back.

Worst of all, what she couldn't feel was anything beneath her.

She kicked her feet around, hoping to knock into something that would give her support. No matter how hard she kicked, or in what direction, she still couldn't feel anything.

There was nothing below her but a sheer drop onto the cellar steps, and a steep tumble onto the bare bricks two stories below.

The only thing keeping her from falling was her own death grip on the rotting wood on either side of her and shredded carpet hanging before her.

"Miranda!"

She turned her head as much as she dared. Del was standing at the foot of the stairs.

"What happened? Did you fall?"

"Not yet. Now get me out of here before I do!"

"Are you hurt?"

"No." She'd never admit she'd hurt herself doing something he'd told her not to. But it did sting. "Well, yes, sort of."

"Hang on."

"Del, there's not much to hang on to up here. You'd better hurry."

"I'll get you out." He tried to mount the stairs. The creaking grew loud and ominous, but he continued up two, three, four steps.

The closer he drew to Miranda, the worse he realized the situation was. All the stairs between them had collapsed under her slight weight. They must have been really rotten to give way under a tiny thing like Miranda, he thought, worried.

He looked at what was left of the stairs—a few broken pieces of wood attached to the wall on one side and to the banister on the other. Neither would be sturdy enough for him to walk on to go up and get Miranda.

Several pieces of wood knocked loose from around her. She felt the pressure ease on her ribs as the wood plummeted into the cellar, clattering loudly all the way down. But she also felt the support that had wedged her in slipping away, too.

"Hurry, Del! The stairs are falling apart!"

"I can't climb the stairs."

"Why not?"

"They're gone. They collapsed behind you. There's nothing to walk on."

"Well, you better learn to fly real soon, then, and get me out of here."

"How much longer can you hold on?"

"As long as I have to," she said with a gasp.

She'd do her best, but she could feel the splinters of

wood digging into the palm of her hands, and the threads of the carpet cutting into her fingertips. She could feel her arms and fingers weakening.

"The real problem is not how long I can hold on to the stairs, but how long the stairs will hold on to me."

"Just hold on as long as you can. I'm coming to get you," he promised.

He studied the staircase again. He certainly couldn't go up stairs that were no longer there. It was too wide of a gap to jump. Even if he could jump it, when he landed, the weakened stairs on the other side would probably collapse under his weight.

The stair to which Miranda clung so desperately groaned with increasing fatigue. It could give way any second. He didn't have time to run to the barn for a ladder or a piece of wood to stretch across the gap.

If he couldn't go up the inside of the stairs, maybe he could go up the outside.

He rested the outside of his foot on the small edge on the outside of the banister. He bounced up and down. The stair held him. He tugged at the banister. It seemed sturdy enough. As long as the banister held, and his foot didn't slip, he just might be able to make it.

Gripping the banister, Del started to make his way up the stairs from the outside. The banister creaked and protested the whole way.

His mother had made him go to church every Sunday. But he hadn't been to church since her funeral. That didn't mean he wasn't a praying man. Whatever he'd missed in the past three years, he sure was making up for now as he inched his way toward Miranda.

He looked down. Not a good idea. Standing in the vestibule, the top of the stairs hadn't looked that far away. But hanging from the top of the balcony overlooking the vestibule, that floor seemed a long, long way down.

He inched his way past Miranda.

"Hey, hey!" she cried. "I'm here. Where the dickens do you think you're going?"

"Past you."

"I can see that, you big dummy. What good is that going to do?"

"If I step on the tread holding you, we'll both go down, you little dummy."

"What?"

"So I'm almost to the top," he explained as he reached the final step.

He threw a long leg over the banister and felt with his toe for a sure purchase. When he found it, he quickly slipped his other leg over the banister.

Dropping to his stomach on the floor, he crawled closer to the edge of the top of the stairs. He reached out his hand to Miranda.

"Closer. I can't reach you."

"I'm trying." He inched closer.

"I can't move," Miranda told him. "You have to get me."

"I can't reach you."

"If I move, I'll fall."

He wasn't sure how sturdy these top stairs were. They could collapse, too, sending them both to their death in the cellar. But if he didn't move out onto them, Miranda would fall alone. He'd have to take the chance.

Swallowing hard, and breathing one more prayer before he had to focus all his concentration on saving Miranda, he crawled out over the top two steps. They didn't even creak. He breathed with relief, reached out and seized Miranda's wrist.

"I've got you."

"Don't let go."

Now that he knew the stairs and banister would hold, now that he had Miranda's wrist securely in his grasp, he swung his legs around to brace against the top of the banister. Pushing hard with his legs, he pulled Miranda closer.

She didn't budge.

"Miranda, you have to let go of the carpet."

"What?"

"Open your fingers and let go of the carpet," he said slowly and distinctly.

"No, I'll fall."

"No, you won't. Look, I've got you."

"Oh."

"Boy, you really are confused."

"Want to trade places to see if you can do any better?"

"No, thanks. I don't think you could lift me."

"Now that that's settled—get me out of here!"

He pulled again. This time Miranda began to rise from the hole in the stairs.

She moaned in pain as the wood scraped against her sides.

He pulled harder. Now that she had released her grip on the carpet, he could grab both of her wrists and haul her up that much more quickly.

She was in his arms. He clutched her tightly to him.

"I never want to let you go!"

"I thought I was going to die."

"I thought I was going to lose you. I can't lose you, my love."

"You saved me. Again."

"I had to. Without you I don't have a reason to live."

"It was worse than the snake!" she declared. "That was the scariest moment of my entire life."

"What in the name of all that's holy made you try to go up those steps?" he demanded.

"I . . . I wanted to see the rest of the house."

He gestured around him. "Satisfied?"

"No. I still haven't made it up there."

"You're here now."

"Oh, that's right." She lifted her head from his chest and looked around. Then she rested her head against him once again. "It's worse than the other floor."

"Not worth it, huh?"

She shook her head.

"Lord have mercy, Miranda! Don't ever let your blasted curiosity get the better of you again," he scolded.

"I won't." She cuddled closer to him.

He kissed the top of her head. With her head still resting against his chest, she looked up at him. He pulled her closer to him and kissed her again.

"I just wish I could figure how we're both going to get down from here."

"Back stairs?"

Del shook his head. "Not in this house. Your father's the only one I know who added a back stairs."

Miranda managed a small giggle. "He tried to escape from my mother once at your house, when she was really angry, and there was no way out but through the kitchen, right past her, so he was caught. He never wanted anyone in our house to be in that position, so he added the stairs."

"Good ol' Sam, friend of the fugitive."

"That still doesn't help us."

"Do you think you can climb down the way I came up?"

"Sure."

"It's a pretty tough climb," he warned.

"I'll be going down. Gravity is on my side."

"I don't think you'll see it quite that way once you get the view."

"Anyway, it'll still be easier for me. My feet are a lot smaller than yours."

"Can you stand up?" Del asked her.

"Sure."

He stood and reached down to lift her. Her shaking legs barely supported her. She leaned against Del for strength.

"You're bleeding!"

"Just a little."

She looked down at her legs. There were a few tiny rips in the legs of the jeans. When she lifted the fabric, she could see more damage had been done. Her legs were red from the scratches. Fortunately, the scratches weren't deep and the bleeding had stopped. The trails of blood were already drying to a flaking brown.

Del tugged carefully on the bloodstained shirt at her side.

"This doesn't look so good."

"It looks worse than it really is. Honestly."

"Do you think you can make it, then?"

"Sure." She moved to the balcony and peered over. "I don't see any problem here. I don't know why you were huffing and puffing and complaining so."

"Be careful."

"Relax. When I was a kid, I used to do this all the time."

"Little liar. There aren't any stairs like this in your house. I know you have closed stairwells."

"You're too observant for my own good."

But gravity was on her side. She managed to descend the stairs on the outside more easily than Del would have given her credit for.

"I think we ought to take you in to see Doc Marsh."

"No. He'll tell my mother. Or worse yet, if we go into town, someone might see us, and Charles and Mrs. Lowell will find out I've been sneaking over here."

"Maybe you ought to go to your mother for help."

"How am I going to explain to her why I'm dressed in your clothes, crashing through the stairs at your house? You're going to have to take care of me."

"I think I have some bandages back here," he said as he led her back to his bedroom.

She sat on the side of his bed and began to unbutton her shirt.

"Stop! Miranda, what do you think you're doing?"

"What's the matter? I need to put on a bandage and you're the only one around who can help me. Don't you start sermonizing to me about what young ladies should and should not do."

"But, Miranda," Del pleaded. "Do you know what you're doing to me?"

"Right now you're getting me bandages."

"And then?" Del reached into the top drawer of the dresser and pulled out a bundle of bandages.

"Geez, I don't need a bandage that big. It's just a few scratches. It's not like I'm going to die or anything."

He came and sat beside her on the bed.

"I'm glad you weren't hurt badly. I'm glad you weren't killed."

"Oh, my goodness, yes!" she said with a deep breath. At last the shock was setting in.

She leaned her head on his shoulder.

She looked up at him apologetically. "I'm sorry I ruined your shirt. I think I can still wear the pants."

Del reached over to cradle her chin in his hand. Slowly he lifted her face to his and placed a grateful kiss on her lips.

"I'm so glad I still have you, my love. I don't know what I'd do without you."

"Yes, you do. You'd marry Dorothy Halstead."

Holding her chin just a bit more tightly so that she couldn't look away, he gazed deeply into her eyes.

"I forbid you ever to mention her name again in this house," he ordered. "Without you, I'd spend the rest of my days a lonely old bachelor, a recluse, a man without friends or family, wasting away my lonely days rattling around in this big house like a marble in a rain barrel."

"A what?"

"A marble in a rain barrel. That's what Will said I was like."

"Will's had too much of Mrs. Nichols's punch."

"I'll never have enough of you," he told her, and kissed her again.

"You asked me a question once, Del, I never answered." She moved to face him and wrapped both arms around his neck. "You asked me once if Charles could make me feel the way you do."

"Have you decided on your answer yet?"

"I believe I have. But I'd like to try just once more before I really decide."

"I'll help you with all the evidence you need."

He pulled her gently to him. She'd had a bad shock. He didn't want to hurt her any more. He kissed her tenderly on the lips, then meandered around to her cheek and her tender earlobe.

She responded to his kisses with a fervency he'd never imagined, even from Miranda.

"I've wanted you for so long, Del." She giggled. "But I was just a girl. I didn't know how much I could really want you, in what powerful ways I could want you, until I'd grown up and become a woman. Until you held me and kissed me."

"I still want you, Miranda," he told her. "I've already told you, and it'll never change. Even though I know you're engaged to another man. I'll never interfere. Whatever decision you make, you have to live with it, so it must be yours."

"What I feel for you I've never felt for Charles," she softly admitted.

She held the edges of the shirttail in her hands and twisted them round and round.

"I tried to break our engagement the other night. I just never got the chance to tell him. I never got the chance to give him back his ring. But I took it off, and I'll never wear it again."

"Good. That leaves more room on your finger for *my* ring—when I can get you one."

"I'll never take it off."

"It'll be hard to tell him you don't love him anymore."

"No, it won't. Because I don't think he ever really loved me. I can't even recall him ever saying so, even when he proposed marriage to me."

"Really?"

"I think I was like those animal heads down there to him."

"Dead, and stuffed with cotton."

"No, you big dummy! I was just something pretty to have hanging around him for him to show off what a great hunter he was."

"Does it hurt to think that?"

"No, because I never really loved him, not truly. I thought he was clever, witty, sophisticated—the kind of man my parents wanted me to marry, the kind of man I ought to marry. But he's not the kind of man I could love. I love you, Del."

"I love you, too."

"I've always felt there was something missing between Charles and myself. When you're never experienced true desire, then you never know it's missing. I didn't think it was all that important, anyway. It just wasn't something that a well-bred young woman knew about, or even talked about—much less cared about. Being with you, Del, I know what was missing, and what can never be, between Charles and me."

"But we have it, Miranda, don't we?"

He held her closer to his, running his hands slowly up and down her back, enjoying the feel of each tender curve and swell.

"Of course. Just like I always knew."

"Do you still think you know everything?" he asked, chuckling.

"Nope. I only know I love you."

She moved her hands over his arms and shoulders. His arms were strong. He'd managed to pull her from death's gaping jaws. He had the love and strength to hold on to her for a lifetime.

"And we have something more, too."

"What's that?"

"Desire—that's a part of love."

"You know how I desire you, Miranda," he said.

"Yes. Do you know now that I want you, too, Del?"

"Are you certain, my love? There'll be no going back."

"I won't be going back. Not to Charles. Not to Boston."

Del reached up and slowly began to unbutton the top button of her shirt.

He kissed her lips, then trailed his kisses down her soft neck to dwell in the delicate hollow of her throat. He slowly parted the shirt, revealing her gently rounded breasts, and the tiny tips of pink that crowned them.

He placed a reverent kiss on each nipple. He eased her back onto the bed.

Spreading the shirt wider, he carefully kissed each scratch and bruise while she ran her fingers through his hair.

"Are you sure you want this, Miranda? It'll be tough on me, but it's still not too late to stop. I'll stop if you want me to."

"Del Williams, I will not chicken out on you now."

"It . . . it doesn't have anything to do with that, Miranda."

"I know, but I'm too nervous not to make bad jokes. All right?"

"I should have known." He groaned with resignation. "Miranda, you will always keep me on my toes, won't you?"

"You bet!"

She wrapped her arms around his neck and drew him closer to her. Just when he thought she'd kiss him, she reached up and began unbuttoning his shirt.

Their shirts lay in a heap on the floor at the foot of the bed. One pair of jeans joined them. A second pair of jeans joined the first.

He moved to tuck himself into bed beside her.

Very quietly, whispering into his ear, she made her demand. "I want to see you naked."

"What?"

"You've seen me."

"Yes." He nodded.

She cuddled up closer to him and ran her warm, smooth hands the length of his body.

"I want to see you naked," she insisted in a husky whisper.

"What? Here? Now?"

"No, noon tomorrow in front of Quinn's." She laughed. "Yes, here, now. I can't think of a better place."

"You've always had some very bizarre ideas, Miranda," he told her.

"What? That I love you and want to see all of you? Don't tell me you're one of those old stick-in-the-muds that thinks ladies shouldn't look at naked men, but men can look all they want at naked women!"

"No, no."

She kissed him passionately on the lips, then moved back to rest on her elbow and gaze down at his body, spread the length of the bed. Her eyes swept his body, devouring the sight of him, that she'd so longed for.

"You're . . . beautiful!" She sighed. "You're more than I'd ever dreamed. I love you, Del. I love all of you. Every magnificent inch of you."

"I love you, too, Miranda. Every agitating, irritating, inquisitive inch of you." He chuckled.

He flipped over onto his side and threw his arm across her waist.

"Now, are you happy with what you've seen?"

"Yes." She drew in a deep breath. "Make me happier, Del."

"You know I want you, Miranda."

"I want you."

Poised over her, Del bent down to whisper quietly in her ear, "I'll warn you, Miranda. This . . . this might . . . this is going to hurt a bit . . . the first time."

"No, it won't."

"I'll try to be gentle, but it'll still smart."

"Nope."

"Why? What? Have you . . . done this before?"

"Good lord, no! Not with Charles Icebox Coldfish the Third!" she said, making a horrible face. "Not with *anybody*."

She kissed his cheek, his throat, then ran her kisses down his body.

"All my life, I've never wanted anyone but you, Del. Never have. Never will."

"It'll hurt just a little," he warned her one last time as he waited above her.

"No, it won't. I won't let it. I'd do anything for you, Del."

She'd always said that. Now it took on a special meaning.

She closed her eyes. She waited as his warmth drew closer to her. She held her breath as she waited their ultimate union.

"Hey! That hurts!" Her eyes flew open. She almost took a swipe at his head. "Well, just a little," she stubbornly amended, and stroked his cheek instead.

Del laughed.

"Miranda, my love, you will always keep my life interesting! I love you."

He kissed her again and again, then settled into a rich rhythm of love and life.

She closed her eyes, moving with him. "I love you, too, Del. With all my heart."

She breathed deeply as he sent a warm glow through her body.

Sending Miranda home again was the hardest thing he'd ever had to do. But he knew he had to. And she must. She had a ring to return to Charles.

15

$\mathcal{D}$EL HAD A little more work to do yet, too. Somehow he had to block off the staircase so that no one would mistakenly go up them during the party. That could be disastrous for anyone.

He pulled a sofa and table from the parlor and placed it in front of the stairs. It didn't look too bad there, and the crowded parlor didn't look as if it were missing anything. Now he was almost ready.

He took the last of the rat traps to set them out in the cellar. He hadn't seen any of the obnoxious critters. He really didn't think there were any in his cellar. But some kind of rat—the two-legged kind—had been there. Maybe getting a big toe stuck in a trap would be just the thing to discourage hammer-toting, snake-sneaking, floor-creaking intruders.

Darn, Del cursed as he watched his step descending the cellar steps. These stairs sure were a mess after Miranda had almost fallen through.

After he'd set the traps, he started picking up the broken wood from the stairs. At least he could use the splintered pieces this winter for kindling.

He looked a little more closely at one board. That was a pretty big piece of wood to rot away like it had. He looked at it even more closely. It wasn't much of a rot and splinter. It looked more like a pretty clean break.

Dang if it didn't look as if the end of that board had been sawed. Del bent down to examine the mess on the steps a little more closely, too. It was a darn shame he'd already trampled over a lot of it. But there were still some places where the boards lay over the coating of dust on the stairs.

He lifted the board. He'd seen trees axed, rails split, boards cracked, burned, and even a chair broken over the back of a guy's head in a bar fight. But not a single one of those ways of making two pieces out of one piece of wood ever resulted in making sawdust. And dang if there wasn't sawdust on those stairs!

There was only one way to make sawdust. Somebody had to saw something.

Del got the ladder out of the barn and propped it up on the stairs. It was a precarious perch, he knew, but he had to see for himself. He sure as shooting wasn't going to try to climb the stairs again, not yet. So looking at it from the bottom was his only alternative.

"Yep, that's what they did," he told himself as he brushed his fingers against the damaged wood.

The board was such a clean slice he could almost match the board in his hand with the stair from which it had been cut. When he looked closer at the underside of the stairs he could see that the top few steps had all been sawed like this one. No wonder they'd all given way. The surprising thing was that they hadn't collapsed completely and killed Miranda.

It wasn't just a mistake in the construction of the house that had finally shown up. Only the top steps were sawed. Only the highest steps, that a fall from would do the most damage. Someone had very carefully planned this. Someone very recentlly.

"Who did this?" Del demanded angrily, slamming his fist against the wall.

The same person who left the hammer? The same person with the noisy footsteps from nowhere? The same person who had put the rattlesnake in the pantry? Why would they want to harm Miranda?

Who else knew Miranda was coming here? Himself, Miranda.

Sally, but she was Miranda's best friend.

Dorothy was probably jealous of Miranda, but she had no way of knowing Miranda was coming here.

Will must have his suspicions, or he wouldn't have gone shooting his mouth off about Del being alone, but he'd never hurt Miranda.

Widow Crenshaw and Miss Barber would never try to get even with Miranda for exposing their literary alter ego. They were having too much fun being celebrities.

Mrs. Cartwright had seen her here and wasn't too happy about it. Did she think that by eliminating Miranda she could finally get her old job back?

Charles and Mrs. Lowell had seen Miranda here once and weren't too happy about it. Del guessed that there were probably occasions when Mrs. Lowell would like to strangle Miranda, but the lady would never countenance a scandal to touch her house.

But everybody in Grasonville knew Del was in this house every day.

But he'd been gone for three years. How could he possibly have that many enemies? With that much skill at carrying a grudge?

Sally was good at carrying a grudge, and she could get awful riled with him. But, shoot, if she killed him, she wouldn't be able to have any more fun badgering him into doing all the work he'd neglected while he was away.

Mrs. Cartwright was angry that Mr. Richardson had left the house to him instead of to her, and had sworn to make him sorry for not hiring her. But killing him wouldn't get her her job back.

Jasper and Daisy Richardson wanted the house, and they had been acting awfully nervous and suspicious the day he and Miranda had met them in town. Killing him might make their lawsuit a lot easier and cheaper if he wasn't around to contest it.

Charles and Mrs. Lowell hadn't made any open threats against him. They didn't want his house. But Miranda would probably be a lot easier for them to handle if he were out of the picture. Del chuckled at the thought. Those two still didn't know Miranda very well, did they?

Miranda claimed she'd given up all hope of ever owning the house, but he knew she still wanted it. Why would she kill him for it when all she had to do was marry him? A much more pleasurable way of getting it. Unless all this talk of love was just a trick.

No, he couldn't believe that of Miranda. She couldn't have been the one who sawed through the steps. She wasn't any good with tools, and she couldn't have gotten up that high, even with a ladder. Why would she put her own life in danger when poisoning him would be so much quicker and neater? And white arsenic was so readily available at Quinn's. Should he start watching what he ate a little better?

No, Miranda might be pigheaded and bossy, but she was honest and true.

If Max weren't so busy with the train robbers, he'd talk to him, have him come out here and investigate. He wasn't sure what good having Widow Crenshaw and Miss Barber investigate the scene of the crime would do, except make them happy, and provide them with more tales to put into their books. On the other hand, he didn't think he was quite ready to hire a Pinkerton man.

Why did everyone want this darn house, anyway? Who would want it badly enough to kill him for it? It might be a nice house, but it wasn't worth that much. Mr. Richardson might have made a good deal of money predicting the railroad coming through so many years ago, but he was no dummy. He kept his substantial fortune in the bank. Just like Del did. There wasn't anything in this house worth killing for.

"No, I do not want to go into that stupid cellar one more time," Miranda protested.

"I just want you to see where they sawed the steps in half," Del insisted.

"You know I hate that cellar. Why do you want to torment me like this?" she demanded with a deep sigh of resignation as she followed him to the cellar door anyway.

He opened it. "See, see up there?"

"Where?"

"Up close to the edge." He pointed. "There."

"If I say I see it, will you stop this stupid search?"

"All right. If you don't care that someone's trying to kill me, that someone almost killed you trying to kill me—fine!"

"Come on. You're just all riled up because of all the work you've been doing for the house and the party," she said, trying to sound calm and soothing. "Sally hasn't stopped complaining about the food since she started cooking—even though you and I both know she's tickled to be doing this."

"Yeah. I guess."

"Mrs. Cartwright and the strange Richardsons are still on your mind. There's got to be some other logical explanation for the stairs."

"Like what?"

"Like, maybe Mr. Richardson started some repairs long ago, then got sick and couldn't finish them, and then forgot all about them until we found them."

"I don't think so. Henry Richardson never handled a tool in his life."

Miranda released a sigh. "I guess not, but it sure beats the alternative. Someone really is trying to kill you."

Creak, creak.

"What's that noise?"

"I didn't hear anything. You're carrying this way too far now, Del."

Creak, creak.

"You must have heard that."

"Well, yes, I did," she was reluctantly forced to admit. "It sounded as if it was coming from the kitchen."

"It always sounds like that when you're in the cellar. When you're in the parlor, it sounds like it's coming from the cellar. I still haven't found any kind of rhyme, reason, or logical system to it."

"It's not coming from the kitchen," Miranda said. "It's coming from over there."

"Where?"

Mice or no mice, Miranda quickly descended the cellar steps and headed toward the back of the house. She came up against the brick wall that enclosed the cellar.

"There's nothing there," Del told her. "I've told you before. There's just crawl space under the rest of the house."

"Over here," she insisted, looking up at the bottom of the floor. "By what I'll bet is the kitchen, upstairs."

Del looked up. "Yeah, yeah. I suppose as far as I can tell, this is where the kitchen starts."

"There's got to be more under here," Miranda insisted.

"Where?"

"Here."

She started to run her hands along the rough brick wall.

"It's cold here."

"Of course it's cold. We're underground in a cellar."

"No, I mean the wall is colder here than anywhere else along this wall. Here, feel."

She seized his hand and flattened it, palm down, on the wall.

"See for yourself, hard-head. Colder."

"Don't be silly," he said, moving his hand over the bricks. "How can it be colder here?"

"I have no idea. It's your house. All I know is, it's cold here."

She was so insistent, Del reached out again and placed his hand closer to Miranda's on the rough wall.

"See."

"Yeah, you're right."

"Hey, don't ghosts make cold spots when they materialize?"

"No, Miranda. It's a draft. The cold air's got to be coming from somewhere. That means there's got to be some kind of opening—somehow, somewhere."

Del started pushing against the wall. He heard a slight scraping sound of brick against brick.

Miranda looked at the floor.

"This part's moving," she said. "Push here some more."

"Give me a hand."

"It's heavy."

"Don't worry, you won't get your skirt caught in it this time."

Miranda placed her shoulder against the wall, dug her heels in and pushed with Del.

The bricks scraped even more loudly. The wall slid inward a few feet, leaving an opening just wide enough for one person to slip through.

"It's probably a root cellar for the kitchen," Del said.

"Fiddlesticks! What root cellar wouldn't have an opening into the kitchen? What root cellar hides behind a secret door in a brick wall? It's a secret room!" Miranda exclaimed. "Wait until Widow Crenshaw and Miss Barber hear about this."

"Mr. Richardson must have had more imagination than I'd ever have given him credit for," Del said, scratching his head in puzzlement.

He searched the workbench for a lantern, struck a match, and lit the kerosene wick.

"You have to show this to Mrs. Crenshaw and Miss Barber," Miranda insisted. "They'll be so hurt if you don't include them. And it'll probably show up in one of their books. Maybe you will, too."

"I'll go in," Del told her. "You wait out here, just in case . . . well, just in case I need you to go run for help."

"Like you ran for help for me when I was stuck in the staircase?"

"I couldn't leave you just hanging there. Now, guard the door while I'm in here."

"Are you expecting to find a nest of snakes?"

"Jiminy, I hope not!"

"Are you expecting to find a pile of gold?"

"If I do, I'm not telling you. You'll make me share. I'm not saying a word, and leaving it there and coming back for it later."

"So generous of you, Del."

"If you're good, I'll give you a tip. Now wait here."

"Are you expecting someone to shut you in and not let you out?"

"Maybe."

"Bye, Del."

"What?"

"Just checking to see if you were paying attention."

"Just shut up and stand guard, Miranda."

Holding the lantern before him, Del poked his head into the room.

"Well, I'll be jiggered!" His voice sounded hollow and resonant as he disappeared completely behind the sliding wall.

"What is it? What is it?" she cried.

"I'll be double-dog sheep-dipped, and birch-switched."

"What is it?" she demanded, clenching her fists in frustration.

Del stuck his head out the door. He was grinning from ear to ear.

"Money."

"Money," she repeated.

He nodded. "More than I've ever seen all together in one place in my life."

"Where did it come from? How did it get there?"

"Didn't we ask the same things about the snake, and Jasper and Daisy?"

"I don't think they all came from the same place."

"Me, neither."

"What are you going to do with it?"

"That depends on where it came from," Del told her. "If it was hidden here by Mr. Richardson, I'd say it's mine. If it somehow got here because it was stolen from the Railroad Employees Widows and Orphans Fund, I'd say it's got to go back."

"Good decision."

"No, bad decision."

"Why do you say that?"

"Because knowing Mr. Richardson was the bank president for many years, do you honestly think he would've left this much cash lying around his house, not earning interest for him?"

"Good point. So, how do we go about finding out whose money it is?"

"Good question."

"And who put it there."

"You can't get away with this, you know," Mr. Hendricks said, his hands raised high over his head.

He glanced at the clock. Right after closing time. Now who'd come in and save his hide from getting aerated?

"The town's full of lawmen."

"No, it's not," Jimmy said. "Seein' as how they couldn't find the train robbers, they all went back this mornin'."

"That just leaves my dumb ol' brother lookin' out for things." Allen laughed. "Cripes, what good can he do?"

Jimmy trained the barrel of the gun directly on the high, wide forehead of the bank president.

"So just shut up, Mr. Hendricks. Keep your hands up where I can see 'em, hand over the cash, and no one gets hurt."

"I can't," Mr. Hendricks answered in quaking tones.

"What do you mean, you can't?" Allen demanded, pointing his revolver at the bank president's chest.

"Well, make up your minds," Mr. Hendricks wailed. "Either I keep my hands up or I hand over the money. I can't do both at the same time. If I move to give you the money, you might think I'm going for my gun—"

"You got a gun!" Jimmy exclaimed.

Mr. Hendricks heard the click of the hammer being drawn back.

"No, no! No gun. Honestly. No gun. Never. Not me."

"Shut up," Allen ordered.

"Yeah, shut up, hands up, and give us the money."

"Let me ask one question. Is that fair enough?"

"Yeah, I guess."

"If I don't give you the money, you'll shoot me?"

"Yep."

"If I move my hands, you'll shoot me?"

"Hey, that's two questions. You can't do that," Allen protested.

"Shut up and let him talk," Jimmy said. "This is gettin' interestin', all this talk o' shootin'. It's almost as good as Captain Jackson Armistead's stuff."

Jimmy waved his gun at Mr. Hendricks again. "What were you sayin', old man?"

"If I move my hands, you'll shoot me?"

"Yeah."

"Then how can I give you the money?"

"That's three questions," Allen protested. "He's really takin' advantage of us, Jimmy."

"Yeah, don't push it, old man. Just give us the money."

Mr. Hendricks released a sigh of exasperation. He'd either die by gunshot, or of an excessive exposure to stupidity. He figured he might just as well give them the money and get them out of here. Then they'd be Max's problem.

"Tell me, how many banks have you boys robbed?" he asked as he reached into the cash drawer.

"This is our first," Allen declared proudly.

"But we're not greenhorn amateurs," Jimmy informed him. "Not us, no, sir."

"Oh, what have you boys done before?"

Mr. Hendricks felt as if he were asking for the résumé of someone he was interviewing for the position of bank teller. He almost laughed, but he didn't believe these fellows' senses of humor had survived the large quantities of alcohol Jimmy and Allen had subjected them to.

"You know that train that was on its way to St. Louis?"

"Not personally, no. But I've heard of it," Mr. Hendricks said as he put the money in a large canvas sack.

"We did it."

"Yeah, that was us."

"Just the two of you? My, my, I'm impressed."

"No, we had a little help with that one," Allen admitted.

"You don't say."

"Yeah. We got them goofus Lansing brothers from over in Willoughby to help us with that one," Allen continued his confession.

"But that train that was headed for Omaha, that was all ours, just the two of us," Jimmy declared proudly, as if chagrined that they'd ever needed help on any of them.

"I'm impressed by your fatuous audacity and utter flapdoodle."

Jimmy and Allen grinned at him broadly. "Yeah?"

"Oh, indeed. I think—indeed, it is my fervent hope that someday more people—why, the whole country, the entire state—will be able to acknowledge your heinous exploits."

"Yeah!"

He passed the bag over the top of the counter. Jimmy snatched it up quicky and backed away.

"With a public hanging," Mr. Hendricks mumbled to himself.

"You know, old man, we like you so much, we're gonna let you live."

"Oh, too kind, too kind," Mr. Hendricks murmured, making a series of obsequious little bows, while wiping the perspiration from his bald pate. "I'll . . . I'll sing your praises to everyone I meet."

"You do that! Yahoo!" Jimmy yelled as he fired a few shots into the ceiling, sending down a shower of plaster.

Mr. Hendricks ducked down behind the counter, covering his head with his hands.

Jimmy and Allen ran out the door.

"You're doggone right I will," Mr. Hendricks muttered angrily as he peeked over the counter to make sure they were gone. "I'll sing to the sheriff, to the U.S. Marshall, to the judge, to the state prosecutor, all the way up to the governor himself!"

Shots rang out again. Mr. Hendricks ducked back down again, until he realized the sound had come from outside. He quickly ran to the window and peeked out.

"Stop, in the name of the law," Max commanded. He trained his gun on Jimmy and Allen as they ran down the steps of the bank.

Jimmy and Allen stood there and laughed.

"Didn't anybody ever tell you, you mule-eared jackass? Sticks and stones'll break our bones, but names'll never hurt us?"

"I don't believe you two would be stupid enough to pull a stunt like this," Max said.

"Well, we are," Allen taunted.

"I know *you* are, Allen. I'm danged ashamed to call you my brother."

"I ain't too fond o' you, neither, you piss-ant little nose-wipe. You always were a pain in the ass, followin' me everywhere, snitchin' on me to Ma."

"I didn't take this job because I wanted to be popular."

"Well, good, 'cause you ain't."

"Throw down your guns, and the money, and we'll cart you off to jail. Seeing as how nobody's been hurt yet, maybe we can get the judge to be lenient."

"I ain't throwin' down my gun," Allen insisted.

"Then just drop it real gentle," Max said mockingly. Then his tone grew deep and commanding. "Get rid of the gun. Now."

"No."

Allen swaggered a bit, straddling his feet a bit farther apart. Jimmy did the same. Who did they think they were, the Clantons? This sure as hell wasn't the OK Corral. Max hoped it wouldn't turn into that.

"There's no reason for gunplay, boys," Max said. "Not for one holdup."

"Yes, there is," Jimmy said. "You really are stupider

than you look if you ain't figured out yet it's been us breakin' into them stores."

"Two hats and a hammer are nothing to get shot over," Max said. "I guess Liz Englemeyer'd even settle for you just replacing the windowpanes you broke. Don't make it any worse on yourselves by robbing the bank."

"Too late, you big dummy," Jimmy said.

"You're right, Max," Allen told him. "Two hats and a hammer ain't nothin' to get shot over. Couple o' hundred thousand dollars might be, though."

Jimmy stared in disbelief at the canvas bag. "Wow! You reckon there's that much money in there?"

"No, stupid! In our hidin' place."

"Oh." Jimmy paused for a moment, as if trying to remember exactly where their hiding place was. Then he nodded vigorously. "Yeah, yeah, that might be worth it."

"See, Max, while you and them other lawmen were off chasin' train robbers halfway 'cross the state, you never thought to look right under your own snotty nose." Allen laughed. "It was us all the time. You just thought we spent all our time drinkin'."

"And visitin' Miss Sadie, Allen. Don't forget Miss Sadie—and Miss Blue," Jimmy added.

"How could we afford all them drinks and good times without money? Did you ever ask yourself that?"

"I thought—"

"Yeah, I know," Jimmy said. "You always thought like the rest o' the folks in this town. Me and Allen was just a pair o' losers, never amount to nothin', just scroungin' drinks from our friends. Well, we done proved you all wrong."

"Yeah, we got close to two hundred thousand Yankee dollars stashed away in our hidin' place, just waitin' for us. We figured we'd rob the bank as sort of a goin' away present before we collected it all and headed out to Californy."

Allen spit at Max.

"See how many people vote for you for sheriff next time when they find out how you botched this up."

Allen turned to mount his horse.

"Don't move," Max commanded.

Allen laughed.

"Back away fro the horse, Allen, or I'll have to shoot you for an escaping bank robber."

"You're full of it, Max. You won't shoot your own brother. You're too much of a Goody Two-shoes."

"Don't get on that horse, Allen."

Allen turned to Jimmy. "He's gettin' on my nerves. Shoot him."

Jimmy fired.

Max shot back.

Jimmy fell backward against the bank steps.

Allen sprang into the saddle. As the horse reared and bolted, Allen fired at Max. Max's arm burned as if he'd been branded. He felt sick to his stomach. He fired, but Allen and the horse were growing blurry as they galloped out of town.

16

"*It's amazing!*" Mrs. Nichols exclaimed.

"Unbelievable!" Mr. Quinn declared.

"I can't believe what you've done to this house, Del," Widow Crenshaw told him.

"I can't believe I'm actually standing in that old miser Richardson's house," Miss Barber said. "He sure as shooting never let anybody in it while he was alive."

Widow Crenshaw drew Del a little closer and whispered in his ear, "Thank you so much for inviting us. We'll do our best to keep an eye out for anything suspicious looking."

"Thanks."

Everyone was milling about the downstairs of the house. Doc Marsh would have a full schedule tomorrow, treating all the wry-necks from people who couldn't see enough of the statues, paintings, and hunting trophies.

"Just stay off the stairs, please," Del announced. "We had a little mishap the other day, and we're missing a few steps. I don't want any of you thinking to take a tour of the second floor and ending up suddenly and unexpectedly in the cellar."

"Oh, Sally, did you do all the cooking?" Mrs. Nichols asked.

Sally nodded modestly.

"Absolutely wonderful, I must admit," Mrs. Stanley agreed. "I'd never imagined a bitty little thing like you could be such a good cook. You must come visit me and Harriet sometime. We'll exchange receipts. Won't that be fun?"

Sally nodded wisely.

"Charles, this is preposterous!" Mrs. Lowell complained. "I cannot for one minute imagine why I agreed to come here."

"Because you didn't want to sit home alone," he replied. "Mr. and Mrs. Hamilton can hardly refuse to attend their neighbor's son's party. I certainly did not intend to allow Miranda to come to this place alone again. You had the choice of coming here or staying home with the cat."

"The place might be just a little cleaner, although I can't imagine anything short of flooding the place with lye soap and carbolic acid would improve it."

She ran her gloved finger along the chair rail in the dining room, seeking damning evidence. Finding none, she moved on.

"But the furnishings are still so woefully out of fashion. And where on earth did he get those draperies?"

"My friend Liz Englemeyer made them. Isn't she talented?" Sally replied as she passed by. She didn't stop to chat. She just kept moving through the crowd.

Mrs. Lowell moved into the dining room. She picked up a small piece of cake.

"The food's not much better, either. Imagine, eating with one's fingers!"

"Ah, but the Lord made fingers before man invented forks," Reverend Knutson proclaimed, and popped a piece of cake into his mouth.

Mrs. Lowell might refuse to associate with everyone else in town, but even she could hardly disdain the company of the minister. Seeing the woman properly occupied, Miranda sought out Charles.

She approached him very slowly.

Come on, Miranda, she chided herself. It's not as if he's a bomb that's going to explode.

"I've wanted to talk to you about this before, Charles, but the opportunity never . . . well . . . and all right, I'll admit, I'm a big coward.

"What is it?"

She reached into her purse and pulled out the engagement ring.

"What's it doing there? Why aren't you wearing it?"

She stared at him sadly. "Is this the first time you've noticed? I haven't been wearing this for . . . oh, I don't know how long. That's why . . . Charles, about our engagement. I really can't—"

"All right. Nobody move!"

"Who said that?" Miss Barber demanded.

"I did," Allen declared from the doorway. "Now, nobody move or I'll blow you all to Kingdom Come!"

Miss Barber turned to Widow Crenshaw. "Janet, did we write that line in *The Clue in the Cavernous Cave* or in *The Gambit of the Gregarious Gambler*?"

"No, it was in *The Mystery of the Magnificent Mohican* or maybe in *The Adventure of the Ambidextrous Archer*."

"They do all sort of tend to blur together after the first fifty or sixty," Miss Barber lamented.

"Oh, everything blurs together to you, Catherine."

"I said shut up and don't move!" Allen growled.

"No, you didn't," Miss Barber argued. "You said not to move, and we didn't. You didn't say a thing about shutting up. Really, young man. If you hope to make a truly successful career at robbery, you must have a plan. You can't just go making stuff up as you go along."

"Why not, Catherine? You do," Widow Crenshaw grumbled.

"I do not! My books are always very carefully plotted."

"They are *not*. You're always changing the plot on me just when I get—"

"Shut up!"

Allen fired a shot into the ceiling. The two elderly ladies stopped bickering. The guests screamed.

"This is a holdup! You're all goin' to line up against the walls in this here room—"

"It's called a vestibule," Miss Barber corrected. She waggled her finger at him. "Perhaps if you'd been more attentive in school, young man, you would be gainfully employed now and wouldn't have to resort to a life of crime and degradation."

"Shut up!" Allen shoved the gun directly into Miss Barber's nose. "I know you can't see no further than the end of your nose. Can you see this?" he demanded. "Can you feel it, then? 'Cause it'll be the last thing you feel when I blow your dang fool head off if you don't stop flapping your jowls!"

Turning to the rest of the crowd, Allen continued, "Now, does everyone here understand that I'm not foolin' around? I mean business. I've shot and killed three men to get the money I want, so one or two more of you ain't gonna make much difference to me."

While Allen was occupied with Miss Barber, Del slowly made his way to Miranda's side.

"Allen Douglas." She could feel her lip curl in disgust. If she weren't too nervous to work up some saliva, she'd have spit in his face—or at least on his shoe. "They should've killed you long ago when they had the chance."

"Friends of yours, Mr. Williams?" Charles asked with a sneer.

"Yeah, and he owes me a favor, so watch your mouth."

Charles clamped his lips together and leaned back against the wall, probably trying to look as inconspicuous as possible.

"Hey, hey, Del, my good buddy!" Allen called to him. "Hell of a party, man!"

"Thank you."

"Hate what you've done to the house."

"Sorry."

"It don't make much of a hideout now."

"Sorry."

"'Course, it don't make much difference, 'cause I ain't gonna be needin' it for my hideout much longer anyway."

"I should've figured it was you two. Where's your buddy?"

"Jimmy? Hell, I think Max shot him dead. So then I had to go shoot Max."

"Oh, blast. There goes the writing career!" Miss Barber exclaimed.

Sally slumped to a heap on the floor.

"Hey, somebody get her," Allen ordered, jerking his head in Sally's direction.

"We can't. You told us not to move," Miss Barber said.

"Yeah, you two." He waved the gun back and forth between Mrs. Baldwin and Mrs. Nichols. "Do somethin' with her."

Mrs. Nichols dug in her purse for smelling salts while Mrs. Baldwin tried to drag Sally back to lean against the wall.

"You shot your own brother? You swine!" Miranda sneered at him. "You have got to be the lowest form of life on the planet!"

"Shut up."

"You're worse than a cretin. You're lower than a worm. Even worms don't kill their own brothers."

"How do you know, you snot-lickin' little sow?"

"Because I've got a brain, something you obviously lack."

"Hey!" He stuck the gun under her nose. "I believe I'm the one with the gun here, and right now that makes me the smartest man in the room."

"Or the biggest jackass."

"That does it! You, take this bag." He pushed a canvas bag into Miranda's hand. "I'm makin' you my accomplice."

Miranda stood there, trying to look at the bag without going cross-eyed trying to see past the gun.

"I think I'd make a better accomplice if you got rid of this." She slowly reached up and, with her index finger, tried to push away the gun barrel stuck to the end of her nose.

"Nope. I still need this aimed directly at you."

With the gun still pressed into Miranda's temple, he pushed her toward the cellar steps.

"We're goin' down these steps, and you're goin' to fill this bag with as much of my money as you can. Then we're comin' back up again. If anybody tries to shut that door, thinkin' like he was so smart and could trap us down there——" He gave Del a sharp sneer. "Well, I'll just have to shoot this fine lady."

"Don't shoot her, Allen," Del said. "It's my house. I'll make sure no one in this house does anything until you come back up."

Del held his breath until he saw Miranda reappear at the top of the stairs. Allen had two saddlebags stuffed full of bills slung over his shoulders. The bag Miranda carried looked pretty heavy, too. But it wasn't completely full.

"Yeah, okay, okay, okay!" Allen yelled. "Ladies and gentlemen, if I may have your attention—ha! Like I ain't already got it. This here beautiful young lady is now goin' to be comin' around amongst you all. I would be mighty gratified—and you would, too, 'cause then I won't have to shoot you—if you'd drop your valuables— no, no, gentlemen, I mean your negotiable valuables—into the bag. And I do mean all of them, too. Just 'cause you're in Henry Richardson's old house don't mean you all got to be stingy old bastards like he was."

Miranda circulated among the guests. How could all the wonderful work she and Del had done to make everything beautiful turn out so ugly?

At last she returned to face Allen.

He snatched the bag away from her and gave it a shuffle.

"Sounds good, folks. Sounds real good to me. But you forgot something, Miranda." He shoved the bag back into her hands.

"What?" She answered quietly, but she knew he had to see the hatred for him in her eyes.

"I happen to know you are engaged to be married to this real rich city feller. I also believe that rich city fellers are in the habit of givin' the girl they're gonna marry a nice, big, expensive engagement ring. So where is it?"

Miranda pulled the ring from the palm of her glove and dropped it into the bag.

"Thanks. Now, hold on to that bag real good and tight 'cause it's got lots of nice things in it, and if you drop it, I'm gonna shoot you."

Allen reached up and grabbed a hank of Miranda's hair. Then he looked directly at Del.

"She might be engaged to that city feller, but I know you two is still real sweet on each other, so I'm tellin' you, Del."

He tugged on Miranda's hair. She had no choice but to follow him toward the door or wear wigs for a long time.

"I don't want no one followin' me, understand?"

"Yes." Del was trying to keep his voice very calm.

"So I'm takin' her with me for a while. If I see any sign of anyone followin' me, I'll shoot her."

Del took a single step forward.

"Don't be a bigger fool than you already are. I'll do it, and you know I will."

Allen dragged Miranda out the front door and down the walk into the darkness. Del listened hard as he heard the horse's hooves clatter away.

"I got a gun at home," Mr. Hamilton offered.

"I've got one of my own. Thanks anyway."

"I'll bring it back anyway. I used to be a pretty good shot."

"I'll get my hunting rifle," Hal Danvers offered.

"I got a shotgun," Mr. Nesbitt told him.

"He's gone and killed the sheriff. We'll have to form a posse ourselves and go get the varmint!" Mr. Quinn declared.

"No!"

Everyone turned to look at Del.

"All Allen needs to see is the cloud of dust a posse this size will raise, all he needs to hear is one voice or horse whinny, and he'll kill Miranda."

"He's right," Mr. Hamilton admitted with a sigh.

"But we've got to get her back," Mrs. Hamilton insisted.

"I know, Mrs. Hamilton," Del said, wrapping a consoling arm around her shoulder. "No one wants her back more than I do. But I'll have to go after him alone."

"Shucks! I missed him."

All eyes focused on the door. Max stood there, his arm dripping blood.

"You're not dead!" The cry went up from a thankful crowd. Most thankful of all was obviously Sally, who rushed to Max's side.

"Sit down. What happened?" Sally danced attentively around Max while Hal and Isaac helped him to the sofa. "We thought you were dead. You have to let me bandage that for you."

"I take it Allen has been and gone," Max said weakly.

"Don't talk too much," Sally scolded. "You've lost a lot of blood and you're very weak."

"What happened, Max?" Del asked.

"Tarnation, Del! I just tell him to stay quiet and you've got to go asking him questions," Sally grumbled. "What are you trying to do? Allen missed, but are you trying to kill him, too?"

"No, but I've got to know what happened."

"Those two robbed the bank. I shot and killed Jimmy. I'm after Allen now. He said he was going out to California."

"No, *I'm* after Allen," Del corrected. "He took Miranda as a hostage. I'm going to bring her back. But I've got to go alone."

Del strode toward the doorway. Will had already run to the barn, saddled his horse, and brought him around front. Several of the men had packed rifles in his saddle and pressed revolvers into his hand.

"May God go with you, Del," Reverend Knutson said in his best pulpit voice. "All our hopes and prayers go with you, too, to bring Miranda back alive and well." He gave a little cough and, in a slightly lower tone of voice, said, "I don't particularly give a damn what you do with Allen."

California. max had told him Allen was heading for California.

Del figured even Allen wasn't dumb enough to go back to Grasonville and wait for the eight o'clock morning train. Del also figured Allen wasn't a man of much imagination, so he must be taking the only road going west out of town.

Allen didn't have much of a head start. He couldn't have much of a horse, either. Del was glad now that he'd been extravagant enough to buy the best horse Simpson's had to offer.

The mare was fast. In the distance Del could see a rider. He'd have to get close enough to make sure it was Allen and Miranda, without letting Allen see him.

Allen slowed his horse to a walk. Del matched his gait and continued to follow at a steady distance.

Del was glad the mare was a quiet, steady one, too, not one of those horses that shies and whinnies at the slightest movement or sound. He wouldn't have been able to continue following Allen this closely without being noticed if the mare hadn't been quiet.

Even though they were heading westward into the setting sun, the sky was growing too dark to do much further traveling. Allen's horse was wearing down. He'd have to stop soon for the night. Del had to make sure he paid attention. He couldn't let Allen see him.

"You'd better let me go, you bird-brained coward," Miranda told him. It was so uncomfortable hanging over the saddle this way. "You think you got away, but Del's coming for me. I know he is."

"Shut up. Why don't that sissy boyfriend come after you?"

"He probably will, too. My father's coming after you, too. So is Mr. Pickett."

"They're old men!" Allen said with a sneer. "They can't do nothin' to me."

"They can still hold a gun. Del can do a lot of damage to your bloated hide all by himself. I don't need anyone else to come get me. Just Del."

"Shut up. He's still waitin' back at that big fancy house o' his, tryin' to figure out which way I went with you."

"Del's smart. He'll figure out which way you went."

"Hey, I'm smarter."

"Oh, yeah, that's right. You're the one with the gun, and that makes you the one with the brains. Just be sure you don't blow your puny little brains out."

She laughed harder.

"If brains were bullets, you'd be out of ammunition."

"Shut up. They always said you was too smart for your own good, and they was right."

"Del's leading the posse that's coming to take you back to Grasonville. They'll put you in jail for robbing the trains and the bank. They'll put you in jail for killing those other men and the sheriff, too."

"They've got to catch me first."

"They will." She nodded with certainty. "Then, while you're in jail, right outside your one and only window, they'll start building this big wooden platform. Do you know what that'll be, Allen, or are you too stupid?"

"I'm not stupid."

"It's a gallows. They're going to stretch your neck there really good."

"Shut up."

"Every day, all day, until it's done, that's all you'll hear is the hammering, hammering, hammering, constantly reminding you that you're going to die when the hammering stops."

Miranda wondered how much longer she could keep this up. The jogging of the horse was battering her already bruised ribs.

She knew in her heart, even if she couldn't see him

with her eyes, that Del was following her. When would he catch up to them? When would he save her again?

Was it because she was closer to the ground that she heard the hoofbeats before Allen did?

She tried to look behind them. Someone was coming up on them at a gallop. It had to be Del!

She still had to believe it was Del as the rider came up swiftly on the other side from her head. She was glad he had, otherwise he'd have knocked her head off as he slammed his horse into the side of Allen's.

The horses screamed in fright. Allen went tumbling from the saddle. She went sprawling headlong into the dried grass at the side of the road.

She rolled until she crashed into a tree stump.

Dazed, she grabbed her head with her hands to stop the spinning. She tried to sit up. She tried to focus.

She blinked hard and shook her head hard to clear her vision. She had to be awake and fully aware of every-thing that happened.

Del and Allen were tangled in a full-scale brawl. Fists flailing, they pounded at each other. She couldn't just sit there, watching them.

Leaning on the tree stump, she pulled herself up to stand. They were still pounding each other. She couldn't just stand there watching them, either.

Del was holding his own. She drew in a deep breath of relief. She knew he would.

They were fighting so closely, she couldn't have gotten in to take a swing at Allen no matter what.

Dell almost had Allen pinned. The other men would be following soon. Then they'd take them all home.

Allen squirmed in Del's grasp. He was wiggling and stretching like the worm she already knew he was. It would have to take a worm or an eel to get out of Del's strong grasp. But suddenly Allen was on top, pounding into Del's face with his fist.

He dragged Del off the road, down the embankment, and to the edge of the river that ran beside the road.

"Del!"

Allen turned back to her. "Don't worry, Miranda. I ain't forgotten you."

"Del!"

She could see Del trying to wipe his face to retain consciousness. He was digging his heels into the sand along the river to stop Allen from dragging him in.

He wasn't succeeding.

Allen threw Del down into the river. The water wasn't very deep. It didn't need to be. Only a few inches was enough to drown a man.

Allen slammed Del's face into the sandy bottom. He jabbed his knee into Del's back between his shoulder blades, pinning him down.

"Del!"

"He'll never get up," Allen answered.

But Del was still struggling. Allen turned his back on Miranda, concentrating on finishing Del.

Miranda rushed up behind Allen. She hit him hard along the side of his head.

He only flinched. She should've figured after taking Del's battering, she'd only be about as effective as a buzzing fly. He swatted her off as easily.

She fell into the sand. All around her rocks as smooth as pebbles offered themselves to her. She chose the largest. If Allen couldn't feel this, she . . . no, she didn't want to think about what would happen if she failed to stop Allen this time.

She had to be quick.

She smashed the rock onto the top of his head. He buckled, but remained upright. She hit him again, this time with a more sideways, glancing blow.

Allen toppled into the sand.

Del sprang up, gasping for air. Miranda threw her arms around him and pulled him onto the sand. She didn't want to take any chances that in his weakness he'd topple back into the water.

"Allen?"

"I think I killed him."

Del just nodded. He kept drawing in deep breaths and

coughing to clear his lungs. After a few minutes he reached over to wrap his fingers around Allen's wrist.

"No, he's still alive, darn!"

"We'll tie him onto one of the horses and take him back."

"Max'll be real glad to throw him in jail."

"Max?"

"Jimmy only winged him."

"Good."

"Sally thinks so, too."

"Let's go home."

17

*D*EL STUCK HIS hand in the canvas bag. He pulled out a large cameo brooch.

"I believe this is yours, Mrs. Nichols."

"Oh, my grandmother's brooch!" Mrs. Nichols cried, clasping the piece of jewelry to her ample bosom. She sniffed loudly and wiped away a tear from the corner of her eye. "I never thought I'd see it again. You really are our hero, Del."

Del shot her a sheepish grin. He reached into the bag again. "Why do I feel like Santa Claus?"

"You don't look like him," Miranda told him.

He pulled out a gold and seed-pearl bracelet.

"Oh, that's mine," Miss Barber said. "I'm so sorry Janet and I couldn't figure out who the culprits were before they did all this damage."

"Not at all, Miss Barber," Del hastily assured her. "Why, if it weren't for you and Mrs. Crenshaw staging that mock argument, we'd never have been able to stall Allen long enough for Max to arrive and tell us which direction he was heading.

Del held the drooping bag up so everyone could see it was now empty. Since all the loot had apparently been returned to its rightful owners, the guests all began milling around. They were all congratulating themselves and each other on their parts, no matter how small, in Miranda's rescue and Max's predicted recovery. It was almost as if, now that the stolen goods were recovered, everyone had forgotten about Del and Miranda.

Miranda huddled beside Del. She didn't need protection now, but she still felt safe beside him. And secure. She felt as if, after much aimless wandering, she'd finally returned to where she truly belonged.

Through the noise, she heard Del whisper in her ear, "You know, there's still one more thing left in this bag."

She looked into his eyes. "What is it?"

Reaching all the way to the bottom, he pulled out her engagement ring.

"Oh, I'm sorry I asked," she remarked with a grimace.

Still holding the ring, he flung the empty bag into a corner.

"I have to give this back to you," he told her. "You know that, don't you?"

She shook her head, then quickly changed to a nod.

"You know I love you."

"I love you, too," she quickly responded.

"But it's your life, Miranda."

"It's yours, too," she protested.

"I've already made my decision. Whatever happens, I'll love you for the rest of my life."

He reached out and took her hand. Slowly he pressed the ring into her palm. When she tried to pull back, he folded her fingers over it.

"But this is the rest of *your* life you're deciding on now," he continued. "Only you can make that decision."

"I've already made my decision, Del. I guess I really knew it all along. There's no one else in the world for me but you."

A wide smile lit Del's face. He wrapped his arms around her and drew her closer.

She held her hand in front of her, stopping him.

"No. Not . . . not yet. Not until I feel I'm really free. It's . . . it's only fair."

Del released his embrace. "I understand."

Miranda made her way through the crowd to Charles. As usual, Mrs. Lowell was standing beside him.

While he appeared to be laughing and drinking with the rest of the guests, his eyes still held the detachment and scorn that Miranda had come to know too well. And, while all her childhood friends and neighbors saluted him cordially, she knew Charles would never truly be part of her world of farms and barn dances, just as she knew she would never truly be a part of his life of yachting clubs and polo ponies.

"Please, Charles," she said very quietly. "I'd like to speak to you in private."

He glanced about. "That might be a little difficult here at the moment. Just tell me what it is."

Miranda released a deep sigh. She extended her hand, holding out the diamond engagement ring.

"Charles," she began hesitantly, "I can't marry you."

He blinked in surprise. "What do you mean, you don't want to marry me?"

"I'm not in love with you," she stated more firmly. "Not anymore."

"Oh, balderdash!"

"You know it's true," she insisted. "I think I was in love with the promise you presented of living an exciting life. But . . . that's not the right reason. I . . . I used to like you. I think I could still tolerate being around you. But I don't love you. I can't . . . I *won't* marry a man I don't love."

"A week before the wedding? This is a fine time to tell me." He glanced about with open scorn. "And here—of all places!"

"I tried and tried to tell you before, but you wouldn't listen. That's the trouble. You never actually *listen* to me."

Charles lifted his chin indignantly. "Well, I suppose it has something to do with that Williams fellow."

"It has *everything* to do with him."

He struck an heroic stance—chin up, one hand on his

out-thrust hip, knee cocked. "But I'm handsomer than he is."

"I'm sure when you return to your own kind of people in Boston, there'll be hordes of young ladies vying for your attention who'll think you're very handsome."

"Yes! Yes, indeed. But I still don't see how you can prefer him to me. I'm richer than he is."

"Money isn't as important as love," she stated very emphatically. "You don't count love and money by the same measure. I know you've got more money, but . . . you and I have never—will never—have as much love as Del and I do."

"This is preposterous!" Mrs. Lowell exclaimed. "You can't do this to me . . . to my son!"

"Mrs. Lowell, mind your own business," Miranda told her and felt extremely satisfied.

"Oh, the shame! The scandal! The embarrassment and ridicule!" Mrs. Lowell cried in despair.

"The attention you're drawing to yourself," Miranda noted.

Confronted by an increasing number of curious, prying eyes, Mrs. Lowell hushed. "How will we ever explain this when we return to Boston?" she fretted to Charles.

"Why not tell them the truth?" Miranda suggested. "That I decided to marry for love. Or make up some tale that suits you. I really don't care. Social obligations will never be as important to me as following my own heart."

She held out the ring to Charles. When he refused to take it, she grabbed his hand and pushed the ring into his palm.

Charles tightened his lips and glared down his nose at her. Lately she'd seen him do that quite often with so many of her friends. Now he looked at her with that same expression. She'd truly grown to despise that look.

With great relief, she turned away from him—away from his overbearing, domineering mother, away from their entire life. She knew she'd definitely made the right decision. She only spared a brief moment to note that

Charles and his mother made a rapid and unlamented exit.

She walked over and stood beside Del. "I did it," she announced quietly.

"I didn't hear an explosion."

"An explosion is not . . . proper," she offered with a grin.

"This isn't proper either," he declared, "but it's darn good fun!" He scooped her up in his arms and kissed her soundly on the lips. With a loud whoop, he swung her around.

"Oh, merciful heavens!" Miss Barber cried, so shaken that she jostled her punch out of the cup and over her fingers. "Is someone kidnapping Miranda again?"

"You've *got* to get a pair of spectacles, Catherine," Widow Crenshaw insisted. "It's only Del."

"Del's kidnapping Miranda?"

"No, no. I think she's going to go very willingly this time," Widow Crenshaw said.

"Oh, so the silly thing finally realized she ought to be marrying Del all along," Miss Barber said with great finality, and turned back to her punch.

"We're getting married!" Del declared. "Miranda and I are getting married!"

Will started to cheer, and the rest of the guests joined in.

"Oh, it's just the way I always felt it should be," Mrs. Hamilton said. She sniffed and dabbed at her eyes with the edge of her handkerchief. Tom and Sam started clapping each other heartily on the back. Miranda saw Max lean over and whisper something in Sally's ear that made her blush profusely.

"I think I ought to be old-fashioned and ask your father's permission to marry you," Del said.

"I think you ought to be modern and ask my *parents'* permission," Miranda corrected him with a grin. "On the other hand, if I were to be truly modern, I suppose I needn't ask anyone's permission to marry the man I love."

Del gave a deep, theatrical sigh. "Taking an educated woman for a wife. Oh, what have I gotten myself into?"

"The time of your life!" she whispered.

With gentle pressure against her shoulder, Del began to draw her along. Instead of leading her toward her parents, as she expected, he guided her out the front door.

He closed the door behind him. The laughter and cheers of the guests, the bright lights, and the clinking of the glasses all seemed very far away.

They stood alone together on the porch in the pale moonlight. Del placed his arm around her shoulder.

"The streets are so deserted," she whispered.

"Everyone's at our party."

"It seems as if we're the only two people in the world—in the entire universe."

He drew her closer to him. She rested her head on his shoulder.

"We are. It's like we're before the very dawn of time, ready to make a new life together, just the two of us."

"No. We'll just be continuing what should have been our lives from the very beginning. We got interrupted a little when your mother passed away and I went off to school in Boston. But now we're back together again, just as I knew we'd always be."

"Oh, you did, did you?" he challenged.

"You know very well I did. I told you from the very beginning I was going to marry you, Del. And we were going to live in this house."

Del laughed and shook his head.

"Yeah, I guess you did, didn't you? How did you know?"

"I just made up my mind that's what I wanted. I'm not the kind of woman to let anything stand in my way."

"I sure can see that now." He chuckled. "You were such a rascal when you were a little girl."

"You were dull and boring," she countered. "But I still loved you, even then, I guess."

"You've turned into quite a lady, Miranda," he admitted with admiration. Turning her to face him, he placed a kiss on her forehead.

"I've always thought you were quite a man, Del." She cuddled more deeply into his embrace and wrapped her arms around his waist.

"Are you certain a lady like you won't be bored in a little town like this?"

The admiration in his eyes had turned to concern.

"You know I've always made my own fun."

"And your own mischief."

"I've *never* been bored here," she assured him. "I missed everyone so much while I was in Boston—my parents, my friends, all the people in town with their stores and houses."

"Not me?"

"Especially you!" She gave him an extra squeeze. "You have no idea—"

"Yes, I do. I missed you all when I went to Texas. But now there's no need to go away ever again. I'll always have all the love I need right here with you."

Del reached up to cradle her chin in his hand. He lifted her face to his. Slowly, in the moonlight, he kissed her. Gently, tenderly, sealing their fates, bonding their lives together forever.

Miranda nestled her head against his chest until she could hear his heart beating. "I can't think of any place I'd rather be than here with you, with our children someday, all together in our house."

FREE
Romance
(a $4.50 value)

Send in the Coupon Below

To get your FREE historical romance and start saving, fill out the coupon below and mail it today. As soon as we receive it we'll send you your FREE Book along with your first month's selections.
